AF451162

Kashmir-e-Taliban
2032

Kashmir-e-Taliban 2032

Anant Joshi

Title of the novel: **Kashmir-e-Taliban 2032**

Author's Name: Anant Joshi

Language of Original Work: Marathi (Regional Indian Language)

Translated by: Mrs. Jayashree Naidu

Book Cover – Raja Graphics, Nagpur

Copyright Holder: Anant Joshi

 Publisher: Anant Joshi

ISBN --- 978-93-5980-424-8

Disclaimer: This is a work of fiction. Names, characters, incidents, places, institutions and conflict mentioned in this work are either the product of the author's imagination or used fictitiously. Any resemblance to real persons, living or deceased, events, locales, or institutions is purely coincidental. Most of the information on military prowess has been derived from google only and other created with imagination.

DEDICATION

Dedicated to the memory of
My elder brother
Vasant P. Joshi alias Tatya

Preface

My debut work, a collection of Marathi poetry titled "Ek AavegalaMrityu," was first published in 1996. In 2013, my first Hindi novel, "Geeta Chali Gai," was published. "Beg Your Pardon," my third book, was originally published in Marathi by Vijay Prakashan, Nagpur, in January 2015.The novel has also been published in Hindi, English, and Bengali languages. Another novel "On the banks of Damodar "wasoriginally written in Marathi andpublished in Hindi and English languages.

On 15th August 2021, Talibanis forcefullytook over Afghanistan, after American forces took exit. The president of Afghanistan had to flee for life. There weredisturbing scenes on TV. At that time, I thought that Talibaniscould invade Kashmir province in India. This thought brought me to the conception of this novel. This imaginative picturization was not possible without the help of Google for information on geopolitics and the military of countries,and then phantasy ultimately could be penned on paper.

This novel was originally written in Marathi and subsequently translated into English.

I am deeply grateful to my relatives and friends who have consistently encouraged me in my writing endeavours. Special thanks to Mrs. Jayashree Naidu for her translation. I also thank Raja Graphic Centrefor a nice book cover.

I sincerely pray that readers will find this book engaging and thought-provoking.

Thank you to all who have supported me in this journey.

January 2032

The sun had set on the streets of New Delhi, and a chill permeated the air. Seated in the back seat of their SUV, Buddhadeva Trital and his wife, Vijaya, were en-route to the Rashtrapati Bhavan, the Presidential palace. Their vehicle had been stopped at three security checkpoints, with a Security Officer in the front seat handling all the necessary procedures. The van escorting them from the rear had also undergone security checks. At the first gate, separate passes were issued: two passes for the two vehicles, and individual passes for the Tritals, and their entourage. The staff at Rashtrapati Bhavan were well-acquainted with the Tritals and greeted them with smiles and salutations as they dutifully performed their security duties.

At the final checkpoint, the lady security officer felt a bit embarrassed subjecting Mrs. Trital to a body check, but she carried out her duties in a matter-of-fact manner. Mrs. Trital, in turn, cooperated without any fuss, pulling her warm shawl away to allow the officer to scan her with the electromagnetic device. The staff knew that Mr. and Mrs. Trital were on a personal visit. Mr. Trital walked towards the halls, instructing his security staff to stay at a safe distance. Only one security officer walked with him inside.

It was the day of Makar Sankranti, January 14, 2032, an Indian festival. In the State Drawing Room, located in the right corner of the Durbar Hall, the President's wife awaited their arrival. The security officer escorted the couple into the room. Vijaya Trital quickly moved forward, touching the feet of the First Lady, who held her close. "Didi" (elder sister), said Vijaya, embracing her sister. Buddhadeva also stepped forward respectfully, touching the First Lady's feet and offering Makar Sankranti greetings.

Then, they all proceeded to the rear of the room and took the elevator to the first floor, where the President was waiting in a stately, warm room with electric heaters. There was a fireplace, but President Shiv Kalyan Singh and his wife, Vinaya, preferred electric heaters to avoid unnecessary deforestation. On the uppermost terrace of the courtyard, there was a small solar plant providing lighting to the entire premises.

Vijaya took a quick step forward toward her brother-in-law (Jijaji) and touched his feet as a mark of respect. Trital did the same. Vinaya sat down beside her husband on the sofa, and Buddhadeva and Vijaya took seats on the opposite sofa.

The President playfully asked Vijaya, "Have you brought my favorite sesame laddoos (an Indian sweet dish) or not?"

"How could I ever forget that, Jijaji? I have made them just the way you like them, with cashew and almond powder and jaggery."

Trital took out a packet from his briefcase and handed it over to his wife. She opened the packet and offered the sweet to her brother-in-law. The President picked up one and took a bite, and Vijaya then offered the sweet to Vinaya.

Meanwhile, the housemaids brought out a tray full of sesame and jaggery sweetmeats and some cashew fudge, along with glasses of water, and arranged them on the tea table.

Both the President and Buddhadeva had dark complexions, but their heights differed greatly. The President, over six feet tall, towered over Trital, who was just about five and a half feet tall. Both had solemn expressions. The President had a longish face, a pointed nose, shrewd eyes, and a muscular body. Trital had a round face, an eagle nose, and deep-set, alert eyes. Despite his corpulence, he was quite agile on his feet due to his former military life.

They settled down to the usual banal talk about the day's weather. Aware that Trital had something important to discuss, the President asked his aide if the heaters were on in the adjoining room. Just as they got up to go to the room, Vinaya gently intervened, "Will you keep your discussion short? Dinner will be served soon."

After giving instructions to the cook, the sisters engaged in a tete-a-tete. Vinaya had a fair complexion, a round face, a slender frame, and very expressive eyes. She spoke softly. Vijaya had a wheat-brown complexion, a round, attractive face, and large eyes. She used a lot of makeup and was slightly plump but still curvaceous and light on her feet. Both were cousins on their maternal side.

Meanwhile, in the privacy of the room, the President asked, "Yes, tell me, our Deputy Chief National Security Advisor, what news have you brought?"

Trital replied, "The news is rather serious and disturbing."

"Tell me,"Said the President.

Trital continued, "We are receiving intelligence inputs that the Taliban is planning an attack on Kashmir."

"This has been the case for the past five years."

"Well, yes, but this time it seems they have a solid plan."

The President inquired, "If your information is authentic, then I am sure other agencies are aware of it too. Has this come from Mossad?"

Trital nodded in affirmation.

The President said gravely, "If the Prime Minister's Office is aware of this, surely the Defense Department would know as well. Some steps must be in progress..."

"Yes, we are getting prepared, but..."

"But what?"

"In light of the current happenings in the government, there might be..."

"Okay, we will have to keep an eye on it."

Trital mentioned that the Minister for Home Affairs was hosting a grand party that evening at his mansion. The President remarked on the coincidence that Eid and Makar Sankranti, both festivals, had occurred on the same day. Just then, Vijaya knocked on the door and inquired if they were ready for dinner.

"Yes," said the President. To Trital, he added, "Keep me informed on a weekly basis."

Dinner was set out in one corner of the large dining table. The President asked Vijaya if she would like to listen to some devotional music first. She agreed, and the President said, "Alexa, start the *Hanuman Chalisa* chant," and the words of the Hanuman Chalisa began to play. "*Shree Gurucharan Saro..Jai Hanuman DnyanGunasagar, Jai Kapish..*" Everyone sat still with hands joined in reverence as they listened to these words. As the Mantra came to an end with "*Ki Jai Hruday Man Dera,Ramlakhan Seeta Kahee Hruday Sur Subahu,*"they opened their eyes and began to eat their dinner.

After dinner, they all proceeded to the State Drawing Room located at the right corner of the Durbar Hall, where they engaged in an expansive conversation for a while. Vinaya asked the Tritals when they would be visiting again, and the President made a pointed comment that they would have to be summoned again very soon. Trital did not miss the significance.

The Tritals bid their farewells and prepared to leave. Vinaya insisted on seeing them off at the door and invited them to pay another visit soon. Just then, Trital's mobile phone beeped, indicating that someone might have been listening on spyware. Trital felt the need to speak with the Chief Security Officer, Joseph Daniel, immediately but decided to postpone it until the next morning. The couple took leave of Vinaya and departed after having complied with all the security formalities.

Trital switched on the TV set before retiring for the night. The news was that the dollar had been devalued. The Chinese currency had also suffered the same fate. There were riots raging in two European nations, as a consequence of some religious places being under demolition. Vijaya quickly switched off the TV with the remote button and asked her husband to go to bed rather than hear such dismal news.

The following day Trital called up Joseph and expressed his suspicion. He said that fifteen days ago he was on a vacation in Kerala for Christmas and perhaps in his absence an attempt had been made to render some jammers ineffective. He added that before going on leave he had given permission for some painting work to be done on some outer walls where the paint had peeled off. It was likely that something had gone wrong inadvertently or deliberately during that time.Trital disconnected the phone. He knew that without support from some influential person, most likely from someone in the Home Ministry, such a thing was not possible. He was worried about the motive behind this and resolved to get to the root of the matter and also place new jammers immediately.

&&&&&

17.01.2023

"Hello, Ilyas, this is Majid Khan speaking." "Hello, Adaab (greetings), I'm calling from Srinagar. Brother Ozair is also joining the meeting."

The Zoom meeting commenced at 10:30 pm that night. Mohammed Majid Khan was speaking from the Sheraton Hotel in Kabul, where he served as the right-hand man to the defence minister in the Taliban Government. Ilyas Zaibuddin, the leader of the Azad Kashmir Organization, had joined the call from his room at the Blooming Windows Hotel in Srinagar. The Pakistani ISI officer was connecting from the Embassy Hotel in Lahore.

They were discussing the construction of a hotel in Kashmir. Ilyas posed the question, "Should we build it in Anantnag or Rajouri?" Majid Khan suggested it should be in a place attracting a large number of tourists and asked for Ozair's opinion. Ozair recommended Baramulla, citing the availability of gravel and sand and a constant flow of tourists.

Ilyas expressed concern, saying, "Working under the watchful eye of government officials there might be problematic."

Majid Khan responded, "Dealing with those officials is your responsibility. We must construct the hotel in a prime location." Ozair assured them, "Funding won't be an issue; we'll arrange the necessary funds."

Majid Khan concurred, saying, "Yes, we don't need to worry about finances. We are generating substantial income from medicines, with a lot of cash coming in from Africa."

Ilyas mentioned that he would hire an architect to create a plan, emphasizing the need for a solid foundation due to the crumbly ground.

Unbeknownst to them, the entire discussion was being monitored by Soshe Dayan, a Mossad agent. He had planted a bugging device at the Embassy Hotel in Lahore, Pakistan, and had assumed the identity of Nazir Mehmood, living in Pakistan as a Kabuli. He had even undergone circumcision to blend in with the Islamic tradition. A few years prior, he had successfully rescued Mulla Akhtiyar, a Taliban leader previously held captive by ISIS(A terrorist organization). Mulla Akhtiyar had risen to the position of Vice President in the Afghan government, granting Soshe Dayan the full support of the Taliban. He had managed to infiltrate the team sent by the Afghan government to Pakistan to learn nuclear technology and had set up a small lab at the Research Centre in Pakistan.

Soshe Dayan, alias Nazir Mehmood, was adept at deciphering the cryptic discussion. It appeared that there was a plan to launch terrorist activities from Baramulla, with a solid foundation being laid for these operations. The money supposedly coming from medicines was actually derived from narcotics like marijuana, opium, cannabis, and other intoxicating drugs.

Soshe Dayan maintained contact with Buddhadeva Trital, albeit indirectly through Tel Aviv. He had to create special message capsules hidden within packets of powdered drugs (medicines), which would then be airlifted to Saudi Arabia. The capsules would be codified and often went unnoticed, especially if concealed within small white pellets in the powder. These packets containing the message capsules would be sent to Tel Aviv, from where the information would eventually reach Trital. On occasion, the capsule would reach Tel Aviv directly.

It was only a matter of time before Trital would become aware of where the impending encroachment would begin.

&&&&&

23.01.2023

It was evening in Hyderabad, and in the home of Prakash Reddy, his children, Ojas, aged thirteen, and Swapna, aged twenty-two, were engaged in a casual conversation.

Ojas began, "Sis, our Social Science textbooks have been updated."

Swapna inquired, "Which books are you referring to?"

Ojas replied with a hint of frustration, "What do you mean, 'which'?"

Swapna clarified, "I mean, are you talking about online books or the printed ones?"

Ojas explained, "Both."

Swapna responded nonchalantly, "Well, what's so new about it? During our school days, these books used to change in the middle of the course."

Ojas continued, "This time, they've added more pages on Mughal history to our history textbook, covering from Babur to Aurangzeb."

Swapna remarked, "Even during our time, there was a significant focus on the Mughal era."

Ojas added, "You might find it interesting to know that many women warriors were included in last year's history books. Our teacher had promised we would learn more about these brave women the following year. However, all of them, like Rani Laxmibai, Rani Chennamma, Chand Bibi, Zalkari Bai, etc., have disappeared from the books this year."

Swapna exclaimed, "That's a clear injustice to women. I must raise this issue on a social platform. It needs to go viral. I'll also post it on the Women Lawyers' Forum."

Ojas continued, "You know, the history of ancient Indian kings that was part of the previous books has vanished from the new ones. The history of King Vikramaditya, the Cholas, the Chalukyas, the Vijayanagar Empire, and the Travancore Empire has been completely omitted. Among these, the Ahom kings of the North East were remarkable; they never allowed the Mughals to enter their territory. Would you like me to share their operational strategies?"

Swapna, busy with her work, replied, "Please don't overwhelm me with those details. I'm preparing a brief for a trial legal case tomorrow. Let me focus on my work."

Ojas offered, "Alright, *Akka*, I'm going to have some leftover cake. Would you like me to get you some?"

Swapna eagerly accepted, "Sure, I'll have some. And please don't call me *Akka*. Also, remember to save a piece of cake for Mom."

"Okay," said Ojas.

Ojas and Swapna were the children of Prakash Reddy and Aruna Reddy, both Chartered Accountants by profession. They resided in Hyderabad. Being in the same profession, they would leave for work together and return together. Usually, Prakash would handle meetings outside the office. On that particular day, he had attended a meeting with Mr. Ramkrishna Rao, an automobile dealer. Ramkrishna Rao was the proprietor of an electric vehicle agency and had gifted an EV to Prakash a few years ago. As Prakash anticipated a late return, Aruna took a taxi home. The taxi driver mentioned taking a longer route to avoid traffic jams, saving them half an hour. Aruna had no choice but to agree.

&&&&&

26.01.2023

Raj Path was all set for the annual Republic Day festivities, with elaborate security preparations in place. Anti-missile defences had been strategically positioned, and rigorous security checks were being conducted.

The Home Minister, Avdhesh Singh, had initially requested the President to deliver his Republic Day Address from a bullet-resistant enclosure. Initially, the President declined, but when the Prime Minister, Rajendra Kaul, made the same request, the President acquiesced. It was customary for the President to comply when such requests came directly from the Prime Minister himself.

The heightened security measures and troop mobilization were warranted due to a recent failed attempt by Pakistan to carry out an aerial bombing in Srinagar, Kashmir. The target was Lal Chowk, where the Chief Minister was scheduled to hoist the national flag. Thankfully, the bomb was diverted and exploded harmlessly in an uninhabited area, thanks to the use of drones.

Supervising all security arrangements was the Chief Security Advisor, Radhakrishnan, and Buddhadeva Trital. Trital had personally overseen the preparations at Raj Path on the 24th and 25th of January and played a key role in the deployment of anti-missile defences.

Upon the President's arrival in his carriage, he was greeted by Prime Minister Rajendra Kaul, Home Minister Avdhesh Singh, and Defence Minister Ravindra Prasad.

After the unfurling of the national flag, the National Anthem played, followed by a 21-gun salute. The President's speech followed. In the five days leading up to the event, the draft of the speech had undergone multiple revisions between the Home Ministry and the President's office before its finalization. The President's office had recommended that the draft avoid unnecessary political commentary, although there was initial resistance to this advice. All editing was conducted digitally. However, in keeping with tradition, the President delivered his speech from a printed sheet, even though he was prepared to use a tablet. This preference for tradition came at the request of Subhash Singh, a senior and respected leader in Parliament, who held the number two position in the Cabinet, just below the Prime Minister, and also managed the Finance portfolio. The President and Subhash Singh had a strong and enduring rapport, often serving as a bridge between the Cabinet and the President in times of potential disagreements.

Earlier on that day, Prime Minister Rajendra Kaul paid his respects at the Amar Jawan Jyoti (Memorial for Soldiers) and observed a two-minute silence.

Rajpath, the expansive venue for Republic Day celebrations, came to life with the presence of numerous dignitaries. Ministers and leaders from all political parties, both in government and opposition, were in attendance. The Chief Guest for the event was the King of Bhutan, who was personally welcomed by the Prime Minister.

During the ceremony, seven soldiers received the Param Veer Chakra gallantry awards from the President, while five soldiers were honoured with the Ashok Chakra. Four of these were posthumously received by their wives. Eleven children were recognized with the National Award for Bravery for their courageous acts. Different units of the Indian Army, as well as contingents from the Navy and Air Force, conducted a grand march, with the President taking the salute each time. Twelve units from paramilitary forces and a platoon from the Delhi police also participated in the parade. National Cadet Corps (NCC) cadets from various states and a group of schoolchildren joined the march past. The recipients of the Children's Bravery Awards were paraded on the back of an elephant, and the President warmly greeted each one.

At this moment, Trital discreetly moved away toward the rear of the grounds. The President, sharp-eyed, noticed this but deemed it of minor significance and decided not to disrupt the proceedings.

It was then time for the colourful floats representing different states to pass by the President. These displays showcased the cultural and artistic heritage of each state. A total of twenty-seven floats participated, with the northeastern states putting considerable effort into highlighting their unique ethnic cultures.

As the grand finale, thrilling motorcycle stunts were performed by Army personnel, capturing everyone's attention. The skies were graced by a spectacular aerial display, featuring both imported aircraft such as Jaguars, Rafales, and Sukhois, as well as indigenous ones like Rudra, Dhruv, Abhimanyu, and Tejas. The highlight of the day was the unveiling of the newly commissioned "Vayu Putra" supersonic jets. These fifth-generation Advanced Medium Combat Fighter jets, known as AMCA, were manufactured domestically and boasted cutting-edge stealth capabilities and a powerful 110-kilounit, Mark-2-grade engine, developed by General Electric Co. They were on par with international counterparts like the American F-35, Chinese Chengdu J-20, and Russian Sukhoi-57.

This concluded the grand Republic Day celebrations.

That evening, the President hosted a state dinner, inviting not only the Prime Minister and cabinet ministers but also high-ranking officers from the Army, Navy, Air Force, Police, and Paramilitary forces. Chief Security Advisor Radhakrishnan and Buddhadev Trital were among the guests. The Home Minister had excused himself due to health reasons. The atmosphere was relaxed and informal, with even the wives of dignitaries in attendance. Official matters were scarcely discussed, and it was past 11 p.m. when the event concluded. Vinaya and Vijaya, who had assisted, were on their feet all evening. Vinaya insisted that Mr. and Mrs. Trital spend the night at the Rashtrapati Bhavan and made suitable arrangements for them, a suggestion that the President endorsed. Since January 26th fell on a Saturday that year, Trital faced no work-related pressure the next day, which was a Sunday, although he would have to attend to official calls.

Before retiring for the night, the President requested Buddhadeva to join him in a room and inquired, "What prompted your departure from your seat?"

Buddhadeva sensed that the President had an inkling of the situation and replied, "A group of three potential suicide attackers had infiltrated the grounds. Since we had received prior intelligence, I had positioned our personnel strategically, with plainclothes agents keeping a vigilant eye. They had identified three individuals who had passed security checks, indicating they weren't carrying weapons. Although they were seated in the distant rows, they frequented the temporary bathrooms. These restrooms had undergone thorough checks."

"Why weren't they apprehended earlier?" queried the President.

Trital explained, "They possessed VIP passes, and taking them into custody prematurely would have caused a commotion and drawn excessive attention."

"So, what happened then?"

"Well, a bit farther away, there was a refreshments area where drones were delivering food from a nearby hotel. Our agents observed that these three individuals were continuously eyeing the drones. Consequently, our agents began inspecting each drone landing. This irritated the canteen manager, fearing a shortage of supplies, but our agents had no choice."

The President listened intently.

"I was aware of all this from my seat. But when I received word that one of the suspects had approached the canteen manager, I intervened and detained them. We silenced them with rags and placed them in a van. Guards were stationed around the canteen, and we took the canteen manager into custody only after the event concluded."

"Were the drones meant to transport weapons and ammunition?"

"Yes, although I doubt the canteen manager was aware. The plan was to redirect the drones toward the bathrooms and seize the weaponry."

The President sighed, "Good Lord! What's our plan of action now?"

"First, we need to ascertain who recommended these three for VIP passes. We suspect it's one of the twenty members of parliament from the Hyderabad political party supporting the government from the outside."

"Next, we must scrutinize the credentials of the food supplier agency and the canteen itself. Additionally, we need to identify the vulnerabilities in our intelligence system. As of now, the media is unaware of the incident, and we must ensure it remains that way. I've instructed the Information Ministry to keep this under wraps. We'll require the cooperation of the Ministry of Home Affairs."

The President remarked, "Extreme caution is imperative from now on."

"Absolutely, Sir," replied Trital.

"Now, get some rest. You must be exhausted."

Trital thanked him, and both retired to their respective bedrooms.

Vijaya was still awake when Trital entered the bedroom.

"What happened today?" Vijaya inquired.

"Nothing," Trital responded.

"I'm sure there's more to it, or else Jijaji wouldn't have called you aside."

"Look, I can't discuss every official matter with you."

Vijaya persisted, "I believe your life is in danger, or you're putting yourself at risk. I know that. You've lived as a spy in Pakistan; what more can I say?"

"Listen, I can't delve into everything about my past in Pakistan with you."

"Yes, I understand, I mustn't mention Pakistan. But even so..."

"Even so, what?"

"When I bring up Gujranwala or Kahuta, you visibly change."

"That's not true."

"I know there's a mystery there, something you're not telling me."

"Didn't I just mention that I can't share all official matters with you?"

"Not official matters, but surely you can talk about personal experiences."

"There's nothing personal to discuss."

"Alright," Vijaya acquiesced, "Let's go to sleep."

Yet, Vijaya remained convinced that there was a secret her husband was unwilling to share with her.

&&&&&

02.02.2032

There was a Cabinet meeting in the PMO today. All ministers, except three, were present. The three ministers, who were out of Delhi, had asked forpermission to join the meeting via Zoom conference. Seated to the right of the Prime Minister was Subhash Singh, the finance minister, who held the most senior position in the cabinet. Next to him were Ravindra Prasad, the defence minister, Venkatappaiyya, the Agriculture Minister, Kalavati, the Minister for Social Justice, and Riyaz Mehmood, the education minister. Avdhesh Singh, the Home Minister, was seated to the left of the Prime Minister, while to his immediate left were Basavraj Patil, the External Affairs Minister, Manohar Reddy, the Highways Minister, Bhavna Shinde, the Minister for Communication and IT, S.Subramaniam, the Railway Minister, Salma Heptullah, the Women and Child Welfare Minister, Arvind Kumar, the Minister for Heavy Industries, Shamrao Patil, the Foodgrains and Fertilizers Minister, and Kamlesh Yadav, the Trade and Textiles Minister. Rakesh Pilot, Minister in the Prime Minister's Office (PMO) responsible for the North Eastern Region, sat next to Subhash Singh, near the Prime Minister. The three ministers who joined via Zoom were Joginder Kaur, the Minister of Information and broadcasting, Nambudripad, the Law Minister, and Tribhuvan Singh, the Minister for Civil Aviation.

This government came to power in the mid-term polls held in the previous year in 2031. Rajendra Kaul's Bharatiya Lok Shakti Party(Indian people-powerparty()BLP) formed a minority government with the support of other parties. Pratibha Kaul Khan led the party, while her husband Javed Khan, previously involved in a land scandal, had been released on parole.

While most Cabinet ministers belonged to the BLP, there were representatives from other parties, such as Kalavati from the Dalit Samman Party, S. Subramaniam from the Tamil Munetra Party, Kamlesh Yadav from the Bihar Jana Shakti Party, and Joginder Kaur from the Punjab Kisan Party. Members of other parties held positions as Ministers of State.

Rajendra Kaul, with his fair complexion, still appeared youthful despite being in his sixties. He was always impeccably dressed in formal suits and shoes and possessed a deep knowledge of various subjects. Subhash Singh, at the age of seventy-nine, looked elderly but brought invaluable administrative experience to the table. He preferred traditional Indian attire, typically wearing a white kurta-pyjama and jacket. His eyes remained sharp behind his glasses, and he often paused before speaking.

In contrast, Home Minister Avdhesh Singh spoke rapidly and fluently in both English and Hindi. His prominent eagle nose contrasted with his short neck and small ears. He had a penchant for clothing, sometimes donning Western attire and at other times traditional Indian wear.

Ravindra Prasad, hailing from a humble background in Bihar, had worked his way up the political ladder through perseverance. He possessed a strong physique but a compassionate heart, making it challenging to decipher his thoughts.

The first item on the agenda was the situation in Arunachal Pradesh, where the Chinese had made a ten-kilometre incursion. Despite improved relations between India and China in recent years, this act of aggression required a response. Subhash Singh expressed his confusion about China's actions, given their amicable relations.

Trade and Textiles Minister Kamlesh Yadav added, "We've offered them export discounts and reduced customs duties."

All were in agreement that military forces from other parts of the country needed to be redeployed to Arunachal Pradesh. However, Defence Minister Ravindra Prasad raised a concern, mentioning the presence of Pakistani and Taliban forces in Kashmir. He emphasized that withdrawing troops from Punjab and Kashmir would create vulnerabilities.

Subhash Singh concurred, "Yes, that's a valid point."

Home Minister Avdhesh Singh proposed, "Let's recall CRF and BSF units deployed in various states for maintaining law and order. We can retain only what's absolutely necessary."

Defence Minister Prasad suggested, "The southern regions are relatively peaceful now. We can bring back some units from there, as well as from Maharashtra, Madhya Pradesh, Rajasthan, Chhattisgarh, and Orissa."

The Prime Minister agreed, nodding his head. He appointed a three-member committee, consisting of Avdhesh Singh and Ravindra Prasad, chaired by Subhash Singh, with instructions to submit their report in two days. Additionally, they were tasked with assessing the situation in Kashmir and suggesting any necessary tactical improvements. This decision ensured that the three senior ministers, often with differing views, would collaborate for this cause, although the Prime Minister was aware of their individual reservations.

Next on the agenda was a discussion about the law-and-order situation. There was general satisfaction that conditions were improving in Gujarat and West Bengal.

The Cabinet then moved on to the topic of nationalization. It was decided to form a committee to oversee the re-nationalization of Railways, Banks, and Textile Mills. The Prime Minister took the lead and formed three committees under his chairmanship, one for each sector, involving various ministries. He set a one-month deadline to carry out the necessary actions and directed relevant orders to be issued to the concerned ministries.

The discussion then shifted to how to respond to the questions raised by the opposition parties during the forthcoming Budget Session. Kamlesh Yadav emphasized the need to counter the opposition, especially due to ongoing troubles in Bihar, where his brother Suresh Yadav served as Chief Minister. The challenges faced by Suresh Yadav were detailed, and everyone listened attentively.

The Prime Minister was well aware that the Chief Opposition Party had been restless since losing power in 2029. The RashtriyaVicharmanch Party/National Thinking-tank party (RVP) had held power for several years and now found themselves frustrated. This frustration led them to challenge the ruling party at every turn, which included PM Kaul's Party and other parties in power in states like Bihar. The PM cautioned his Cabinet ministers to exercise caution, knowing that the RVP had a knack for quickly uncovering corruption cases within their party. It was likely that they had informants or loyalists within the bureaucracy.

Minister Rakesh Pilot then asked if anyone had any additional matters to discuss with the Prime Minister. The Minister from Tamil Nadu raised concerns about a fertilizer shortage in the state and requested additional supply. The Prime Minister promptly issued orders for immediate action.

The ministers expressed their gratitude to the Prime Minister, and the meeting concluded. Rakesh Pilot was tasked with calling a press conference to brief the media on the decisions made during the meeting.

&&&&&

05.02.2032

In the basement of an opulent mansion in Kabul, Razia Begum and Nadira Begum were having a private conversation. Their masters were away at that time, leaving the house under constant surveillance by CCTV cameras. The only discreet place for them to gossip was a corner in the basement, permeated by the strong scent of marijuana. Weapons, gunpowder, and other arms were scattered around the basement, mostly near the staircase. There was a room filled with opium, along with more weapons and hand bombs stored there.

Razia inquired, "How are you feeling today?"

Nadira replied, "I'm much better now. Undergoing an abortion is never easy. I can't fathom why they don't opt for a hysterectomy instead."

Raziya said, "Nurse Rashida must have visited you and provided the necessary medications. You'll start feeling better in a few days."

Nadira sighed, "Yes, Nurse Rashida does make regular visits, but on the occasions, she misses, we are left without birth control pills and have to endure the consequences. Whether we take the pills or not, suffering seems inevitable."

Razia agreed, "Indeed, these birth control pills often result in stomach discomfort. And then, they coerce us into consuming foreign liquor. To make matters worse, they take all sorts of Viagra pills and use our bodies as they please."

Nadira confessed, "Sometimes, I feel like grabbing a weapon and ending it all. But there are moments when I hold on to hope, the hope of escaping one day and reuniting with my son."

Razia shared her thoughts, "As for me, I can never hope to see anyone again, except perhaps in the afterlife (*Jannat*). I did want to end it all too, but not now. I want to do something different before my time comes."

Nestled in the mansion were three brothers: Afzal Khan, Ashiq Khan, and Salman Khan. They had various business ventures, some in common and others separate, and their bond of brotherhood was unbreakable. Afzal Khan, the eldest among them, was the leader.

In 1995, at just fifteen years old, Afzal Khan had joined the Taliban during the height of their movement. Now, at 52 years old, he remained a formidable force, capable of taking on multiple men single-handedly. He had eliminated countless adversaries and was the linchpin of the drug trafficking enterprise, extending his influence to multiple countries and establishing a thriving narcotics trade in Africa. He enjoyed political protection and had even taught himself English through private lessons. In Afghanistan, he typically wore traditional Afghan attire*PerahanTunban*, which consisted of loose tunic, pantsand turban, often complemented with a sheep fur *Karakul* cap or a *Chapan* coat in winter. Abroad, he occasionally donned suits, and anything seemed to suit his imposing 6.5-foot-tall, well-built frame. Despite his fair and scarred complexion, his eyes bore a cruel and fierce demeanour.

His carnal desires matched his physical prowess, and he had an appetite for expensive foreign liquors and various meats. He was insatiable in his pursuit of women, adhering to a primitive and archaic view of women as objects of pleasure.

Ashiq Khan shared many traits with his older brother. Though not as physically robust, he was tall with a muscular build. His indulgence in food and drink had started to show, with an expanding girth and belly.

He typically wore Afghan clothing and primarily handled domestic affairs while assisting his elder brother.

Salman, the youngest at forty, was slender and full of energy. He held a government position in the Intelligence department of the Home Ministry, wielding considerable influence that he used to benefit his family's businesses. His attire varied, from Afghan clothing to Western suits.

The three brothers jointly owned an estate near Asadabad, where they cultivated marijuana and opium. Their harvest was subject to Business Receipt tax and hefty export duties, but it remained an exceedingly lucrative enterprise. The family's primary residence was in a village near Asadabad. Shahrukh Khan, Afzal Khan's son, managed the operations in Asadabad. Afzal Khan's wife, Aseefa, kept a watchful eye not only on the business but also on her two sisters-in-law, whom she managed with diplomacy and pretended to be warm and affectionate toward. Saira, Salman's wife, was the youngest sister-in-law and particularly beautiful, requiring extra attention from Aseefa. Although Salman spent most of his time in Kabul with Raziya, who was even more stunning, he occasionally visited the family home to see his daughter Salma.

Razia and Nadira were engrossed in their conversation when the doorbell rang upstairs, signalling the arrival of masters by Shama Didi. Hastily, they made their way upstairs with some refreshments. Ashiq and Salman, the brothers, had entered the house. The women quickly stepped forward to offer them a glass of water.

Shama Didi inquired, "What flavour of sherbet would you prefer?" However, the men preferred alcohol, and preparations were underway to serve them their preferred liquor.

&&&&&

09.02.2032

Three days had passed since Superintendent of Police, Bhargav, had arrived in Hyderabad from Uttar Pradesh. His team of five officers had checked into various hotels and were conducting a covert investigation. Two of them had the privilege of concealing their identities, while the remaining three were tasked with visiting several offices as part of the probe. These officers carried copies of a letter that had already been received by the Director General of Police (DGP) and the Chief Secretary of Telangana, which they presented at the various offices they visited.

One of the offices under scrutiny was the government registrar's office for Charitable Trusts. The officer in charge initially declined to share any information with Police Inspector Shyam Prasad, as he had not received authorization from higher authorities. Eventually, he agreed to forward a copy of the letter authorizing the investigation to his superior. Only after receiving approval, he wouldprovide the requested information. Given the time this process would take, he asked Shyam Prasad to return the following week. Similar encounters with resistance were faced by the other four investigating officers, prompting the entire team to temporarily withdraw, with plans to resume the inquiry in 15-20 days.

Shyam Prasad's specific task was to identify the names of trustees and the sources of funding for several Trusts. The ostensible reason for this investigation was national security.

However, there was significant pushback from the Hyderabad government in sharing information about certain Trusts due to their political affiliations. The Deccan Awaam Party had gained substantial influence in the northern states of India. Many members of this party were associated with Trusts, and the sources of their funding were closely guarded secrets. Any leak of this information could have dire consequences for the Trust officials. While they enjoyed protection from powerful figures in the government, public exposure through the media would create a storm.

The Intelligence Bureau (IB) of the Government of India had issued reports indicating threats to the life of Uttar Pradesh Chief Minister Mahant Surajnath. The Anti-Terrorist Squad (ATS) in Uttar Pradesh had been actively investigating and had discovered links between certain Trusts in Uttar Pradesh and Hyderabad. Superintendent Bhargav's team was in Hyderabad to delve deeper into these connections. However, their progress in Hyderabad had been limited, and they had temporarily suspended their mission, informing the Uttar Pradesh DGP of their situation.

The Chief Minister of Uttar Pradesh belonged to the Rashtriya Vichar Manch Party (RVP). Until 2029, the RVP held power at the Centre, and Mahant Surajnath enjoyed the cooperation of all central institutions. However, since 2029, he had encountered difficulties, with some of his requests being disregarded. He was re-elected in 2031 in a fiercely contested election, with heavy security measures in place to maintain law and order. Negative campaigning against him and opposition from the

Bharatiya Lok Shakti Party (BLP) and other state governments led by the BLP and DeshbandhuSwabhiman Party (Deswap Party) had made his victory a narrow one. Despite securing only 205 seats in the Vidhan Sabha, he managed to reach the magic figure of 220 seats with the support of independent candidates and another party.

The Prime Minister had made concerted efforts to bring his Bharatiya Lok Shakti Party to power in Uttar Pradesh, but Mahant Surajnath had thwarted all attempts. Pratibha Kaul Khan, the President of BLP and the PM's sister, had spent three months in UP in a high-stakes contest. The PM's BLP and the Deswa Party had joined forces, but the Mahant had proven to be a formidable adversary. His victory had elevated his status within the RVP, causing some central leaders in his own party to envy him. He had become a thorn in the side of the Central Government, especially since the election highlighted the importance of maintaining control over Uttar Pradesh, the state with the most parliamentary seats in India.

Mahant Surajnath was a influential religious leader who made frequent pilgrimages to Kashi-Vishwanath and Ayodhya. He lived a life of celibacy and detachment from worldly desires, focusing on the welfare of the people and earning popularity among the common public. Clad in saffron robes, he possessed a well-toned, healthy physique.

Although he had dealt with threats to his life before with composure, he was slightly concerned about the recent threats, particularly because they had been brought to his attention by a central agency like the IB. His party members shared his worries. The gravity of the threats had prompted the investigation, but so far, not much progress had been made.

&&&&&

11.02.2032

Hotel Paradise, a luxurious five-star establishment, graced the bustling city of Mumbai, located near the picturesque Worli Sea Face. Inside one of its well-appointed suites, a discreet meeting was taking place between two prominent leaders from Maharashtra: Ajay Patil, the head of the Chhatrapati Sena Party, and Dilip Deshmukh, the Chief of the Maharashtravadi Party. Although there was no veil of secrecy shrouding this meeting, it had managed to avoid media attention.

Ajay Patil, dressed impeccably in a formal suit, had arrived first, with Dilip Deshmukh following him by a mere ten minutes. Upon entering the suite, Deshmukh warmly embraced Ajay Patil. Patil, with his rotund build, round face, and dark complexion, exuded a refreshing charm.

Deshmukh, on the other hand, was tall and possessed a slender frame. He moved with a sense of agility and grace. A seasoned politician, he had a deliberate way of speaking, carefully weighing his words before uttering them—a trait evident to anyone in his presence.

Both leaders had politely requested their personal secretaries to step aside, allowing them to engage in a private conversation. The two secretaries had made themselves comfortable in the hotel's coffee shop.

"Deshmukh Saheb, it's a pleasure to meet in person after such a long time," Ajay Patil remarked.

"Yes, Patil Saheb, I believe our last encounter was during Diwali," Deshmukh replied.

"That's right. Most of our discussions happen over the phone. Face-to-face meetings like this are becoming increasingly rare," Patil noted.

Deshmukh mused, "Indeed, technology has made communication so convenient. Video calls on large screens have made face-to-face interactions a rarity."

"Earlier, we could only make video calls on mobile phones. Now, we can do so on television screens. It's incredibly convenient," Patil concurred.

Their private secretaries had thoughtfully arranged for refreshments, including food and drinks. Patil broached the subject, asking, "Shall we begin with some wine?"

Deshmukh suggested, "Let's start with a cold beverage, perhaps a fruit punch?"

"A fruit punch it is, then," Patil agreed.

Ajay Patil promptly fetched two bottles of fruit punch, placing them on the coffee table. A bowl of salted cashew nuts and almonds awaited them. As they savoured their drinks, Patil casually inquired, "How is your son?"

His intent was not to cause discomfort but to engage in casual conversation. Deshmukh took it in stride and replied that his son Kunal was currently touring Marathwada in preparation for the upcoming Zilla Parishad elections.

Patil added, "It's good to get back to work after such a long time."

Deshmukh concurred, saying, "Yes, I agree."

Both leaders were subtly avoiding a significant issue that loomed between them. A year earlier, when efforts were underway to include

Kunal Deshmukh in the cabinet, he had unfortunately been caught using drugs during a party on a cruise ship, accompanied by several girls. He had been arrested by a central investigative agency, the Narcotics Control Bureau (NCB), and the incident had garnered extensive media coverage. With some pressure from the central government and substantial bribes, Kunal had managed to secure bail. At the time, Kunal had been newly married, and his bride had sought a divorce. Ajay Patil had assisted Deshmukh during this crisis, and while he didn't wish to remind Deshmukh of his help, he couldn't help but allude to it.

Deshmukh reciprocated with a casual inquiry of his own, "How is Sadhana?" referring to Patil's daughter.

"She's doing well. She's delighted with her appointment as a Minister of State. Her MBA from the USA makes her confident in managing her ministry," Patil shared.

"That's excellent to hear," Deshmukh replied.

Now, they began to sip their wine, both eager to broach the main topic of discussion. However, each awaited the other to initiate the conversation. Eventually, Ajay Patil took the lead. "Have you paid a visit to Delhi recently?"

Deshmukh responded, "Yes, I was in Delhi, but..."

"The Home Minister was away on a tour of the northeast, so you couldn't meet him?" Patil interjected.

Deshmukh nodded, saying, "That's correct. So, what should be our next course of action?"

"That's a decision we need to make together," Patil replied, emphasizing their shared responsibility.

"Indeed, we must act in unison. It's been years since we found ourselves entangled in these investigations by the Enforcement Directorate (ED) and the Central Bureau of Investigation (CBI)," Deshmukh acknowledged.

"Yes, we must find a way to extricate ourselves from this situation promptly," Patil stressed.

Deshmukh proposed, "Let's schedule meetings with everyone. We can request appointments for the second week of March, and they can provide convenient dates."

"By 'everyone,' do you mean the Home Minister, Finance Minister, Prime Minister, and Pratibha Kaul Khan, the President of BLP?" Patil sought clarification.

Deshmukh affirmed, "Yes, precisely. And meeting Pratibha Kaul Khan may require exerting political pressure, if you catch my drift."

Patil concurred, "Of course. Our parties hold positions in both Central and State governments, after all."

"Meeting everyone will inevitably alert the media," Deshmukh pointed out.

"Agreed. We can divert their attention with other stories, such as farmer suicides, the heavy debt burden on the Maharashtra government, or the production of new electric armoured tanks," Patil suggested.

"You're absolutely right. To disentangle ourselves from the ED and CBI, we must take a proactive stance," Deshmukh emphasized.

Deshmukh concluded, "So, it's settled. I'll instruct my party's MP at the Centre to book Maharashtra House for our stay in Delhi. You can do the same with your party."

Patil readily agreed to this plan, and they departed from the hotel separately. Both leaders were visibly agitated because the cases against them had reached the charge sheet stage. However, now that their coalition government had come to power, they felt a renewed sense of confidence. The previous administration led by Lalita Chatterjee, which also relied on their party's support, had shown little interest in resolving their legal issues. Deshmukh and Patil had made numerous appeals to her, but she had remained stubborn. With Rajendra Kaul as Prime Minister, they were more hopeful of obtaining favourable outcomes in their cases.

&&&&&

19.02.2032

The Chief National Security Advisor's office was located within the Prime Minister's complex in Central Vista, where Radhakrishnan and Trital were currently in a meeting. They were engaged in discussing several pressing national issues, including conflicts in the northeast region, a letter from the Chief Minister of Uttar Pradesh, Chinese incursions in Arunachal Pradesh, and the looming Taliban threat.

Radhakrishnan possessed an impressive personality. He had a slender physique and a fair complexion, which was somewhat unusual for someone hailing from South India, specifically Kerala. His convent education had bestowed upon him a remarkable command of the English language. Topping the Indian Administrative Services (IAS) examination, he was erudite, well-informed on a variety of subjects, and a voracious reader.

Throughout the day, Radhakrishnan and Trital were engrossed in reviewing dossiers related to these pressing matters. Periodically, Radhakrishnan would summon his secretary to prepare documents, while Trital would request his own secretary for additional papers.

Their busy schedules had caused them to overlook lunch, but a timely reminder from Trital's secretary prompted them to open their lunch boxes and sit down to eat. Radhakrishnan, a pure vegetarian, declined the egg curry from Trital's lunch box, and they each consumed their respective meals.

Trital remarked, "The last three years have been incredibly challenging, Sir."

Radhakrishnan agreed, saying, "Yes, Trital. Governments change, people change, and policies change, but individuals like us who retain our positions must constantly adapt to the preferences of our superiors. It's quite the exercise."

"It's peculiar that we're still in our roles. Perhaps they've struggled to find replacements for us, or we've managed to earn their trust," Trital suggested.

Radhakrishnan pondered, "You are the President of India's co-brother, so perhaps they hesitated to remove you."

"Maybe," Trital acknowledged.

"By the way, what about the incident on January 26th? Whose recommendation allowed the suicide squad access, and what actions have been taken since?" Radhakrishnan inquired.

"They are still detained under the national security law. However, the Member of Parliament from Uttar Pradesh who endorsed their entry passes had to be released. He belongs to the Hyderabad political party, which supports the central government. The Home Minister advised us to let the matter regarding him slide, as the political party in Hyderabad had already issued a warning to the MP."

"It's regrettable, but there's little we can do," Radhakrishnan lamented. "We've compromised on matters of great national security multiple times over the past three years. The political landscape has been in turmoil during this period; we should reflect on these times."

He recalled some incidents and discussed them with Trital.

The election in 2029 had been historic. RVP (RashtriyaVicharmanch Party) was in power at the time of the elections. Nation-building activities were in full swing and the national infrastructure had changed tremendously. A network of airports, highways, expressways, and factories was created. Things that were earlier imported from China were now being manufactured indigenously. The nation was becoming self-reliant on lithium batteries, semi-conductors, solar panels, chemical intermediates and pharmaceutical products. The Opposition parties could not tolerate the privatization of the defense sector and banks. As if this wasn't enough, Uniform Civil Code had been implemented. This gave the opposition parties the ammunition to fight their battle—they claimed that because of the Code, Secularism was in danger and instigated communal riots everywhere. In 2028, they had organized long lasting agitations in many places. The consequence of all this was an impending change in power at the Centre. The real catalyst in the situation was the sting operation on the sons of two ministers. The son of Manoj Mitkari, the highways minister and the son of Uday Patel, the defense minister, had in an inebriated state, blurted out something that exposed the corruption in the government. The matter was given a lot of media coverage. The image of the Prime Minister suffered a setback. The PM, Surendra Dhami would not have given up his power easily, but he lost badly in the elections.

No single party received a clear majority in the 2029 elections. The BLP (Bharatiya Lok Shakti Party) got 152 seats and the RVP got 164 seats out of 542 seats. Many Regional parties had captured other seats. The real winner turned out to be Lalita Chatterjee, whose DeshbandhuSwabhimaan Party, DESWAP won 76 seats. They had made headway in West Bengal, Bihar Orissa, Assam and the north eastern states and few other places. BLP, under the leadership of Rajendra Kaul, could not form the government. Lalitaji had managed to unite the regional parties and form a powerful coalitionwith 135 members.

Lalita Chatterjee had a striking personality. Only five feet in height, she always wore a white saree and simple chappals on her feet. But she was a gifted orator and a feisty woman and was nicknamed 'Mulukh Maidan Tof(Cannon). She would lace her speeches with quotes from writers and poets. She knew by heart poems of Poet Laureate Rabindranath Tagore. She had read the writings of several Western politicians and administrators. She would refer to these writings in her speeches and so she was the darling of the intelligentsia.

The SamajikSamarasata Party of Avdhesh Singh had been merged with the BLP and then dissolved. Rajendra Kaul had to give his support to Lalitaji from the outside. Many could not understand this change of stance. Many thought that had he given open support, Rajendra Kaul would have been the PM and Lalitaji the Deputy PM. But Rajendra Kaul's party, BLP had avoided even joining the cabinet. It was a strange coalition government that assumed power.

Meanwhile, ex-PM Surendra Dhami had unfortunately met with an accident and died thereof.

The RVP strength was going to dwindle then onwards.

Hence, Lalitaji had started keeping the RVP leaders on tenterhooks. She had the ED, CBI, NCB investigating cases against them. It was obvious that she was getting back at them for hounding her son Ashutosh Chatterjee during the previous regime of RVP. This did not go well with the public in general and her image began to suffer. The DESWAP and the RVP had taken to the streets. The RVP had launched protest marches and the DESWAP held meetings in support of the government. The newspapers were full of these events. Although the print media had gone digital, there was a sizeable number of newspaper- reading public. People were getting fed up with the news. The nation's economy was crumbling. Industrialists and businessmen were subjected to extortion and threats for funds. For this, DESWAP had opened offices in several cities. Many were suffering huge financial losses due to these extortions.

At this time, Pratibha Kaul, the President of BLP began nationwide tours, and especially concentrated on the southern states. She had begun to make an impression on the masses. While supporting Lalitaji's government from outside, she was also campaigning against Lalitaji. Lalitaji could not pull the leash on her, so she began to adopt her own election strategy. People felt that the present government would not last long and this is what happened in reality.

The government lasted for just twenty months. Lalitaji had introduced a different Citizenship Amendment Bill in the Parliament. It allowed the Rohingya and Afghan Muslims living in India, the facility to become Indian citizens. RVP party quickly took up this issue to start nationwide protests against the Bill. RVP leaders like the leader of the Opposition in Lok Sabha, Namrata Rupani, leader of opposition inRajyasabha, Rameshwar Singh, the RVP President Ashok Chadda, Dilip Wadhwa, Keshav Shah and Venkatraman were at the forefront of the protests. However, other leaders of the RVP, particularly theChief Ministersof the states likeMahant Surajnath CM of Uttar Pradesh, Pramod Joshi from Karnataka, Abhay Patel from Gujarat, Banwarilal Gupta from Rajasthan and Sundarlal Mishra from Madhya Pradesh did not actively take part in the agitation but gave their tacit support.

There was a lot of dissent amongst the BLP members. Avdhesh Singh and a few leaders were for the Bill while some senior leaders were against it. They felt that the Hindu masses would not favor the Bill and the RVP would get political advantage. It was better not to support the Bill. Lalitaji had tried her best to convince Rajendra Kaul and Pratibha Kaul Khan but to no avail. The BLP received the support of some other parties in the government. The Dalit Party, the Chhatrapati Sena, Punjab Kisan Party and the Tamil Munetra Party gave the BLP full support.

When the Bill was first introduced in the Lok Sabha, it created a furore. There was a lot of high- pitched drama in Parliament. The RVP had torn apart copies of the Bill and shouted slogans. BLP leaders appealed too Lalitaji to withdraw the Bill and save the government, but she had been adamant. Either she wanted to emerge as a global leader or because the Muslim voters held sway over her, or for reasons best known to her, she remained obstinate. She was defeated in the Lok Sabha and had to resign.

No Party had a clear majority. There was a tripartite division—The DESWAP, the BLP, and the RVP. President's Rule had to be imposed and it paved the way for re-elections.

The country went to the polls again in 2031. The BLP won a decent number of seats, 221 in all. Lalitaji's party won only 17. The BLP had received huge support in the South from Telangana, Andhra Pradesh, Karnataka and Kerala. Since BLP had an alliance with Tamil Nadu Munetra, it was victorious in TN as well. In Maharashtra, Gujarat, and Rajasthan BLP had outnumbered RVP. In Madhya Pradesh, Uttarakhand, Uttar Pradesh, and Himachal Pradesh, RVP had triumphed over BLP. Because of alliances with Parties in Punjab, Orissa Bihar, and some northeastern states, BLP was able to garner enough support. RVP ended up with just 172 seats.

The BLP had come to power and formed the government but they were still in a minority. The allied parties would sometimes threaten to withdraw support or sometimes insist on some issue. The Deccan Awaam Party was not part of the government, but it gave external support, so despite Deccan Awaam Party's objectionable activities, the government could not take any action against it.

The RVP had a fair success with the constraints. They had hopes of winning in the next elections so they were picking up public issues and raising debates in Parliament and the Rajya Sabha over them. The cases slammed on them under Lalitaji's rule was also a sore point with them. The BLP had to cope not only with this nuisance by RVP but also the looming attacks of China, Pakistan and theTaliban government in Afghanistan.

Radhakrishnan and Trital were discussing all these matters.

Radhakrishnan said, "I think we are going through a very difficult period."

"Yes, we are, but I am sure we will find a way out all this mess," replied Trital.

Radhakrishnan doubted it, "Our national and international security is under a serious threat. We have to be extremely watchful at all times."

Trital said with confidence, "Ataljee , late Prime Minister used to say that our country is a Super country (Rashtra- Purush), Our country will prove more than a match for all of them."

"Let us hope so. By the way, please do not randomly use quotes by our national leaders like you did just now."

"Sorry sir. I dare to say such things only to you, that too only after years of association with you. I keep my mouth shut otherwise."

"That's Okay."

The meeting on that day ended on this note.

&&&&&

24.02.2032 to 26.02.2032

Superintendent of Police Bhargav arrived in Hyderabad from Uttar Pradesh to resume his investigation. This time, his team had secured the cooperation of the National Security Advisor, Trital. Mahant Surajnath had briefed the President of India about the matter, which prompted the PMO and NSA to be informed. With Trital's involvement, the Home Ministry of Telangana was more willing to assist. These procedural steps had consumed a considerable amount of time, delaying SP Bhargav's arrival in Hyderabad.

He initiated his investigation based on information from the NIA and the Uttar Pradesh ATS, which had apprehended some sleeper cell members in Rampur and Gorakhpur. Initially uncooperative, these individuals started revealing information when threatened with raids on their relatives, property confiscation, and property demolition.

The 'Bewaa Janana Khushamadi Trust' (Widow Welfare Trust) in Hyderabad came under scrutiny. SP Bhargav's team, with the necessary permissions from the Telangana Home Ministry, conducted raids on the trust's offices. Enforcement Directorate officers were also involved, and four teams conducted simultaneous raids on the trust's four offices, two in Hyderabad, one in Secunderabad, and one in Khammam. The teams discreetly seized numerous documents and made photocopies before the media could catch wind of the operation. Members of the Deccan Awaami Party rushed to the locations but were halted by CRPF personnel. This intervention by a central agency like the CRPF would later lead to a heated dispute between the Telangana Home Ministry and the National Security Advisor.

The trust received funds from various sources, including foreign organizations and individuals and organizations within India. A list of sixteen prominent donors had been compiled, with nine of them residing in Hyderabad. These nine individuals were summoned for questioning, causing a sense of unease among the city's elite business class.

SP Bhargav's team was tasked with bringing all the gathered data back to Lucknow and awaiting further instructions on the course of action. Given that this was an inter-state matter involving two states governed by opposing political parties, any actions were expected to face delays and generate political manoeuvring and criticism. Nonetheless, the terrorists' morale had suffered a temporary setback, and the political atmosphere in Hyderabad was heating up.

&&&&&

27.02.2032

In Kabul, Nurse Rashida arrived to deliver the monthly supply of birth control pills, a routine she often carried out. On this particular day, the male household members were absent, and after a thorough security check, the guards allowed her entry. Nadira, who was experiencing a stomach ache, rested, while Raziya and Shama Didi were present. They guided her upstairs through the staircase situated to the right of the drawing room.

Expressing her urgency, Rashida remarked, "I'm a bit pressed for time today."

"Please be patient," responded Shama Didi. "I'll fetch you some snacks and a refreshing sherbet."

Curious to hear any updates, Raziya inquired, "What information do you have for us today, Rashida?"

"Ensure the CCTV is turned off, or else our conversation might be inadvertently recorded," Rashida cautioned.

"Of course, I've disabled it. Please share your news quickly, before Shama Didi returns," replied Raziya, displaying her impatience. Raziya, who had previously worked as a receptionist in a large hospital, was well-versed in handling CCTV systems and computers.

Rashida continued, "We need to exercise extreme caution now. Government agents have caught wind that sensitive information is being leaked. They are actively searching for the source, and houses like yours have not yet been thoroughly investigated."

"I hope you're not in any danger," expressed Raziya.

"My dear Rajjo, we are fully aware of the risks associated with this job. These heartless individuals brutally took the lives of our family members right before our eyes. They spared us only because of our appearance. My ten-year-old son was right there..." Tears welled up in Rashida's eyes as she recounted this painful memory.

Raziya embraced Rashida and shared, "My son was just five years old. I miss him terribly." Tears flowed down Raziya's cheeks as well.

"Let's compose ourselves," urged Rashida. "Shama Didi will be coming up shortly. Kindly pass me the piece of paper." Raziya tucked the note into the medicine packet that Rashida held.

After wiping away their tears, both women regained their composure. Rashida retrieved the packet of pills and handed them to Raziya. She had also brought vitamin tablet bottles for Nadira. Shama Didi offered Rashida a plate of fried chickpeas and a glass of sherbet. After enjoying the refreshments, Rashida bid them farewell.

&&&&&

28.02.2032

The central government's annual budget was presented on this date. This year, February 29th, which was a Sunday, led to a rare occurrence where the Lok Sabha and the Rajya Sabha convened on a Saturday, typically a parliamentary holiday.

With the Speaker of the Lok Sabha's approval, Subhash Singh, who had recently undergone heart surgery, delivered the budget speech from his seat. According to the fiscal report presented the previous day, the country's economic condition appeared robust. The GDP stood at a commendable 8.2%, and foreign currency reserves were ample. The budget aimed to appeal to both the common man and the middle class.

Substantial loan waivers were granted to farmers, and numerous agricultural development plans were outlined.

Tax reforms were announced to tighten the reins on tax evaders. A software system had been developed to track the tax liabilities, wealth, and shares held by each family member. This would reveal the family's overall tax liability and any instances of tax evasion. It was anticipated that this reform would trouble several affluent individuals and politicians. However, the Reserve Bank had long been working on this issue, and it was a much-anticipated reform.

The Defence Budget received a significant boost, and the proposal to manufacture electric armoured vehicles and tanks in Nagpur and Jabalpur received approval.The budget also included provisions for soft loan facilities for the unemployed, and start-ups could access interest-free loans for up to three years. Tax incentives were offered for solar, hydrogen, and electric vehicles, and factories using these alternative energy sources were eligible for tax rebates.

The Prime Minister asserted that this budget would set the nation on a path to prosperity, while opposition parties argued that the unemployment situation would remain unchanged. Heated debates on the budget's pros and cons dominated television channels that night.

&&&&&

05.03.2032 to 09.03.2032

On the 5th of March, a video went viral on television channels in India and abroad. The video depicted the former MP of the RVP (Rashtriya Vichar Manch Party), Suresh Dutt, in conversation with his party officials in Pune. Speculations arose that the video might have been created by one of his own party members, either voluntarily or for a bribe.

Suresh Dutt was notorious for his controversial remarks and had a penchant for seeking publicity by any means necessary. Despite warnings from his party seniors to refrain from making reckless comments, he paid no heed.

In the video, he was seen discussing China, Pakistan, and the Taliban with his party members. He praised the previous government for keeping China in check and claimed that the RVP government had repelled a Taliban attack five years ago, even downing their airplanes. While boasting, he criticized the present government, insinuating that it was helpless and vulnerable to Chinese and Taliban threats. He referred disrespectfully to the Prime Minister, saying, "This Rajendra Kaul is a useless fellow. He's incapable of defending the country. He must be removed somehow. If necessary, someone should 'takecare' of him."

The phrase "someone should 'take care' of him" caught the attention of all channels, although only one or two bothered to show the complete video. The country reacted strongly, with protests erupting everywhere. Over a hundred FIRs were filed against Suresh Dutt, and arrest warrants were issued from various locations.

Suresh Dutt went into hiding, and numerous agencies were on the lookout for him. He sought bail in the Supreme Court, leading to heated arguments between the opposing lawyers. The Supreme Court denied bail but transferred all the FIRs against him to Pune, withdrawing some charges.

This incident tarnished the reputation of the RVP. BLP party members organized protests outside RVP offices, with protestors in Lucknow pelting stones, causing significant damage. Police had to resort to baton charges to control the crowds, creating an atmosphere of unrest in the nation. Avdhesh Singh had previously established a group of young activists called the 'Social Equality Group' (SamajikSamrasta Dal or SASAD), initially operating only in Uttar Pradesh and Uttarakhand but later expanding throughout India. Avdhesh Singh's son, Raj Narayan Singh, held the position of Vice President in this group.

In response to SASAD, another group called the Hanuman Shakti Dal was formed, consisting of young activists, some of whom were RVP members. Suresh Dutt's remarks ignited a fierce rivalry between these groups, resulting in violent clashes that were difficult for the police to control. In states where RVP held power, SASAD members faced beatings, while in BLP-controlled states, Hanuman Dal activists received similar treatment from the police. Ultimately, both Rajendra Kaul and RVP President Ashok Chadda had to appeal publicly for peace.

The protests and clashes persisted until Suresh Dutt surrendered to the court. However, the situation calmed down once he was incarcerated, except for sporadic incidents, mostly instigated by Avdhesh Singh's son, Raj Narayan Singh.

RVP expelled Suresh Dutt from the party, but BLP leaders continued to seize the opportunity to tarnish RVP's image. News channels used this incident to debate Rajendra Kaul's competence, exposing his weaknesses and inefficiencies. Activists from the SamajikSamrasta Dal launched protests against these news channels, sparking nationwide debates on

Freedom of Expression and Tolerance, ultimately contributing to a state of unrest in the nation.

&&&&&

11.03.2032

As per the scheduled plan, Iliyas Zaibuddin waited in his room at Hotel Blooming Windows in Srinagar for the Zoom meeting to commence. At this moment, he was deeply contemplating the Kashmir issue and the Azad Kashmir organization. His organization had incited numerous uprisings in Kashmir, with many young individuals actively participating in these rebellions. Even though the situation in Kashmir had evolved significantly, there were still some who clung to their pro-Pakistan beliefs. They aspired for liberation from India, and some young men from various families had taken up arms as terrorists to achieve this goal. Tragically, they often lost their lives in anti-terrorist operations conducted by the Indian army. The families of these young militants harboured deep resentment against the army, and this cycle continued as more young men underwent training to become terrorists.

At this time, Kashmir had a tripartite government, led by Chief Minister Shahnaz Khan from the BLP party. The three parties did not share a common agenda, and the government operated on shaky ground. Two of the parties were restless, aiming for 'Azad Kashmir,' although they were aware that the Constitution did not permit this. Kashmir had two opposing viewpoints, with one faction advocating separation from India, while the other wished to remain within the Indian Union.

While several industries and businesses had thrived in Kashmir over the years, some had closed due to terrorist threats. Notably, the textile industry continued to flourish. Handlooms were a common sight in many households, and there was significant demand for Cashmere woollen clothing both domestically and internationally. These woollen and silk fabric industries, both cottage and factory-based, provided employment opportunities to locals. Additionally, three mobile assembly manufacturing units are operated, with two located in Jammu. The discovery of rare metal lithium in Kashmir led to mining operations and the establishment of lithium battery manufacturing facilities in three factories—two in Kashmir and one in the Jammu region. While several plastic industries had initially emerged but subsequently closed down due to security concerns, most thriving industries were situated in

Jammu and Ladakh, where terrorism was minimal, and young men from the valley sought employment.

The Central Government had also set up a Fertilizer Industry and a Railway Coach manufacturing factory in the region. International giants like Amazon and Alibaba had established depots in Buchpura and Hafizbaug in Srinagar, despite previous security incidents. These companies now operate under tight government-provided security. The presence of these depots had a positive impact on the local textile cottage industry and raised the standard of living for residents. Consequently, more than half the Kashmiri population did not desire separation from India, a matter of concern for Pakistan as they grappled with severe hunger and unemployment issues. Pakistan saw an opportunity to use the Taliban's assistance to gain control of Kashmir, with its well-established infrastructure, potentially improving Pakistan's economic situation. The Taliban, too, sought a chance to engage in battle after a period of inactivity, and this bleak situation gave rise to nefarious plots.

Iliyas attempted to initiate the Zoom meeting but encountered technical difficulties with the link, causing frustration. After some time, he successfully connected with Majid Khan in Kabul, but not with Lahore. Iliyas and Majid exchanged pleasantries until they managed to bring Ozair Bhai into the conversation from Lahore. Initially, they discussed the availability of mules and donkeys, as Iliyas mentioned that construction had begun at the Baramulla hotel site, and they needed mules for soil transportation. Ozair assured them of a ready supply of mules from Muzaffarabad, Abbotabad, and Skardu.

Majid Khan pointed out that many of these mules were their own, and they could send additional ones if necessary. They proceeded to discuss the mules' route, agreeing that Uri Road was the most suitable option. The mules would be dispatched in batches from different locations, with those in Skardu sent using whichever route was available. Iliyas mentioned that they had received ample funds from Kabul and Pakistan to support mule fodder and camping arrangements during the hotel construction.

Unbeknownst to them, an Intelligence Bureau (IB) agent was monitoring their conversation at Hotel Blooming Windows, not particularly interested in the mules but realizing that some nefarious plan was unfolding. The agent diligently recorded every word.

Subsequently, the three individuals discussed a "langar" (community kitchen). Uzair explained that a large langar was to be prepared in a mosque in Delhi, with lime juice served initially. While salt for the lime juice had already been sent, they needed to purchase lemons from a Delhi bazaar.

The IB agent inferred from their discussion on mules and lime juice that a sinister plot was being devised in Delhi. He intended to share these recordings with his superiors.

In Pakistan, a contact of Soshe Dayan was also recording this conversation, but it would take two days for Soshe Dayan to access it. Upon decoding the conversation, he wouldsuspectthat "mules" referred to terrorists from Kabul and Pakistan, indicating a looming threat to India. The mention of lime juice and langar suggested that the life of an important individual was in danger, possibly even that of the Indian Prime Minister. The reference to salt in the lime juice implied arms and weapons, and buying lemons in Delhi indicated a plan to approach the Prime Minister closely. The term "langar" hinted at the possibility of instigating widespread violence. The agent believed that this information needed to reach Trital promptly, but he lacked direct access and would have to relay it through Tel Aviv.

&&&&&

12.03.2032

At Prakash Reddy's residence in Hyderabad, Prakash, Aruna, and their daughter Swapna engaged in a conversation. Swapna inquired of her father Prakash whether he was facing any issues.

Aruna asked, "Why do you think that, dear?"

Swapna replied, "I can sense it. You seem tense."

Prakash responded, "No, it's not a major concern."

Swapna persisted, "There is something bothering you, isn't there? It's alright if you don't wish to share it with me."

Aruna adopted a conciliatory tone and said, "Well, there is a minor issue. Perhaps it's not a big problem, but it has made your dad quite restless."

Swapna interjected, "You can tell me if you want. I'm old enough to understand."

Prakash objected, "Don't trouble her."

Swapna insisted, "Why not? Am I not part of this family?"

Aruna tried to explain, "You see, we manage people's financial accounts. Money flows into and out of these accounts."

Prakash added, "When money is withdrawn from an account, the record only shows where it was paid or to whom it was paid, right?"

Swapna nodded in agreement.

Aruna continued, "Out of the many accounts we handle, we've been informed by an official that there are concerns about four of them."

Swapna asked, "What seems to be the problem?"

Prakash replied, "I don't believe there's a legal issue, but I have some doubts that there might be an issue."

Swapna urged, "Why don't you tell me the whole story?"

Aruna clarified, "There are four accounts with us that have raised suspicions. Authorities suspect that the money sent to two social organizations from these accounts may be used for purposes other than what is claimed."

Swapna inquired, "What other purposes?"

Prakash confessed, "Possibly for terrorist activities."

Swapna reacted, "That's dreadful. But you know there are strict laws against this, and bail is often denied."

Aruna exclaimed, "Oh my goodness!"

Prakash tried to justify, "My role as an accountant is to oversee their balance sheets, tax compliance, GST, income tax, customs tax, and so on. I'm not involved in their other activities."

Swapna empathized, "But, as you always say, there can be collateral damage, Dad. We can't predict what the police might do."

Aruna suggested, "Should we consider hiring a good lawyer?"

Swapna proposed, "Let me consult my senior advocate. You two should be cautious until then. Keep all the necessary documents ready and continue monitoring the account entries for that firm."

Prakash agreed to follow his daughter's advice.

That night, Ojas, Swapna's brother, approached her and said, "I overheard what you all were discussing."

Swapna inquired, "What did you overhear?"

Ojas responded, "You see, *Akka*..."

Swapna corrected him, "Not *Akka*, call me Sister."

"Okay, okay, Sister."

Swapna asked, "So, what did you overhear?"

Ojas explained, "I'm worried about Dad."

Swapna concurred, "So am I."

Ojas suggested, "I have an idea."

Swapna inquired, "What's your idea?"

Ojas mentioned, "Tricorder-X-3."

Swapna remembered, "Yes, we discussed it a few days ago."

Ojas reminded her, "Didn't you mention that your friend has one?"

Swapna acknowledged, "Yes, Ajita has one."

Ojas proposed, "Why don't we ask her to lend it to us?"

Swapna pondered, "I can try, but I'm not sure how to approach Dad about it."

Ojas suggested, "Let's tell him that we need to buy one for future use. Then we can say we borrowed Ajita's for a trial."

Swapna agreed, "That's a good idea. Dad won't suspect anything then."

Ojas shared, "I found information about Tricorder-X-3 on Google."

Swapna appreciated his effort, "Thank you. But I already know what it is. It's a device that can be connected to our mobile phones. It can measure our breath, conduct a retina scan, and take a blood sample. The blood sample is just a slight prick, and it's not invasive. It can provide information on twenty-four biomarkers like diabetes, heart problems, stroke risk, cataracts, lung conditions, and more. Dad might get annoyed and claim that he's perfectly healthy and doesn't need to know these markers."

Ojas offered a diplomatic solution, "Let's involve Mom in our plan. It'll make things easier. First, we can get tests done on Mom and then ask her to persuade Dad to get tested."

Swapna agreed, "That's a good idea. I'll talk to her tomorrow. We can try our plan this coming Sunday."

Ojas extended his hand, "Deal."

Swapna shook his hand, "Deal."

&&&&&

14.03.2032

Ajay Patil and Dilip Deshmukh convened a conference at the Maharashtra House (Sadan) in New Delhi, accompanied by two of their trusted members of the Lok Sabha/Parliament.

Dilip Deshmukh expressed, "I believe our mission won't be accomplished anytime soon."

Ajay Patil concurred, saying, "Even if Pratibha Kaul gave us a patient hearing, others have not granted us proper appointments. We might have to return after ten days."

Arvind Kolhe, the MP who had Deshmukh's full trust, assured, "Don't worry. I've been closely monitoring this entire situation. Subhash Singh, the finance minister, is a meticulous individual. He is always vigilant and insists on reviewing all the documents before taking any action."

Ajay Patil acknowledged, "Well, ultimately, we have to rely on him. The Income Tax department discovered assets worth 135 crores, including documents related to undisclosed properties. It's going to be challenging to extricate ourselves from this predicament."

Arvind Kolhe added, "Bharati Shinde's brother faced allegations of holding undisclosed wealth too, but his case was resolved long ago. Of course, she belongs to BLP Party and was even appointed as a cabinet minister."

Deshmukh commented, "Ah, yes."

Ajay Patil pondered, "I think it's time to consider the threat of withdrawing support from the Maharashtra state government."

Kolhe suggested, "As the Hindi saying goes, *'Tedhiungli se ghee nikalnapadega.'* (We have to find a clever way to do it.)"

Ajay Patil agreed, "We might need to level a corruption allegation against a minister in the Lok Sabha. That way, they will approach us for a compromise."

Deshmukh raised a concern, "But that might lead to a lot of infighting and could impact the government in Maharashtra."

Arvind Kolhe reassured, "The Chief Minister of Maharashtra is from the BLP. He should handle it. He ought to know how to manage senior leaders within their party. We need to demonstrate our leverage."

Ajay Patil concurred, "Yes, it's a sound idea. But we must exercise caution. We don't want to harm ourselves in the process."

Arvind Kolhe suggested, "Yes, let's begin with a more moderate approach."

Deshmukh and Patil shared a hearty laugh and affirmed their commitment to remain in Delhi for a few more days.

&&&&&

15.03.2032

Ashutosh Banerjee, the Chief Minister of Bengal, was enjoying a two-day break at Digha Beach. He had chosen to stay at Mohana Resorts, owned by a well-known politician and a friend. While it lacked the opulence of a five-star resort, the ambiance was lively. He had arrived the previous evening, and now, at 8.00 a.m., the beach was bustling with tourists.

Periodically, tourists would venture into various resorts for a cup of coffee. On this particular morning, three tourists entered Mohana Resorts one after the other. The first to enter was Kalpak Sanodia, a guest at Doltin Hotel. He had presented his pass to the security officer at the resort's gate and was permitted to enter only after receiving a nod of approval. He proceeded to the restaurant, sipping coffee while waiting for permission to access the hotel. Once granted, he underwent another security check before being allowed to enter the Chief Minister's suite. Kalpak Sanodia held the position of Vice President in the Praja Dharm Party, which had previously held power in Delhi, Punjab, and Haryana but had since lost influence. Their support for the Rohingyas had tarnished their reputation, and although they had aided Lalita Chatterjee's Party in securing power at the Centre, the party now had only three members in the Lok Sabha, causing concern and worry.

The second person to enter was Habib Khan, a prominent Rohingya leader who had played a significant role in agitations both within the country and abroad, advocating for Rohingya citizenship. He received substantial support from various quarters, and the previous year, he had come remarkably close to achieving his goal. The bill for granting citizenship to the Rohingyas had almost passed in the Lok Sabha. However, political upheavals led to the withdrawal of BLP's support for Lalitaji's government, causing the government's downfall and the bill's demise.

The third entrant was Mustafazur Khan, the leader of displaced Afghan people. While some displaced Afghan Hindus and Sikhs had obtained citizenship, Muslims like him remained excluded. Mustafazur Khan was not aligned with the Taliban; in fact, he harboured disdain for them. All three individuals were desperate to obtain citizenship.

Ashutosh Chatterjee, the Chief Minister, was informed of their arrival, and they stood as he entered the room. He welcomed them to take their seats and ordered refreshments. The resort staff promptly served a variety of dishes, with most guests favouring egg preparations such as omelettes, boiled eggs, or half-fried eggs. The conversation remained amicable during the meal. Afterward, at the CM's request, the staff discreetly left the room, and the discussion commenced.

The CM disclosed, "You can speak freely now. I've had the CCTV cameras deactivated, ensuring our conversation remains confidential within this room."

Habib Khan expressed gratitude, saying, "It's a wise precaution to have the camerasand audios turned off."

Sanodia shared their predicament, saying, "We are in a tight spot. Our party has very few members left in the Lok Sabha. There was a time when we ruled Delhi, but the BLP and RVP have taken away our power."

Mustafazur added, "Yes, sir, you and CM Sabarwal Saheb have supported us significantly. We are deeply thankful to you."

Habib Khan elaborated, "Our Rohingya community is facing difficulties. With Allah's grace, we have enough to eat and drink, and thanks to people like you, earning a livelihood isn't an issue. However, without citizenship, we can't participate in elections. Although we've managed to acquire Aadhar Cards and Voter IDs, they become invalid digitally, triggering alarms when inserted into the voting machines. Something needs to be done about this."

Ashutosh Chatterjee concurred, "Indeed, we must address this issue. That's why we're having this confidential meeting. We can't rule out the possibility that central agencies are monitoring us. We never know what RAW and IB are up to, and the NSA is quite shrewd."

Sanodia stressed, "It's imperative that we bring down the Rajendra Kaul government."

Ashutosh shared his anguish, saying, "The loss was devastating when the government under my mother was toppled. She has never fully recovered from the shock. Her blood pressure spiked, leading to a paralytic attack, and she remains bedridden. It pains me greatly."

Habib Khan's emotions flared, "All because of that wretched Rajendra Kaul. He must be dealt with."

Sanodia cautioned, "Lower your voice. If someone overhears, we'll be in deep trouble."

Ashutosh expressed his willingness to support but emphasized the need for utmost secrecy. "I can provide financial assistance, but my name must remain concealed."

Everyone nodded in agreement.

Habib Khan urged, "The DeshbandhuSwabhiman Party must assume power in Delhi, no matter what."

Another round of coffee followed, but none spoke until the waitstaff were at a distance.

Ashutosh Chatterjee concluded, "Please be discreet when leaving this room, leave one by one."

With that, they exited the room, ensuring a five-minute interval between their departures.

&&&&&

17.03.2032

Major Ranbir Singh, the Chief Minister of Punjab, embarked on a visit to the Tirupati Temple, a prominent political heavyweight within the BLP. His close friendship with Party President Pratibha Kaul had been an open secret among party members for several years. The gathering of three Chief Ministers from the same party had ignited curiosity and discussions, both within and outside the political sphere. While there was no specific agenda for the meeting, it had garnered significant political importance, drawing news reporters to Tirupati in search of a scoop.

Back in Chandigarh, Trital had alerted Major Ranbir Singh to security concerns. Consequently, upon his morning arrival in Tirupati with his wife, he paid little heed to the media presence and proceeded directly to the Tirumala Padmavati Guest House. Dr. Shekhar Reddy, the Chief Minister of Andhra Pradesh, and his wife were already present to welcome them. Kerala's Chief Minister, Shri Ganeshraman, was expected to arrive later. After freshening up, both couples opted for an early morning darshan (prayer offering) at the temple, having already had breakfast on the flight. The two couples received VIP darshan at 11 a.m. and later explored the temple premises before returning to their guest house suite at noon.

Coincidentally, at noon, an SQ ship from the Chinese Navy and a Chinese warship departing from Coco Islands in Myanmar began to enter the territorial waters of Bangladesh. Initially, the Indian Navy paid limited attention, but as the warship pointed toward India, the information swiftly reached official channels, including CDS (Chief of Defence Services) Maj Gen Ashok Bhat and NSA chief Radhakrishnan. The NSA chief relayed the situation to Trital, who promptly contacted Naval Admiral Balwinder Singh and the Sriharikota Naval base.

This communication placed Vishakhapatnam on high alert, and deployments were made accordingly. Four warships, including a Guided

Missile destroyer and an anti-submarine naval ship, entered the Bay of Bengal. INS Sarayu and INS Sumedha were also dispatched to the region. INS Baaz was placed on alert and preparedness to deploy submarines in the high seas.

Chinese satellites had detected these movements by the Indian Navy and relayed the information to the SQ ship, prompting it to change its course. Speculation regarding the Chinese Navy's intentions abounded, with questions about whether it was an attempt to intimidate India or a planned missile attack.

Trital suspected that a missile attack was planned near Tirupati, but to the Chinese's misfortune, the attempt had been thwarted. A couple of days later, when the three Chief Ministers were apprised of this incident, it sent shivers down their spines.

In the afternoon, Kerala CM Ganeshraman arrived in Tirupati. The three CMs and their spouses were treated to a lavish lunch featuring a blend of northern and southern cuisines, all vegetarian due to Tirupati's status as a temple town. Mrs. Ranbir Singh particularly enjoyed the sambar, sweet-sour vegetable curries, and *paranthas*(wheat bread), but only nibbled at the rice. Mrs. Ganeshraman relished the *Punjabi chole* (chickpeas) and *sarson ka saag* (mustard leaf curry).

After lunch, the two ladies were invited to Mrs. Reddy's room to browse through sarees she had brought to gift them, allowing them to make their own selections.

Major Ranbir Singh harboured ambitions of entering national politics, a secret motive behind his visit to Tirupati.

They began discussing national security issues, primarily in English.

Reddy remarked, "Being a border state, your security concerns must be quite high."

Major Ranbir Singh acknowledged, "Indeed, and given my military background, I insist on receiving all pertinent details from the armed forces, including the Air Force."

Reddy shared, "I received a message just yesterday warning of a possible attack on Tirupati. Consequently, I've implemented heightened security measures, with central forces stationed here."

Major Ranbir Singh noted, "An aerial assault is also a possibility. Therefore, all missile units have been placed on alert. Trital apprised me of the situation."

Ganeshraman cautioned, "Extra vigilance is crucial."

Reddy stressed, "Central agencies should coordinate more effectively."

Major Ranbir Singh promptly suggested, "The Home Ministry should take a stronger stance."

Ganeshraman discerned Major Ranbir Singh's ambition for the Home Ministry, indicating ongoing political maneuvering within the party in Delhi. However, he simply replied, "Yes," outwardly acknowledging the suggestion.

Reddy expressed his discontent, saying, "Suresh Dutt was wrong in his earlier statements. The matter was already sub judice, and the political fracas between the two parties escalated unnecessarily."

Maj Ranbir Singh understood that Reddy was also not happy with the Home Minister, but he decided not to pursue the topic.

&&&&&

22.03.2032

The nation was celebrating Bakri-Id. It was peaceful everywhere. Trital remembered an old friend in Pakistan, Sadaqat Khan and sent him a *Bakri Id Mubarak* message on Facebook messenger. Sadaqat Khan had also responded with a 'Thank you, *Bhaijan*' message.

&&&&&

27.03.2032

It was the day of Holi, and Mr. and Mrs. Trital had arrived at Rashtrapati Bhavan in the morning to meet the President. The atmosphere was festive as the President's son, Sushant, daughter-in-law Sushma, and granddaughter Ananya had come all the way from New Zealand for a visit.

The Tritals underwent the necessary security checks before being escorted to the second floor by a lift. There, they were greeted by the President's wife, Vinaya, who warmly embraced Vijaya. Both ladies took their seats on the sofa, while Trital sat in an opposite chair. Vijaya requested the valet to inform the President and their son Sushant of their arrival.

Vijaya playfully applied a touch of pink colour to her sister's cheek, and Vinaya followed suit. Trital also showed his respect by touching Vijaya's feet and lightly applying colour to her cheek. Just then, the

President entered the room with his son and remarked, "Playing Holi all by yourself, Vijaya?"

Vijaya quickly moved forward, touching the President's feet and adding some colour to him. Trital did the same. In return, the President took some pink colour from Trital and applied it as per tradition.

Sushant then approached and respectfully touched the feet of both Buddhadev and Vijaya. Vijaya inquired, "Where is my daughter-in-law and granddaughter?"

"They are on their way here," replied Sushant.

The President, in a playful tone, asked Vijaya, "Tell me, what sweets have you brought?"

Vijaya replied, "*Jijaji*, I've brought your favourite*khoyagujiyas* (deep fried pastry stuffed with solidified milk).

"Oh, nice! Let's all enjoy them at the dining table."

The two sisters made their way to the dining room, followed by Sushant. Vinaya suggested that the gentlemen could have their private conversation.

After the ladies left, Trital took a seat near the President. The President inquired, "Tell me, what's the latest news?"

Trital responded, "Pakistan continues to plot and conspire against us."

"Hmm. What about the Taliban?"

"They were preparing actively, but for now, they appear to have restrained themselves. They are still fortifying positions around Kashmir and seem to be receiving assistance from within Kashmir."

The President remarked, "Kashmir seems peaceful on the surface."

Trital added, "Yes, but there's a faction within Kashmir's government that seeks the reinstatement of Article 370. We are monitoring their activities, but there are limitations since they are part of the government. The 'Azad Kashmir' organization openly protests against India, and the Kashmir government takes no action against them."

The President expressed his frustration, "These separatist elements and their secessionist stance are getting on my nerves."

Trital sympathized, "Years ago, many young men turned to terrorism, and hundreds were killed. Even today, occasional incidents occur. Their families harbour hatred for India, and they continue to have affection for Pakistan."

The President agreed, "That's the problem. Despite all these years, we have failed to foster a sense of belonging to India among them. Pakistan has brainwashed them into desiring a separate Kashmir state. They fail to realize that Pakistan has been attempting to integrate it into Pakistan-controlled Kashmir for years. Now, even the Taliban is trying to influence these separatists."

Trital concurred, "Sir, you are absolutely right. The Kashmir issue has remained a political quagmire for India for too long. The military believes we should reclaim POK, but an attack would be costly, and international pressure from China and Russia would mount."

"Yes, that's true. What about the national parties?"

Trital replied, "The Prime Minister still holds the reins of his party. Subhash Singh is a respectable man, so he is not in any danger. However, the Defence Minister and the Home Minister appear to have conflicting agendas."

The President speculated, "The Home Minister might be resentful that the Defence Minister is close to the PM. I've known him for a long time."

Trital suggested, "There may also be internal rifts within the ruling party. Some state chief ministers, like Major Ranbir from Punjab, have been quite active."

The President inquired, "And what about the opposition parties?"

Trital elaborated, "Things seem calm on the surface, but there are undercurrents. The President of the opposition party, Chadda, is influential, but the leader of the Lok Sabha, Rupani, is ambitious. Surajnath may not be ambitious, but he has a significant following within the party. The next Lok Sabha elections are still far off, and the situation will become clearer by then."

The President reflected, "I suppose regional parties are taking a cautious approach these days."

Trital explained, "Yes, indeed. Former PM Lalitaji is bedridden due to a paralytic stroke. The Punjab Kisan Party, despite being in the opposition in Punjab, supports the government in the Lok Sabha. Regional parties in Maharashtra have been marginalized, and Bihar parties are aligned with the government. Only in Tamil Nadu do regional parties hold significant sway."

The President noted, "We must pay special attention to safeguard our sacred places like Tirupati, Ayodhya, and Kashi. They might be on the radar. I mentioned this to PM Rajendra Kaul in our recent meeting. Even Jama Masjid in Delhi needs protection."

"Understood, Sir."

"I believe our country is going through a significant upheaval. Events are unfolding rapidly. In this age of technology, human beings seem to have lost their significance. Compassion for humanity is dwindling. There's destruction and hatred everywhere."

"Indeed, Sir."

The President continued, "Look at the situation in Europe, where there is religious conflict and unrest. When they initially accepted displaced people, it was an act of compassion. But what happened? Compassion should be mutual. Even the slightest provocations, like a tweet, can ignite large-scale conflicts and riots. It's as if the whole human race is governed by Newton's law, 'Action and reaction are equal and opposite.'"

At that moment, Vijaya entered and announced that Vinaya Didi had called them for dinner.

The President mentioned, "we will join in a couple of minutes."

Before leaving, he inquired, "Has the NSA budget been approved?"

Trital confirmed, "Yes, to a large extent. It was possible because you spoke to the Finance Minister."

The President nodded, "Subhash Singh is a reliable man."

Then, in a lighter tone, he suggested, "Let's head to the dining table and enjoy the gujiyas you brought."

Once they were seated at the dining table, Sushma approached Buddhadev and touched his feet, while Vijaya held 18-month-old Ananya in her arms, amused by her babbling. Buddhadev asked Sushant about his job.

Sushant humorously replied, "Uncle, you're the one who got me into this police job."

Buddhadev chuckled. Sushant held a degree in Information Technology. Three years prior, Surface Technology Inc. had assigned him to a project in New Zealand, where he was tasked with developing spy software for the New Zealand government's police department. Upon completing the project, the New Zealand government offered him a job, contingent on obtaining a No Objection Certificate from the Indian Government, which Buddhadev had facilitated. It was a mere formality, as the Indian Government would have readily issued one for the President's son.

The President was well aware of Buddhadev's ulterior motives in securing this police job for Sushant, eliminating the need for special security. The prevailing circumstances posed a risk, with terrorists potentially kidnapping Sushant to leverage the Indian government.

Buddhadev rose and approached Vijaya, producing two Cadbury chocolate bars from his jacket pocket. Ananya reached out for them eagerly, and Buddhadev turned to Sushma, seeking her approval. She responded with a warm smile, and Buddhadev took Ananya in his arms, presenting her with the chocolates. Turning away from the others, he gently swung the little girl. His eyes brimmed with tears, though he managed to hold them back.

Vijaya observed him closely, sensing that he was reminiscent of another young girl. Buddhadev and Vijaya did not have children of their own, leaving Vijaya to wonder who he was recalling. She thought it was perhaps her imagination, but she couldn't help but associate his tears with Gujranwala city.

Holi traditions included ordering sweets from shops and distributing them to the staff and officials at the Presidential palace. This had already been accomplished. Some sweets were procured and arranged on the dining table alongside samosas and kachoris prepared by the cooks.

The President had Alexa recite the Sundarkandpaath from the epic Ramayana. He noted, "Traditionally, we shouldn't eat until the scripture chapter is completed, but today we can ask for Tulsidasji's (Authorof Tulasi-Ramayana) forgiveness."

Vijaya inquired of Sushma, "Do you listen to Sundarkand?"

Sushma replied, "Yes, we also play it on Alexa. Look, even Ananya is mumbling some words from Sundarkand."

The President beamed, saying, "Very good. I am a proud grandfather," as he savoured the delicacies. Vinaya, his wife, mentioned to Buddhadev, "Vijaya tells me you've been neglecting your health lately."

Buddhadev responded with a playful tone, "Oh, she's been gossiping about me, has she?"

Vinaya turned to the President and reported, "For the past ten days, he hasn't been sleeping well. Vijaya took him to the military hospital for a check-up."

The President inquired, "And all the reports came back fine, didn't they? No need to worry; he'll take better care of his health from now on."

Trital expressed his gratitude, saying, "Thank you, Sir." The President praised Vijaya's delicious *gujiyas*, and Trital commended the samosas. They enjoyed some coffee after the snacks.

Vinaya asked if she could play some Lata Mangeshkar songs on Alexa, now that Sundarkand had concluded.

"Of course, no need to ask," the President responded.

Vinaya instructed Alexa to play Lata's "*Ae mere vatanke logon.*" Tears welled up in everyone's eyes as they listened to the soulful lyrics. Vinaya revealed it was her favourite song, and a moment of silence filled the room as everyone sat in reflection.

Trital eventually suggested it was time for them to leave. Vijaya exchanged a glance with her sister Vinaya, who nodded in agreement. As per tradition, the couple touched the feet of the President and his wife. Sushant and Sushma followed suit with their uncle Buddhadev and aunt Vijaya, who planted a loving kiss on little Ananya's cheek before departing.

During the journey back in their vehicle, Trital checked his phone and discovered a Happy Holi message from Sadaqat Khan in Pakistan. Trital promptly responded with a thank-you message, pleased that their friendship endured despite the distance.

Back at home, Buddhadev retired to his study, donned his earphones, and became engrossed in something on his mobile device. Vijaya entered the room and inquired about dinner plans, but he seemed oblivious to her presence and didn't hear her. She removed the earphonefrom mobile, interrupting the sad song from the old movie 'Veer Zara' playing on his mobile: "*tereliye hum hain jiye, haraansoopiye.(For you only I lived , loved each tear)* He glanced at Vijaya, conveying his displeasure at having his earphones pulled away. She asked, "I came to ask if you're ready for dinner."

He responded coldly, "You go ahead. I'll eat later."

"Alright," said Vijaya as she left the room, the lyrics "*kyakahun, duniya ne kaisekiyamujhsebair... kitnesitam hum pe sanam logon ne kiye...*"*(how can I tell ,my dear , this world has become enemy for me and how many punishments they have imposed on us)* resonating in her ears. She had long understood that there was a deep sadness in his heart, but there was no point in prying; he would not share.

&&&&&

04.04.2032

At Prakash Reddy's residence in Hyderabad, siblings Swapna and Ojas engaged in a conversation. Ojas had a habit of tuning in to the national news on his laptop, and it happened to be during the academic exam season.

He began, "Sis, may I share something with you?"

"Don't call me 'Akka'; call me 'Sis,'" Swapna replied with irritation.

"Alright,dear Sis. Would you like to hear today's breaking news?"

"Please don't bore me," Swapna retorted.

"No problem, just listen. It's related to your profession. IBM Watson is establishing twenty branches in India. They plan to handle all online legal matters themselves, in person."

"So, they'll be managing legal matters both online and offline. Does this mean their employees will now be appearing in courts?"

"Yes, Madam."

"Don't address me as 'Madam.'"

"Now, let me share the rest of the headlines. Germany is gaining power again and might consider leaving the European Union. The Chinese Yuan is being devalued, the American dollar isn't doing too poorly, and there are developments in the relationship between Russia and China..."

"Stop your chatter," Swapna interrupted.

"Alright, I'll keep quiet."

"Were Mom and Dad discussing something important?" Swapna inquired.

"I won't answer that. You always say I bore you."

"Okay, I won't say it again. Please tell me what they were talking about."

"They were praising us."

"That's it? You were acting so smug."

"That's not all."

"Then what?"

"Remember when we used that Tricorder X-3 on Mom and Dad? We learned that Dad might develop a heart problem, so he was prescribed those medications... let me look up their names on Google."

Swapna prompted, "Blood thinners and statins."

"And we also found out about Mom's issue, but you all kept it from me."

"That's not something for children like you to know."

"Okay."

Swapna said, "Thank goodness they informed me about that funding to terrorists. They're vigilant now and investigating the accounts thoroughly."

"I hope Dad won't get arrested."

"I won't let that happen. I've made arrangements. At the slightest hint of trouble, I've arranged for anticipatory bail."

"Do you know that Mahant Surajnath is a powerful figure in that party?"

"Why do you keep reading about these topics on the internet? Try reading some scientific knowledge topics."

He responded, "I read both on the internet."

She asked, "What interests you more?"

He continued, "I have a strong inclination toward history, but I also need to study geography because to comprehend historical events, one must understand their geographical context. For instance, when I read about the accomplishments of Bajirao Peshwa I, I also delve into the location where he met his demise. I discovered that he passed away in Ravarkhedi, a village in the Khargone district. I mentioned to you last year that we had an extensive chapter on Bajirao I, but it seems to have disappeared from the textbook now. There's only a passing mention of Bajirao in another chapter."

"Don't take it so much to heart," Swapna advised.

Ojas added, "You see, I've read numerous articles stressing the importance of accurately recording history. The history of kings and emperors should document their achievements and feats, along with their failures and atrocities, such as Aurangzeb's acts..."

"Alright, that's enough. Please don't bore me further," Swapna dismissed.

"Didn't you promise a minute ago that you wouldn't say that to me? I won't talk to you."

She apologized, saying, "Forget it, kid. I'm sorry."

He smiled at his sister.

&&&&&

07.04.2032

A two-day conference on Islamic Women's Education had been scheduled at *Vidnyan*(Science)Bhavan in Delhi. Eminent figures from various fields attended, including university vice-chancellors, principals, professors, political leaders, and representatives from social organizations. Several knowledgeable individuals spoke about the progress in women's education, with a particular focus on reforms in Kerala. Brief mentions were made about Hyderabad and Bengaluru. The representatives from Kerala presented statistical data illustrating how women's education had flourished since Kalam Women University became an Open University.

Universities unanimously agreed that Muslim women's education was no longer confined but had extended throughout India.

Two prominent political figures found themselves sitting side by side at the conference purely by chance. Sayyed Mehboob Khan, a former BLP Member of Parliament from Malegaon, a powerful figure in both Maharashtra and national politics, crossed paths with Mufti Yunus Khan, Vice-President of the Kashmir Liberation Front. Sayyed Mehboob Khan had recently lost in the elections to a candidate from the Deccan Awaam party. Both of them were staying at The Ashoka hotel and found themselves sitting next to each other during the conference.

On the first day, their conversation revolved around Kashmir. Sayyed Khan had visited Kashmir twice with his family and praised the region's natural beauty, while Yunus Khan had been to Mumbai once for sightseeing and talked about the city's vibrant lifestyle. In the evening, they shared a taxi back to the hotel but chose to dine separately in their rooms.

During the second day, the afternoon session delved into the state of education in Rajasthan, Kashmir, and the northeastern states. Discussions centred on elevating the quality of education and introducing professional courses in these regions. The conference concluded after these discussions. Once again, Yunus Khan and Sayyed Khan found themselves sitting next to each other and conversing during the taxi ride.

Mehboob Khan mentioned that Kashmir had seen significant changes since the abrogation of Article 370. Yunus Khan, however, believed that the changes were superficial, with underlying restlessness and turmoil.

Mehboob Khan asked, "What do you propose to do, then?"

"We aim to liberate Kashmir, to make it a free Kashmir," Yunus Khan replied.

Mehboob Khan tried to convince him that remaining an integral part of India was in the best interest of the Kashmiri people.

"No, we don't want to remain under your subjugation any longer. On the 15th of August, we will raise the flag of Kashmir in Lal Chowk. Just wait and watch," Yunus Khan declared.

"How do you plan to achieve that?" Mehboob Khan asked.

"We will, for sure."

Sayyed Mehboob Khan, in a fit of anger, exclaimed, "Are you planning to create a Kashmir-e-Taliban?"

Yunus Khan replied calmly, "Yes, something along those lines."

By the time the taxi reached the hotel entrance, they had embraced each other and bid each other farewell, saying, "Khuda Hafiz."

That night, Mehboob Khan couldn't shake off his restlessness. He felt that he had made a grave error in mentioning "Kashmir-e-Taliban" in the heat of the moment. He decided to inform his party seniors about it, as such a development was not in the best interest of Kashmir. Kashmir was an integral part of India, and it should remain so. If the Taliban took over, it would jeopardize the education and future of Muslim girls in the region. Kashmiri girls were making progress in fields like engineering, medicine, chartered accountancy, and aviation. Their future should be one of progress, not regression. In Malegaon, Mehboob Khan's hometown, there were numerous social and educational institutions dedicated to the empowerment of women.

The following day, Sayyed Mehboob Khan checked out of the hotel and moved into the house of a Member of Parliament. This MP had a busy schedule, leaving Mehboob Khan with plenty of free time. He decided to contact Salma Heptulla, the Minister of Women and Child Welfare. Her secretary informed him that she would meet him at her ministry office. After breakfast at the MP's house, he took a cab to her office. The ministry office was crowded with visitors, especially given her Bihar background. He had to wait for an hour before meeting her, as there were others in line.

Salma Madam warmly welcomed him and sent her PA to arrange for coffee.

"How are you, Bhai Sahab (Brother)?" she asked.

"Very well, with your good wishes."

"What brings you here?" she inquired.

"It's not a personal matter," he replied.

"Please, tell me."

Mehboob Khan proceeded to narrate the entire incident with Yunus Khan. Her expression turned serious as she listened. She said, "Why don't you convey this to the PM or the Home Minister?"

"It's not that the PM or the HM don't know me. But it may take two or three days to secure an appointment with them. I informed you so that you can take it forward."

She assured him, "Of course, I will raise the issue with them. I am concerned about the women in Kashmir. If the Taliban were to gain control, it wouldn't bode well for them. But for now, rest assured, these Talibanis won't dare to act. As they say in Mumbai, 'You be *bindhast*' (cool and unperturbed).'"

"Yes, I agree that, for the time being, they won't raise their heads. Nevertheless, we should remain vigilant."

Coffee was served, which Mehboob Khan drank quickly.

Salma Heptulla said, "Yes, we should remain cautious. Is there anything else?"

He understood that this signalled the end of the meeting.

&&&&&

12.04.2032

A meeting was underway at Lahore's Sheraton Hotel today. Iliyas Zaibuddin had come to Lahore under the guise of an official visit to Pakistan's educational institutions. He was part of a three-member team, consisting of two government representatives—an MLA and a government official. This "cultural exchange" program had been initiated during Lalita Chatterjee's tenure and was still in practice. The team was on a four-day tour and had been staying at the Sheraton Hotel. It was the third day of their visit.

Iliyas had informed the other two team members that he wished to meet an old friend, and they had no reason to doubt him.

Ozair Ahmed, the ISI officer, had arranged for Majid Khan to travel from Kabul for a joint meeting with Iliyas. They found it safer to meet in Lahore and decided to book the terrace at hotel Sheraton on the spot for their meeting. They didn't pre-reserve it to avoid the possibility of the rooms being bugged. The terrace functioned more like a small hall, and they requested food and drinks to be set up, instructing the waitstaff to only come when they rang the bell.

April brought warm weather with hot breezes throughout the day, but cool breezes in the evening. Air coolers hummed on the terrace.

Majid Khan had arrived first to make the necessary arrangements. He had spent the day meeting with two ISI officers and two high-ranking Pakistani military officers who briefed him on the general situation. When he arrived at the terrace, Ozair greeted him with a hug and a "*Walekum Salaam.*" Iliyas arrived shortly afterward, and the three exchanged hugs. Each of them was dressed in Western suits, and the air was filled with the scent of their colognes.

After refreshing themselves with a cold drink, they began with pleasantries. Majid Khan remarked, "Iliyas Bhai, we are meeting after a long time!"

"That's true. We've had Zoom conversations, but meeting face-to-face after so long is indeed a rare occasion," Iliyas replied.

Ozair passed a bowl of fried cashew nuts to them, and they nibbled on a few. Ozair commented, "This is a historic meeting, no doubt. Meeting in person is a significant step."

Both of the others nodded in agreement.

Ozair turned to Majid Khan and asked, "What did Maj Gen Naqvi say when you met him today?"

Majid Khan replied, "He didn't seem very enthusiastic."

"What does that mean?" Ozair inquired.

Majid Khan elaborated, "He believes that now is not the right time to initiate an attack on Kashmir. The national morale in India is high, and India has developed good relations with both Russia and America. These three nations have collectively impacted the Chinese economy, so we may not receive adequate support from China."

Iliyas questioned, "What about the preparations we've made so far?"

Ozair chimed in, "The trenches we've dug will serve their purpose sooner or later. We will continue training our jihadis."

"And what about those we've already sent in?" Iliyas asked.

Majid Khan advised, "Let them create unrest in Kashmir. They should avoid major destruction but rather focus on harassing the Indian army with hit-and-run attacks, minimizing risks for themselves."

Ozair concurred, "I believe that's the right strategy in the current situation."

Iliyas shared, "Yunus Khan, that idiot, told a leader of the ruling party in Delhi that we were planning to establish Kashmir-e-Taliban soon."

Majid Khan remarked, "That fool!"

Ozair cautioned, "Iliyas Bhai, even though our men in Kashmir should continue with minor terrorist activities, our primary goal should be to ensure minimal casualties among them. Training jihadis is a complex and costly process, and we have to provide financial support to their families. We need to be cautious since many of our men have been martyred by the Indian military. Fortunately, there's no shortage of young men eager to become jihadis, and it's thanks to them that we can still dream of Kashmir-e-Taliban."

Iliyas responded, "Engaging in these activities puts our lives at risk. We are under constant surveillance by the NIA and Indian Military Intelligence agencies. We must be incredibly cautious in our movements, or we would have landed in jail long ago. Without the support of the Azad Jannat party, we wouldn't have achieved anything. They support us because they want to prevent the Rashtriya Vichar Manch party from coming to power in Kashmir."

Majid Khan added, "Our secret service department is aware that India is already informed about our plans for Kashmir-e-Taliban. India likely has the support of Israel's Mossad; otherwise, how could such a top-secret plan leak out? We have an adept agent named Salman Khan who uses satellite surveillance to monitor India's activities. Our superiors are pleased with his work."

Iliyas wondered, "If not now, then when will we implement the plan?"

Majid Khan explained, "Our friends in China need some time to recover from their current difficulties. When we do proceed with our plan, we'll require China's support to thwart India at the UNSC (United Nations Security Council)."

Ozair concurred, adding that in the present situation, minor attacks were the only viable option. Iliyas inquired about the plan to eliminate Rajendra Kaul. Majid Khan mentioned that while they had the salt ready in Delhi, they were still waiting for the other ingredients—the water and lemons.

Majid Khan stated, "We must proceed with even greater caution. Currently, we have a means to exert pressure on Rajendra Kaul." He was alluding to having some material to blackmail Rajendra Kaul.

As the meeting concluded, Iliyas reflected, "It's a blessing from Allah that we could meet in person like this. I wonder when we'll be able to meet on Pakistani soil again."

Ozair reassured him, "Don't worry. Once we have Kashmir under our control, *Inshah Allah*, you'll be able to make daily trips."

The three of them shared a smug laugh.

Unbeknownst to them, Mossad had covertly installed a camera in the air cooler and a bugging device under the table, having bribed a waiter for the task.

&&&&&

16.04.2032

In the office of the Chief Minister in Kolkata, there was a flurry of activity today. All states had received orders from the central government to enhance security arrangements. Meetings were taking place in this context, and Chief Minister Ashutosh Chatterjee was deeply engrossed in his work.

His secretary informed him that a person named Mustafizur Khan from Afghanistan was waiting to meet him. The CM instructed his secretary to schedule an appointment for the following week. The secretary, however, informed him that the visitor insisted it was a matter of utmost urgency.

This urgent request set off alarm bells in the CM's mind. He pondered what could be so pressing. He directed his secretary to attend to the visitor and offer refreshments, while he would expedite the ongoing meeting to meet the man. Furthermore, he requested the secretary to arrange the meeting in the adjacent chamber and ensure that no one entered the main chamber during their meeting. The secretary was to be on standby until summoned.

Mustafizur Khan had no option but to wait since he had come without a prior appointment. He patiently read through all the newspapers laid out, leaving no news item unread, and consumed two cups of coffee during the hour-long wait. Finally, the CM made his appearance. Mustafizur rose to greet the CM, who appeared visibly agitated.

Mustafizur offered an apology.

The CM responded, "We had agreed not to meet in the office, hadn't we?"

Mustafizur replied, "Yes, but the circumstances demanded it."

"Alright, please get to the point; I have another meeting to attend."

Mustafizur explained, "Although our organization opposes the Taliban, we must monitor their malicious activities and schemes."

"I recall you mentioned their plan to target Kashmir some time ago."

"It appears that they have temporarily shelved this plan; it will not be executed immediately."

The CM inquired, "So, what urgent matter has brought you here?"

"We have received information that the Taliban's External Affairs Minister has visited Thailand and requested the Thai government to recognize their organization."

"Go on."

Mustafizur continued, "While in Thailand, he privately indulged in the company of women and boasted about his experiences at massage Parlors."

Ashutosh was growing impatient with these details, but he had no choice but to pay attention.

Mustafizur went on, "We have insider information that the Taliban has obtained a video clip from an old CD, which contains compromising photos of our Prime Minister."

Ashutosh was all ears, "A CD?"

Mustafizur asked, "Do you have any knowledge of this CD?"

"No, nothing. But what is so significant about this CD?"

Mustafizur leaned in closer and whispered, "The Prime Minister is seen with women."

"So what? I've been in the company of women as well."

Ashutosh was aware of the CD's contents, but he wanted to hear it from Mustafizur Khan.

Mustafizur revealed, "It seems that Rajendra Kaul is completely nude in that video clip."

"Oh my goodness!"

"This is the news I had to urgently share with you, which is why I came to your office."

Ashutosh expressed his gratitude, "Thank you very much for this information. You did the right thing by coming directly to me. Do not utter a word about this to anyone else. I repeat, to no one else, or your life will be in jeopardy."

Mustafizur's face fell, "I appreciate your warning. I will keep this a secret."

Ashutosh said, "You can leave now. We will have to meet at a hotel one of these days."

"May God be with you, Sir (*Khuda Hafiz*)."

"Wait a moment. My associate will safely escort you through the back door of the Secretariat building. I will use the other door." He then returned to his own chamber.

His secretary inquired, "Shall we call the people to the conference hall?"

Ashutosh replied, "Wait. Let me have a strong cup of coffee first, and then we can proceed with the meeting."

Sitting alone, Ashutosh began to contemplate what he had just heard. His mind was in turmoil. The video from the CD reminded him of past events, particularly his wife Lily.

He didn't want the CD to resurface. While it had been useful in the past, it had also led to him losing his wife forever.

The secretary brought in the coffee. Ashutosh finished it and proceeded to the meeting.

&&&&&

01.05.2032 to 03.05.2032

The Vice-President of India, Shamsuddin, arrived in Abu Dhabi and was warmly welcomed at the airport by senior officials from the Indian Embassy in Abu Dhabi and the Foreign Minister of the United Arab Emirates (UAE). Accompanied by the UAE Foreign Minister, the VP was then transported to a luxurious five-star hotel. Along the way, he noticed a group of young men on the street, protesting with black flags that bore a message in the local language.

He inquired, "What are they demonstrating about?"

The Foreign Minister replied, "They are expressing their grievances against India."

"Oh, I see. And what's the reason?"

The FM explained, "It's because your country declined to grant citizenship to Rohingyas and some Afghan Muslims."

The VP nodded in understanding and fell silent. The Foreign Minister of the UAE chose not to delve further into the topic.

The Emirates Palace, an opulent hotel, provided a splendid environment for the Vice-President. He took an hour to freshen up and was pleased to have two of his personal secretaries also accommodated at the same hotel, with top-notch arrangements for their stay.

The VP had a three-day schedule in Abu Dhabi. On May 1st, he was to remain in Abu Dhabi and meet with the President of the UAE, Sheikh Khalifa. The discussions during the meeting focused on international affairs and bilateral trade issues, with an assurance from Sheikh Khalifa to increase the supply of crude oil to India.

The VP was elated to visit his son, Salahuddin, in Dubai on May 2nd. The reunion with his grandsons touched him deeply. As a widower whose wife had passed away long ago, he always regretted that she hadn't met her grandsons before her passing.

On the third day, he returned to Abu Dhabi and embarked on a series of meetings. He first met with the Minister of Petroleum and expressed India's request for an increased supply of crude oil. Subsequently, he met with the Foreign Affairs Minister and discussed international relations, particularly focusing on India's stance in the Sino-India conflict. The VP expressed his gratitude to the UAE for its support.

Foreign Minister Sheikh Mustafa conveyed, "I have some confidential information to share."

The VP inquired, "What is it?"

Mustafa cautioned, "It's highly sensitive."

VP Shamsuddin couldn't contain his curiosity and said, "Please, go on."

Mustafa continued, "Representatives from various countries visit our nation, and Dubai, in particular, is a major attraction. Occasionally, they unintentionally reveal information or stories related to their own country or another. I've heard that the Taliban has set its sights on Kashmir, and Pakistan may be involved."

Shamsuddin's face revealed deep concern. "Thank you for sharing this vital information. I will convey it to our government."

Mustafa emphasized, "Please be tactful in how you relay this information and avoid disclosing our name."

"You can trust me on that."

Mustafa assured Shamsuddin of the UAE's continued cooperation with India.

With the meeting concluded, Shamsuddin returned to the hotel. His departure back to India was scheduled for the afternoon flight.

&&&&&

15.05.2032 to 18.05.2032

A series of raids and arrests were carried out in Hyderabad by the NIA and Uttar Pradesh CID, which sent shockwaves through the political landscape of the city. The authorities were diligently uncovering the money trail and the sources of funding for terrorist activities in Uttar Pradesh.

Before these operations, a wave of arrests had already taken place in Uttar Pradesh, with eleven individuals detained in Rampur and

Azamgarh. Their accounts and Hawala transactions underwent thorough scrutiny, revealing that some of the funds originated from Delhi and Srinagar, but the primary source was traced back to Hyderabad. Arrests had also occurred in Delhi and Srinagar.

Officials of the 'Bewaa Janana Khushamadi Trust' (Widowed Women's Welfare Trust) had been apprehended, alongside several affluent individuals from the city who had been contributing to the organization. The two principal donors, Suhail Seth and Anil Rao, swiftly sought bail from the High Court.

Two automobile dealers, Ramkrishna Rao and Aziz Khan, as well as two wholesale medicine dealers, Ravindra Tilsani and Habib Khan, all four associated with Prakash Reddy, found themselves facing inquiry. Anticipating his own turn, Prakash Reddy applied for anticipatory bail in the High Court.

Ramkrishna Rao, Aziz Khan, Ravindra Tilsani, and Habib Khan had not foreseen that their philanthropic acts would land them in trouble. They had contributed funds to the organization in response to earnest requests from certain political leaders and Trustees. They also filed for anticipatory bail, but the NIA prosecutors raised objections, resulting in the rejection of their bail applications.

Swapna, Prakash Reddy's daughter, approached her senior, Advocate Sudhakar Reddy, to represent her father. He successfully argued that merely managing the accounts of an organization did not imply involvement in terrorist activities, securing anticipatory bail.

This brought a sense of relief to Prakash Reddy's household. Although he would still face an inquiry, they had managed to avert an immediate arrest. The family decided to take necessary steps as the case progressed, with Adv. Sudhakar Reddy assuring them that there was no need to worry. The family felt reassured.

In the meantime, Prakash, thanks to the TriCorder-X-3 test results, was on heart medication prescribed by the doctor. This was a relief, as the stress and tension from the ongoing situation could have otherwise triggered a heart attack. Swapna informed her mother that Ojas, being well-read and tech-savvy, had played a significant role in anticipating Prakash's condition. Aruna lovingly patted her son's back.

The potential terrorist threats in Uttar Pradesh became a widely discussed national issue, receiving extensive media coverage. The names of individuals from Hyderabad featured prominently in newspapers and on television. Reporters came to interview Prakash Reddy, but Swapna handled the situation herself.

Mahant Surajnath maintained an unblemished image and had brought about significant transformations in the state. Within his party, he held a high level of prestige. Some central party leaders were envious of him due to his strong backing from the Party Chief, Ashok Chadda. Rameshwar Singh, the leader of the opposition party, competed directly with the Mahant and aspired to be the chosen prime ministerial candidate if the RVP were to come into power. Namrata Rupani, his party's leader in the Lok Sabha, was also his political rival and enjoyed the support of numerous MPs. Nevertheless, he remained hopeful that the party leadership would take appropriate action when the time came.

&&&&&

22.05.2032 to 25.05.2032

Three brothers convened a meeting in Kabul on a balmy evening, with the room's air conditioners providing respite from the heat. The ladies bustled about, tending to their needs.

Shama, an accomplished cook, Nadira, a gifted dancer and singer, and Raziya, a proficient dancer, were the women attending to the brothers. Nadira had been regaling the brothers with her songs and dances, while Shama worked diligently in the kitchen, and Raziya served food and drinks.

When Nadira grew weary, she requested Raziya to take the floor with a dance. Ashiq Khan, the middle brother, consented, saying, "Very well, Raziya, you may dance."

Raziya agreed but asked for a moment to change into something more comfortable. Salman Khan urged her to be swift. Meanwhile, Nadira replenished the glasses, Shama delivered mutton kebabs to the table, and was returning to the kitchen.

Afzal Khan humorously quipped, "Why don't you grace us with a dance too?" directed at Shama, who responded, "My agility isn't as it used to be, unlike these young ladies," eliciting laughter from all.

Raziya soon emerged, clad in a sheer dress that revealed her undergarments. Salman Khan complimented her, saying, "You look absolutely stunning, my dear."

With a tambourine in hand, Raziya began her dance, incorporating belly dance moves, provocatively showcasing her cleavage. The brothers, under the influence of both lust and alcohol, watched with rapt attention, applauding enthusiastically.

In a hushed tone, Afzal Khan whispered to Ashiq Khan, "You've found a remarkable performer and bought her"

Ashiq Khan replied with a respectful nod. Meanwhile, Nadira continued to pour drink after drink.

Afzal Khan inquired of Salman, "Why haven't those individuals arrived to collect their commission from the medicine sales this month?"

Salman assured, "They'll be here, and this time, their demands aren't excessive."

Under the influence of alcohol, Ashiq Khan mumbled, "Has the plan to attack Kashmir inHindustan been scrapped?"

Salman speculated, "The plan might have been postponed."

Raziya, now alert, and Nadira listened intently. Raziya deliberately accentuated her dance moves, emphasizing her belly wriggles.

Shama called out to Nadira, suggesting they serve the dishes. Each lady brought the serving dishes to the table, which featured *Kabuli Pulav, Naan, Korma-e-gosht, and Kofta.* The brothers revelled in the delightful aromas.

Shama Didi declared, "Raziya, your dance has been delightful, but it's time to clean the kitchen now, while I attend to the men."

Raziya was curious about the brothers' conversation, but she obediently retreated to the kitchen, aware that Salman would likely pursue her to satisfy his desires throughout the night.

The following day, Afzal Khan journeyed to a village near Asadabad town, where he received a warm welcome. The wives of the three brothers and their children resided there, somewhat intimidated by his presence. They managed extensive farmlands in the area, with Asifa, Afzal's wife, overseeing the operations, supported by their son.

In their bed at night, Afzal asked Asifa, "Is everything running smoothly here?"

Asifa responded, "Mostly, yes."

Concerned, Afzal inquired, "What's the issue then?"

"We must arrange our son's marriage soon."

Afzal retorted, "We've received a few proposals, and they've all been accepted. Now it's your turn to evaluate and approve a suitable girl."

"He's turned nineteen now, so sooner would be better."

Annoyed, Afzal probed further, "Is there something else? Has he become entangled in an affair? You keep insisting he marries."

Asifa hesitated, saying, "I'm reluctant to tell you when you raise your voice."

After calming down, Afzal remarked, "Alright, tell me."

"Recently, Shahrukh has been spending a lot of time with Saira."

"What? With his aunt (*Chachi*)? I hope they haven't crossed any boundaries. Bring Saira here; I want to talk to her sternly."

"Speak with her tomorrow, and also talk to our son. More importantly, arrange his marriage soon."

"How can we arrange a marriage on such short notice?"

Asifa suggested, "Consider Mehrunnisa, Ashiq Khan's daughter; she's already fifteen and has stopped attending school. Let's have an in-family wedding."

Afzal pondered, "I'll need to consult with Ashiq about this."

"His wife is agreeable. Let's plan the wedding for next week, inviting everyone except those undesirable women (whores). I can't stand to see them."

"I concur. However, I must address the matter with Saira first."

Asifa pointed out, "Raziya is more attractive than Saira, and Salman often spends time with her. Saira is feeling lonely here."

Afzal firmly replied, "That doesn't excuse her flirting with her nephew and influencing him. Besides, Salman is a government employee, and most of our business dealings are in Kabul."

"That's true. I'll proceed with the wedding preparations."

"No, wait until I speak to Ashiq."

"Understood, *Sarkar* (sir)."

&&&&&

06.06.2032

In Mumbai, Ajay Patil, Dilip Deshmukh, and Arvind Kolhe gathered for a meeting at a luxurious five-star hotel. They wore disappointed expressions, as their efforts in Delhi had not yielded favourable results.

Kolhe shared his frustration, saying, "I made numerous attempts. I met with two influential ministers, the Home Minister, and the Finance Minister, but they paid no attention."

Deshmukh asserted, "We need to take action now."

Ajay Patil concurred, "Absolutely, we're facing pressure from all directions."

Kolhe inquired, "What's the plan, then?"

Ajay Patil proposed, "We'll have to bring down the government in Maharashtrastate ; there's no alternative."

Deshmukh cautioned, "We need a legitimate reason for that. We can't topple the government just because our legal cases can't be withdrawn. People will see through it and condemn us."

Kolhe added, "I agree with that."

Patil seethed, "Rajnarain Singh is getting too cocky. So, what if he's the Home Minister's son? His 'Samajik Samata Dal SAASAD' is spreading like wildfire with branches everywhere, and our young cadres are joining them."

Deshmukh inquired, "What's your point?"

Patil continued, "Haven't you seen the recent attack on your party member in Sangli? It was over a minor issue, a by-election for the Zilla Parishad. They caused a major ruckus!"

Kolhe mused, "Are you suggesting we use that attack as a pretext to withdraw our support from the government? I'm not sure it's a strong enough reason."

Patil clarified, "No, we'll initiate protests against the attack and demand action against SAASAD. Our party will stand by your side."

"Are you suggesting we create chaos in Maharashtra, disrupt law and order?" Deshmukh inquired.

"Yes," affirmed Patil, "The legal cases against us have escalated. We're currently out on bail, but it's only a matter of time before we land in jail. We'll be entangled in legal battles for life."

"If the BLP government falls, RVP may come to power," Deshmukh pointed out.

Patil countered, "RVP won't secure a clear majority. Their government would be a fragmented coalition, much like BLP. We'll provide external support and teach BLP a lesson. It's a risky move, but we must engage in cunning political manoeuvres."

Deshmukh suggested, "We should discuss this strategy during the party meeting. We have ministers and deputies in both the State and Central governments; they must be informed in advance."

Kolhe concurred, "Executing this plan won't be straightforward. Let's begin with the protests against SAASAD. We can't allow them to assault our party members with impunity."

Patil emphasized, "As long as they were targeting RVP members and Hanuman Dal activists, it was tolerable. But now that they're attacking us, we need to leverage this situation."

Deshmukh agreed, "Alright, let's develop a long-term strategy."

Having reached this conclusion, the three of them settled in to savour their whiskey.

&&&&&

26.06.2032

On this evening, Trital, accompanied by his wife Vijaya, was en-route to Rashtrapati Bhavan. It wasn't a festive or special occasion, but they had received a cordial invitation from the President's wife, Vinaya. Their car underwent the standard security check.

Stepping out of their air-conditioned car, they both recognized that the weather in Delhi remained sweltering; the sporadic rain showers had done little to alleviate the heat. A security officer guided them to the first floor in an elevator.

The two sisters, Vinaya and Vijaya, greeted each other warmly with a heartfelt embrace. Then, Trital proceeded to meet the President in his study. The President was engrossed in reading something, and Trital humbly touched his feet.

The President shared that he was engrossed in the book "Future Shock" by the American author Alvin Toffler. Toffler had penned this book five decades ago, forecasting the upheavals future generations would encounter. The President remarked, "I believe people are in for even more significant shocks than Toffler had foreseen."

Trital responded, "I've also delved into two of his works, 'Power Shift' and 'War and Anti-war.' He certainly emerges as a profound thinker."

Their conversation shifted to national politics. Trital inquired, "Is everything proceeding smoothly?"

The President admitted, "So far, things are manageable, but..."

"But what?" the President asked.

Trital continued, "Nothing definitive. It's just a gut feeling. Pakistan's relentless focus on Kashmir, with the Taliban by its side, sends shivers down my spine. I've been receiving a slew of intelligence reports."

"Anything from Mossad?" the President inquired.

Trital nodded in affirmation.

The President pressed on, "How is the situation in the states?"

Trital reported, "Not promising. There was an assassination attempt on the Chief Minister of Uttar Pradesh."

"Yes, Surajnath informed me about it. Anything else?"

"As is customary, West Bengal remains a tinderbox. The government in Maharashtra is on shaky ground. Tensions could erupt in Telangana and Bihar as well."

The President confided, "I'm genuinely concerned when the nation isn't at peace. This is something I can only share with you. You see, foreign investments in India are dwindling, and the country's industrial progress is taking a severe hit. I feel quite restless."

"Understood, Sir."

The butler entered to inquire about their readiness for dinner, and both Trital and Vijaya made their way to the dining room.The Alexa wasasked to rant *Hanuman Chalisa*.

On the table, *aamras* (mango pulp), *roti* (bread), and *kachori* were served. Trital, who was diabetic, couldn't resist the *aamras*, and Vijaya watched with concern. In jest, he quipped, "No need to worry. I'll just double my dose of medication." Laughter filled the room.

The President interjected, "In five days, you'll assume additional responsibilities. You'll have to be mindful of your diet."

Vijaya inquired, "What does this mean?"

The President made the announcement, "Trital is set to become the Chief National Security Advisor; Radhakrishnan is retiring."

Vijaya congratulated, "Congratulations, Buddhadevji."

"Thank you very much. It seems my responsibilities are about to expand significantly."

The President affirmed, "Indeed, that's a certainty."

After the meal, everyone reconvened in the drawing room for some casual conversation before the Tritals departed for their home.

&&&&&

30.06.2032

Trital and Radhakrishnan found themselves in Radhakrishnan's office. Trital expressed his sentiments, "Sir, I'll genuinely miss your valuable guidance. From now on, I'll need to exercise great caution in every decision I make."

Radhakrishnan nodded, acknowledging the gravity of the situation. "You should indeed exercise caution. Our roles come with a great deal of sensitivity and responsibility. Every step must be taken with the utmost care."

Trital affirmed, "Yes, Sir."

Radhakrishnan continued, "Our position carries the name 'national,' signifying that all our actions should serve the national interest. I believe I need not reiterate this."

Trital concurred, "Yes, Sir."

"Sometimes, we'll need to exercise patience and observe, while at other times, quick decisions will be required. In both cases, we must remain composed. Panic achieves nothing," Radhakrishnan emphasized.

Trital expressed gratitude, saying, "Thank you, Sir."

Radhakrishnan disclosed, "In August, I'll be relocating to Kerala. I must complete all official procedures by then, including pension, PF, and vacating the official residence."

Trital reassured him, "Sir, if I encounter any difficulties, I will reach out to you directly."

Radhakrishnan assured, "Certainly, feel free to contact me even in Kerala. Though I doubt you'll face such situations. I have great faith in your capabilities."

Trital replied, "Thank you, Sir."

Radhakrishnan had a request, "I have one request. Please cooperate with Kushalram, who will be assuming your position. I understand you may not be entirely content with this choice, but there was substantial pressure from the Home Ministry, and I had to comply."

Later in the day, a farewell party was organized in Radhakrishnan's honor. The event was attended by numerous officials from the PMO, the Home Department, and senior army officers.

That evening, Trital felt somewhat uneasy. It wasn't the new responsibility that troubled him, but rather his own contemplative thoughts. Vijaya noticed his disquiet and brought him a cup of his preferred strong coffee. Outside, a light drizzle had begun, and dark clouds loomed in the sky.

Trital was seated on the veranda. The sentry stationed at the door made his way toward the bungalow's main gate. Vijaya recognized her husband's sombre mood and decided to let him be with his thoughts. She proceeded to the kitchen, where she intended to prepare Trital'sfavourite green pea kachori. She had called for frozen peas from the pantry and left them to thaw. Trital had returned from the office late, and he had expressed his desire to have the kachoris for dinner.

Seated on the veranda, Trital felt a sense of nostalgia washing over him. His desire to retreat to the bedroom and listen to soulful tunes on Alexa was dampened by the persistent raindrops. The rain showers were pleasant but memories were awakening.He found solace in the brisk breeze that caressed him, a welcome contrast to the stifling air-conditioned office where he spent his entire day. As his mind began to wander, it fixated on thoughts of Reshama.

He contemplated, "Thoughts of Reshama are a constant presence in my life. She's woven into the fabric of my existence, a part of every moment. I can't predict what triggers memories of her—perhaps just a bout of emotional solitude can bring forth tears, unexpectedly."

His mind drifted back two decades to the time he spent as a spy in Pakistan. Operating as a RAW agent, a member of India's Research and Analysis Wing, he had infiltrated Kahuta and secured employment at a local hair salon. His journey to this role wasn't straightforward. Previously, while working as a rickshaw puller in Lahore, he had befriended an elderly barber, learning the trade from him, a skill that proved valuable in securing his position at the salon, as alias Sherkhan name.

The salon, named "*Majmua* Unisex Beauty Parlour," catered to both men and women, each with its dedicated sections. Reshama was also employed there.

Trital's mission involved gathering intelligence on the significant nuclear laboratory in Kahuta, Pakistan. When laboratory officials visited the salon, Trital would discreetly attempt to extract morsels of information from them. However, these officials were often tight-lipped, and the task was challenging. On occasion, if two officials visited together, he could eavesdrop on their conversations and glean morsels of information about ongoing research or capacity enhancements. Trital had to exercise patience to collect these titbits of information and memorize them. Without raising suspicion, he also had to discreetly collect hair samples from the officials and deliver them to an Indian agent for testing the extent of nuclear radiation.

For six months, he hadn't even caught a glimpse of Reshama. He had only overheard the salon owners, a married couple, frequently mentioning her name. Although the salon had separate sections for men and women, a common passageway at the rear was only accessible to the owners. Even this passage was located at the far end of the women's section, where the husband and wife would meet in a small room. A large door separated this male section from the open rear area, which remained locked. This open space at the rear served as a laundry area for both men and women, managed by a female servant. A small room had a door leading to this rear open space.

Trital's proficiency in keeping accounts swiftly endeared him to the owners. He had informed the owner that he had completed his matriculation in Lahore and had previously worked as an assistant to a trading company's secretary. Frustrated by the company owner's miserly salary, he had learned the art of haircutting to make some extra money. Naturally, Trital, also known as Sher Khan, was entrusted with accounting responsibilities.

Reshama excelled in her role as the women's section's accountant, and the landlady relied heavily on her. The landlord was pleased that both Reshama and Sher Khan were honest and meticulous in their duties.

The owner, at 41 years of age, and his 35-year-old wife had struggled with infertility for fourteen years until fertility treatment at a clinic granted them the opportunity to conceive. With the owner's wife absent, Reshama's responsibilities at the salon grew, requiring her to present all the accounts to the owner. Through her meticulous accounting methods, Trital began to establish contact with her.

On one occasion, when neither the owner nor his wife could attend the salon, they entrusted the business to Reshama and Trital. Reshama was veiled in a burqa. It was Reshama who opened the salon that morning, with an elderly woman responsible for sweeping both sections. Reshama and Trital communicated through this elderly woman.

Upon closing in the evening and settling accounts, Reshama confidently entered the men's section and requested the day's account statement from Trital, which she was to deliver to the owners. Removing her burqa, she revealed her beauty, mesmerizing Trital. Playfully, she asked, "Hey mister, why are you staring with such wide eyes?" Her words snapped him out of his trance, and he promptly handed over the account statement, a mix of Urdu and some figures in English. She inquired, "Were you educated in an English medium school?" Trital nodded in affirmation.

She requested that he step out of the salon while she locked up the men's section first and then the women's section. Donning the burqa again, she handed him the keys and asked him to pass them on to the elderly woman in the morning for sweeping. The elderly woman would unlock the men's section for him.

This encounter marked the beginning of a series of meetings between Reshama and Trital. The owner's wife's fragile health often necessitated her husband's care, leaving Reshama and Trital to manage the salon. Their interactions deepened, with Reshama, at twenty-eight, and Trital, still unmarried at thirty-four, finding themselves drawn to each other. Reshama had been married for eleven years but had not yet experienced motherhood.

The landlady had suggested that she visit a fertility clinic, which her husband, Azam Khan, an electrician, initially resisted but later agreed to. Both were placed on prescribed medications. Azam Khan, who had been rendered nearly impotent due to an electrical shock, could not consummate their marriage properly. He sought satisfactionoflibido with other women, paying for it, and was plagued by alcoholism and troublesome friendships. He perpetually found himself in debt, often pressuring Reshama for money and resorting to physical violence if she refused. Her mother-in-law, too, subjected her to occasional beatings and taunts for her inability to bear children. Reshama was ensnared in a deeply unhappy domestic situation.

Trital was acutely aware of his role as a spy and the need for his involvement with Reshama to remain brief. It was becoming a distraction from his primary mission, yet he found himself unable to resist, and Reshama played her part in this attraction. Her husband, Azam Khan, was of a slight build, while Trital, with his robust military bearing, was an appealing contrast. She was drawn to him for his physical presence, and she often shed her veil in his company, captivating him with her face. Later, she began to remove her entire burqa, and Trital's gaze couldn't help but drift towards her figure. Trital couldn't comprehend her intentions, but her beauty was undeniable. With her blue eyes, long neck, and graceful form, she possessed a striking appearance. Her long, delicate fingers, he surmised, must work elegantly when giving haircuts. Her waist-length hair, which she usually kept in a bun, was as soft as silk (*Resham*), and Trital found himself falling for her irresistible charm.

As their relationship deepened, Trital learned that Reshama had been married for eleven years and had not been able to conceive, making her perhaps a dissatisfied spouse. He contemplated quitting his job to avoid further entanglement, but his duty required him to stay close to the scientists at the Kahuta nuclear plant. Moreover, his conscience wouldn't allow him to let the salon owner down, especially when the owner's wife was ill. He felt trapped, but his continued role in the agency depended on the information he was providing, which was nearly sufficient for his bosses.

It was monsoon season, and power outages were common. Reshama's husband, Azam Khan, took advantage of these outages to extract money from her, and Trital had seen him in the parlour a couple of times.

Meanwhile, the landlady's pregnancy was progressing, and her delivery was approaching. The landlord spent most of his time at home with her, only occasionally visiting the salon. He would instruct Reshama to handle the accounts and deliver the earnings to him at home. During this time, Reshama and Trital grew closer and closer. They admired each other and shared an undeniable attraction. Trital was cautious, as he knew getting involved with a woman violated his service conditions, but Reshama's increasing intimacy made it hard for him to resist her charms.

He was determined to avoid any physical involvement, recognizing the complications it could bring in a foreign country. He resisted his desires, and though Reshama seemed to encourage him to make the first move, he maintained a respectable distance. Their connection was undeniable, and they found it impossible to stay apart.

As the landlady's complicated pregnancy neared its end, she had to be hospitalized, leaving the parlour's responsibility to Reshama and Trital. The landlord's visits to the parlour became infrequent. During the day, Reshama and Trital would chat on Facebook Messenger, mostly discussing work-related matters. Reshama had taken to wishing Trital "Good Morning" or "Good Afternoon" in English on the Facebook page, while the rest of their messages were in Urdu.

Reshama had convinced her husband to revisit the doctor and continue taking medications. She ensured the doctor gave Azam Khan hope that he could still father a child.

Reshama would occasionally prepare a special dish for Trital in her home and bring it to the parlour to feed him, usually before the other staff arrived or during their lunch break. She asked him about his favourite dishes and would look up recipes on YouTube to prepare them for him. Trital grew fond of these affectionate gestures.

In the gents' section of the parlour, there were four male employees, including Trital. The ladies' section had three female employees. The parlour used to close at 8 p.m., but lately, they have been closing earlier due to fewer customers. In such cases, two of the male employees would pack up and leave by half-past five, while two female employees left by half-past six. Occasionally, officers from the Kahuta plant would visit with their wives, requiring Reshama to stay until they were attended to. Trital was responsible for managing the accounts.

Finally, the landlady gave birth to a baby boy, which brought immense joy to the landlord. He distributed sweets at the parlour, and Reshama took some for her husband, reminding him of their regular medication.

It was early August, and the monsoon was at its peak. One evening, as the parlour's closing time approached, Trital and Reshama were in the back room, settling the day's accounts. Suddenly, the power went out, and it was pouring heavily outside. Using the flashlight on his mobile phone, Trital went to the men's section to turn off the power switches and lock the door. Reshama recalled that the laundry hanging on the clothesline outside was getting soaked. She asked Trital to use his mobile flashlight to guide her outside, explaining that they needed to dry the laundry overnight under the fan to avoid customers using wetor used laundry the next day.

They ventured out to the courtyard together to retrieve the laundry, getting soaked in the rain as they gathered the clothes. A sudden bolt of lightning followed by thunder made Reshama shudder in fear, and she instinctively embraced Trital with one hand, bewildering him. She threw the clothes towards the door and held him with both hands, a passionate embrace that Trital could no longer resist. Lost in the moment, they kissed fervently, and Trital lifted her in his arms, carrying her to a nearby room. When the lights returned after some time, they became aware of their naked bodies and hastily dressed. They gathered the clothes strewn about, wrung them out, and left them to dry under the fan. They closed the parlour, sharing one last kiss and hug before saying their goodbyes.

These passionate encounters continued for a week, during which Reshama, being an experienced woman, unabashedly guided Trital in the realm of love. She expressed her eternal gratitude for the affection he showered upon her, while Trital confessed he was so captivated by her beauty that he couldn't bear to be apart from her.

As the landlady's confinement period came to an end, her mother arrived to assist her. This allowed the landlord to visit the parlour regularly, making it increasingly difficult for Trital and Reshama to find time together. They only had brief moments when the landlord had to accompany his wife to a doctor's appointment.

A month later, Reshama shared the joyous news of her pregnancy, which made her happy. Trital admitted that he should have used protection to avoid this situation, but she welcomed the prospect of finally becoming a mother and no longer enduring her mother-in-law's taunts and mockery. When asked about baby names, she mentioned that if it were a boy, she would name him Yusuf Khan. She left the choice of a name for a girl to Trital. He expressed his fondness for the Hindi film heroine Madhubala and suggested naming their daughter after her. Reshama, a fan of Madhubala herself, agreed, and they decided it was a fitting choice for a girl. She saidshe had seenthe movie*Mughal-e-Azam* twice , which is a 50-year-old Indianclassic. She pointed out that the legendary actor Dilip Kumar's original name was Yusuf Khan, making it an appropriate name for a boy.Madhubala   and Dilipkumar had acted inthat movie.

Trital felt that their love story was taking an unexpected turn. He couldn't bring himself to report this situation to RAW, and he believed it was best to leave the place as soon as possible. However, the agency instructed him to stay and gather more information about the Kahuta nuclear facility. Their affair persisted for several more months, during which Reshama began to trust Trital more deeply, and he, in turn, fell head over heels in love with her. They seized every chance they had to be together, always maintaining discretion. In public, they refrained from speaking to each other and instead communicated through Messenger.

Following the agency's instructions, Trital relocated to Gujranwala and secured a job at a newspaper office. The separation from Reshama was heart-wrenching, and he couldn't bear to part from her. The landlord began to suspect the romantic involvement between Trital and Reshama, but it was his wife, the landlady, who was more certain. She found it odd that a woman who had struggled to conceive for so long had suddenly become pregnant. She voiced her suspicions to her husband, which led to Trital's request to leave his job being readily accepted, as the landlord wanted to avoid any potential trouble with Reshama's husband if he discovered the affair.

As Trital settled into his new role at the newspaper office, he was instructed to keep a low profile, never forming close relationships with his colleagues. His primary role was to listen to reporters for any titbits of information but not to get too friendly with them.

Meanwhile, in Kahuta, Reshama gave birth to a baby girl. Her mother-in-law was disappointed with the girl's dark complexion, which raised questions about Azam Khan's paternity. Reshama had named the baby 'Madhubala,' a choice that displeased her husband and his mother, who preferred the name Noorjehan. Azam's mother continuously badgered Reshama, demanding to know the true father's identity. Reshama asserted repeatedly that Azam was the father, but the abuse and beatings continued.

Two months later, during a heated argument with Azam Khan, Reshama was thrown out of their home due to comments from a neighbour about the baby's complexion. Determined to leave for good, she rushed to the parlour to claim her salary, retrieved her passbook, and informed her landlady that she was quitting. She made her way to her mother's home in a village near Gujranwala, although her brothers initially refused to take her in due to her reputation. Reshama's mother, however, stood by her and brought her to Gujranwala. Both mother and daughter found work as domestic help and brought the baby along with them.

Azam Khan hadn't anticipated her permanent departure. Her income from the parlour was a significant asset, so he had resolved to take her back if she were to return and plead. However, Reshama had left his house for good. Days drifted by, and Azam Khan found himself in dire straits. He lacked the funds for his alcohol, and his mother sought financial assistance to sustain their household.

At the news agency where Trital was employed, there was a staff reporter stationed in Islamabad, covering the political manoeuvrings in Pakistan.The editor of the Gujranwala paper happened to be the reporter's uncle. Consequently, news from Islamabad reached the office promptly. This was a time of political instability in Pakistan. An ex-Pakistani cricketer aspired to become the Prime Minister, a development that could have repercussions on Indian national politics. Amid this turmoil, thoughts of Reshma were relegated to the background.

A friend from Kahuta had informed him that Reshma had given birth to a daughter. In Kahuta, there was a reporter named Sadaqat Khan, who had become Trital's new friend. Trital and Sadaqat had once collaborated on a drug investigation case. During the operation, goons had attacked Sadaqat with a knife, but Trital's military tactics had saved him. In the ensuing skirmish, the goons were wounded and forced to flee. Sadaqat felt indebted to Trital and was willing to go to great lengths to help him. Trital had even lent Sadaqat 50,000 rupees for his mother's heart surgery, which Sadaqat had repaid after some time. While official regulations prohibited close friendships, Sadaqat Khan had become one of Trital's closest friends. Sadaqat had a vague notion of Trital's true occupation but never broached the topic. After returning to India from Pakistan, Trital had found Sadaqat on Facebook, and they had rekindled their friendship, occasionally chatting on Messenger.

Reshama had secured employment in a nearby parlour close to the newspaper office where Trital worked. She always wore a burqa, so Trital was unaware of her presence in Gujranwala. He believed that he was nearly 200 kilometres away from her. Unbeknownst to him, she had seen him multiple times. On one occasion, she sent him a message on Messenger, saying, "You looked very handsome in the green sherwani and white pyjama you wore today." He was thoroughly puzzled and asked, "Where are you?" She replied, "I'm at the parlour nearby." She had never disclosed her suffering, and he had never attempted to contact her, assuming their affair had concluded. The spark was rekindled, but their meeting would have to await the right moment.

Reshama's husband, Azam Khan, remained enraged. His friends further incited him, claiming that the child born to Reshama was not his, yet she continued to use his name as the father. He harboured thoughts of harming Reshama in a fit of rage. Somehow, he learned that she was now residing in Gujranwala.

Reshama's mother would leave the child at a small neighbourhood childcare facility while she and Reshama went to work. They managed to scrape by as Reshama's brothers provided some farm produce like vegetables and grains for their mother. The mother would offer some of these as gifts to the baby caretaker, who was pleased with these offerings.

Several months passed, and Azam found himself restless without his wife and constantly in need of money. He had a friend in Gujranwala, with whom he had completed an electrician's course. This friend had visited Azam a couple of times and worked as a freelance electrician, attending to power failures and fuse changes. In the course of his work, he learned about Reshama and her workplace.

Meanwhile, Reshama longed to meet Trital again. On one occasion, the parlour owner left to tend to domestic matters, leaving Reshma in charge of the business. Seizing the opportunity, Reshma invited Trital to the parlour. This time, Trital was cautious and used protection. Reshama noticed that Trital was not circumcised like a true Muslim, leading her to question his religion. He had to reveal the truth to her under the promise of secrecy. They continued to meet regularly.

Azam Khan's friend got wind of Reshama's meetings with 'Sher Khan' and promptly informed Azam Khan. Reshama once brought their daughter, Madhubala, to meet Trital. The girl was now a year old, and Trital observed a striking resemblance between her and himself. Reshama had kept her promise to name their daughter Madhubala, after the heroine of the movie "Mughal-e-Azam." Trital held the child, gave her a kiss on the cheek, and the little girl sweetly smiled. Her mother said, "Give your father (*Abbajan*) a kiss," and the child placed her tender lips on Trital's cheek. Trital cherished this moment of paternal bliss and even took pictures of her on his mobile phone, later printing them on the office printer.

Azam Khan, furious about his wife's infidelity, harboured thoughts of revenge. He travelled to Gujranwala and stayed with his friend, who also facilitated Azam Khan's access to liquor. From a distance, he pointed out 'Sher Khan' to Azam Khan, who, upon seeing Trital's imposing physique, realized he was no match for him. Azam had brought a large dagger with him, determined to deal with Reshama first and decide how to handle 'Sher Khan' later.

One day, Azam kept a watch on the parlour. That evening, Reshma had invited Trital to the parlour but Trital had to attend some urgent office work and couldn't make it. Trital regretted his decision not to go that day. When Azam Khan realized that Reshma was alone, he forced his way into the parlour. He bombarded her with questions, feeling unsatisfied with her answers, and his anger grew. Consumed by a desire for revenge and fueled by alcohol, he brandished a dagger. Reshma made a run for the door, but she couldn't evade his attack. He stabbed her multiple times. She managed to stagger out onto the street, screaming, but he continued to assault her. Bystanders rushed to her aid and attempted to restrain him. Trital, hearing the commotion from his office, rushed outside. Reshma lay on the street, in a pool of blood. A concerned onlooker checked her pulse and sadly declared her dead. A nurse from a nearby clinic tried to help, but it was too late to save Reshma.

Trital was overwhelmed with grief. He had to exhibit immense restraint and handle the situation discreetly. He was acutely aware of the secrecy of his mission and his responsibilities to his country. He couldn't express his grief in public, as any suspicion could lead to a police investigation. If it was discovered that he was a spy, it would mean immediate arrest and execution, potentially tarnishing India's reputation worldwide.

Trital's friend, Sadaqat Khan, also arrived at the scene. He had a hunch about Trital's relationship with Reshma. The police arrived and arrested Azam Khan. Several witnesses testified that Azam Khan had wielded the dagger.

That night, Trital vacated his room, having already paid three months' rent in advance to the landlord, who was absent that evening. Trital swiftly handed the keys to the landlord's young son, gathered his belongings, and took a train to Islamabad. He reached the Indian Embassy and had to truthfully report the events to the embassy officials. They promptly issued a diplomatic visa for him. Trital shaved off his beard and mustache, discarded his Pakistani attire, and donned a Western suit. He was sent back to India on an early morning flight, accompanied by two embassy officials.

During the flight, he longed to weep, but he had to restrain his tears. He felt deeply unfortunate for not being able to save Reshma. He realized that Reshma had suffered even more due to her association with him. He believed he was responsible for her tragic death and that this sorrow would haunt him for the rest of his life.

Azam Khan was too intoxicated to provide a statement to the police that evening. His confession was recorded the following morning. He admitted to seeking revenge because of his wife's adultery, mentioning "Sher Khan" and leading the police to search for a person by that name. The newspaper had no information about Sher Khan's relationship with Azam Khan. Newspaper officials claimed that Sher Khan had suddenly disappeared. A search of Trital's room proved fruitless. After four days, the police in Pakistan reached Kahuta in search of Sher Khan. The parlour owners there provided statements, but Sher Khan remained untraceable. The Pakistan police never fathomed that an Indian spy had assumed the identity of Sher Khan. They believed he had vanished to avoid a police inquiry and might be hiding somewhere in Pakistan.

Much later, Trital managed to contact Sadaqat Khan and obtain information from him. He learned that Azam Khan had received a life imprisonment sentence. Sadaqat Khan suspected that Sher Khan, or Trital, was a spy, but he kept this knowledge to himself, and their friendship endured. Neither of them said anything that could compromise their countries' interests.

Trital held himself accountable for Reshma's death. He often thought of her and wished he could find out about Madhubala. Seventeen years had passed, and he had no clue how or where to locate her. This thought weighed heavily on his heart.

On that particular evening, he was consumed by sadness. He hardly noticed that Vijaya had prepared his favourite green pea kachori and offered no words of appreciation for her kind gesture. He lay on the bed, absorbed in his thoughts. Vijaya observed his distant demeanour, noting that this wasn't the first time he had seemed lost in thought and wistful. Restless, Trital tossed and turned until he finally fell asleep late in the night.

&&&&&

09.07.2032

The two suites had been reserved at the Radisson Greene Resort in Digha, West Bengal. One was for the Chief Minister, Ashutosh Chatterjee, and the other for a Bengali cinema actress, Karishma Das. A meeting was scheduled at 9 a.m. between Ashutosh Chatterjee and the Afghan leader, Mustafizur Khan, at the resort. The receptionist had been informed about the meeting, and Mustafizur was promptly escorted to the Chief Minister's suite. However, Ashutosh was in Karishma's suite at the time, and Mustafizur was asked to wait in the CM's suite. He was offered some toast and coffee but had to wait for half an hour before the CM arrived.

When Ashutosh finally entered the room, Mustafizur stood up to greet him. Ashutosh responded, "How are you doing?" He wasn't aware of the exact purpose of Mustafizur's visit, so he asked, "How are you?"

Mustafizur immediately expressed, "It's a dire situation everywhere."

Ashutosh inquired, "Why? What's wrong?"

Mustafizur explained, "Our people are restless because they've been denied citizenship. They can't access government facilities and subsidies. Their ration cards and Aadhar cards are swiftly confiscated, and our agents have to spend a significant amount of money to retrieve these documents."

Ashutosh simply nodded, responding, "Hmm."

Mustafizur felt somewhat put off by this response. Ashutosh pondered the issue for a moment and then stated, "It seems we will have to initiate our protests once more."

Mustafizur questioned, "What will that achieve?"

Ashutosh elaborated, "It will exert considerable pressure on the authorities, making it harder for them to seize the cards and documents. If this can alleviate the suffering of our people, it's worth it, don't you think?"

Mustafizur concurred, saying, "Yes, you're right. I'll discuss this with Sanodia and Habeeb Khan and devise a plan."

Ashutosh urged him, "Please do so and keep me informed."

Mustafizur then asked, "Will you support our agitation?"

Ashutosh replied, "You already have our financial support. Our party workers will stand by you, but our party banners won't be displayed openly. It's risky for our party to be directly associated with your ultimate objective concerning Rajendra Kaul. Our government could be jeopardized."

Mustafizur understood, saying, "I see."

Ashutosh then inquired, "Anything new regarding the video clip from the CD?"

Mustafizur responded, "Nothing new. Our contacts in Afghanistan are closely monitoring Najeeb Khan. There's no doubt he will use the video clip from the CD to blackmail Rajendra Kaul. But we're uncertain if this will advance our cause of citizenship."

Ashutosh agreed, "Yes, that's a valid concern."

A brief pause ensued as the waiter served coffee and snacks. Then Mustafizur continued, "It's no longer as favourable as it used to be. Our Afghan and Rohingya leaders are under constant scrutiny by the IB."

Ashutosh admitted, "They keep an eye on me too."

Mustafizur acknowledged, "That's why it's becoming increasingly challenging to execute the plan to remove Rajendra Kaul. We're doing our best despite these obstacles."

Ashutosh encouraged him, "Continue your efforts, but ensure my name remains unconnected to it. You may leave now," he concluded.

Mustafizur left quietly, and Karishma entered the room, passionately kissing Ashutosh. Their intimacy escalated as he caressed her. She then took a seat, sipping her coffee, and inquired, "Who was that peculiar man?"

Ashutosh reminded her, "I've asked you not to get involved in my official matters."

Karishma responded, "Okay, okay," and continued sipping her coffee.

Ashutosh, lost in his thoughts, recalled the 2029 Lok Sabha elections. His party had won 76 seats and wielded influence not only in West

Bengal but also in states like Bihar, Assam, Tripura, and others. The results had led to a coalition government, with neither the BLP nor the RVP crossing the 200-seat mark. Their party, aspiring for his mother Lalita Chatterjee to become the Prime Minister, formed alliances with regional parties to reach a total of 135 seats. However, the BLP insisted on their candidate becoming the PM, with 152 seats and an additional 20 seats from the SAP. Lalitaji could only become the Deputy PM in this scenario.

In this political standoff, Ashutosh's wife, Lily, played a pivotal role. She had returned from her maternal home in Thailand and revealed the existence of an old CD that could be of use to him. When Ashutosh viewed the CD, he was astounded. It contained footage of Rajendra Kaul in a compromising position with two young girls, clearly identifiable. These girls happened to be Lily's cousins and bore a striking resemblance to her aunt.

Ashutosh had a devious plan. He kept the CD's content a secret from his mother, merely telling her he was meeting Rajendra Kaul for one final negotiation. During their private meeting, Ashutosh showed Kaul the CD, enraging him and prompting threats of blackmail charges and jail time. Ashutosh pointed out that even if he were imprisoned, the CD would become public, severely damaging Kaul's reputation. To avoid this, Ashutosh proposed a compromise: Kaul would withdraw his claim for the PM position, ensuring Lalitaji's appointment. In return, Ashutosh would hand over the CD and guarantee its deletion from his mobile. Kaul also obtained a written agreement from Ashutosh, promising that all copies of the CD would be destroyed, and no future blackmail attempts would be made. Ashutosh signed the agreement, and only then was the path clear for Lalitaji to assume office. Months later, he vaguely disclosed the turn of events to his mother.

Tragically, Lily's involvement may have cost her life. The two girls in the video, Lily's cousins, were on a flight with her back to Thailand. The chartered plane they were on met with a fatal accident, resulting in Lily's death and the destruction of the CD in her possession. The Directorate General of Civil Aviation investigated the crash and attributed it to a standard engine failure. The person responsible for the accident remained unknown.

Ashutosh often thought of Lily, and his mother encouraged him to remarry, but he wasn't ready for it yet. Moreover, there were no shortages of willing partners to fulfil his physical needs.

Now, he felt a growing concern about the CD being in Afghan hands and wondered about the potential consequences. Karishma noticed his contemplative mood and inquired about it. He dismissed it with a brief, "It's nothing."

She then pointed out, "Look how it's raining over the sea."

He simply responded, "Nice."

&&&&&

18.07.2032 to 19.07.2032

The monsoon season had arrived, bringing heavy rainfall across India. This year, the monsoon appeared to be exceptionally fierce, resulting in floods throughout the country. Interestingly, Kashmir experienced only moderate rain, while Pakistan also faced flooding.

The torrential rains initially wreaked havoc in Southern India and the North Eastern states. Kerala and Telangana witnessed the National Disaster Relief teams striving diligently to provide assistance to the affected population. Subsequently, Gujarat and Madhya Pradesh bore the brunt of these heavy downpours and sought military support. In the North East, the situation grew increasingly dire, with thousands of acres submerged. To address this crisis, a special cell was established in the Prime Minister's Office, and Home Minister Avdhesh Singh took charge of coordinating relief efforts.

Two days before the events in Uttarakhand, the weather bureau had forecasted a potential cloud burst in the region. Preparations were underway to manage the situation, and Chief Minister Sukesh Rawat was deeply concerned. As predicted, a cloud burst occurred in Chamoli at 6 p.m. on the 18th, worsening the flooding situation. With nightfall approaching, rescue operations became increasingly challenging. An estimated 800 individuals were swept away by the surging waters. The Indian Air Force, Army, Navy, and NDRF teams launched a concerted effort to rescue people.

Upon receiving news of this tragedy, Avdhesh Singh swiftly established a 24-hour helpline at the Home Ministry. By 10 p.m., he had apprised the Prime Minister of the situation, and the Prime Minister insisted on receiving continuous updates.

On the 19th of July, heart-wrenching images of the devastation dominated the media. An outpouring of compassion swept across the nation. The relentless heavy rain posed significant challenges for rescue operations, but the defence forces persevered in their tireless efforts.

Many people had been carried away as far as Maijuju and Mun villages. By 11 a.m., the rescue teams had saved the lives of 215 individuals, while they had recovered 105 deceased bodies. Nearly 6,000 people were left homeless, and their possessions were swept away by the floodwaters.

Chief Minister Rakesh Rawat arrived at the disaster site via helicopter to assess the situation. He maintained constant communication with the Prime Minister's Office and the Home Ministry.

In Delhi, Avdhesh Singh, with the Prime Minister's consent, decided to establish the Uttarakhand Flood Relief Fund. The extent of the loss in terms of both lives and property in Uttarakhand was enormous, making it imperative to commence the rehabilitation process without delay. Avdhesh Singh and Rawat had already discussed this over the phone.

Rawat had requested financial aid for Uttarakhand, and Avdhesh Singh informed him about the Relief Fund. He suggested reaching out to Mr. Subhash Singh, the finance minister, to request financial assistance. Rawat expressed his intention to directly appeal to the Prime Minister to visit Uttarakhand, witness the situation firsthand, and approve immediate aid. Avdhesh Singh responded positively, saying, "That's agood idea!"

By evening, another 30 bodies had been recovered, and approximately 40 people were rescued. The count of individuals carried away by the floodwaters continued to rise. The initial estimate of 800 had swelled to 1000, and there were concerns that over 500 might have perished.

Relief aid poured in from various parts of the country, including airdrops of food grain packets, blankets, and warm clothing. The Home Ministry operated around the clock, diligently addressing the demands of the situation.

Relief work was on throughout the day in Chamoli. Military trucks rumbled in, delivering supplies to the survivors. Avdhesh Singh monitored all the relief work. He arranged to transport all the supplies that some NGOs were providing. The supplies contained food packets, medicines, blankets etc.

It was difficult to console the kith and kin of the people who had lost their lives. The injured were being treated free of cost in the government hospital. The State Government had declared a relief aid of rupees two lakh to the injured and rupees ten lakh to the dependents of the deceased.

In Kabul, that evening, the home of Afzal Khan was bustling with activity. A significant amount of drug money had been received from Africa.

The three brothers indulged in the delectable dishes prepared by Shama. Nadira skilfully moved in and out of the kitchen, bringing piping hot *paneer tikka, chicken tikka, and Chapli kebab* to the table. There was also a spread of boiled eggs, salted cashews, almonds, and groundnuts. Razia's responsibility was to serve these dishes, brought by Nadira, onto individual plates. Salman Khan, with insistence, persuaded Razia to have a few drinks, causing her to become light-headed and intoxicated. She was eager to dance but couldn't do so until the head of the household, Afzal Khan, gave the order. Meanwhile, the three brothers remained sober enough to discuss their business matters.

Afzal said to Ashiq, "Let's move to your room and tally the cash received from Africa."

Ashiq agreed, saying, "Yes, we need to transfer some funds to that Taliban leader who wishes to utilize it in Kashmir."

Razia, feigning ignorance of their conversation, continued to fill Salman's plate with *kebabs*. The brothers were about to rise and leave when Nadira entered with steaming hot *Nargis kebabs*, urging them to try them, mentioning that Shama Didi had prepared them. They sat back down to savour these delectable treats. Nervously, Razia inquired of Afzal Khan if she could pour him some liquor, to which he nodded in agreement.

Ashiq then spoke to his elder brother, "That Taliban leader, Majid Khan, visited me. He is involved in the Kashmir operation and urgently requires financial assistance."

Afzal responded, "Let me discuss this with our superiors. We can decide on the amount to be sent later."

Throughout their conversation, Razia pretended to be oblivious, continuing to serve food. Salman's gaze lingered on her, causing Afzal discomfort.

Afzal and Ashiq retired to Ashiq's room to discuss financial matters, while Salman went to his own room. Razia told him she would change into different attire and join him in his room. When she returned, she was dressed in a sheer, long gown without anything underneath.

Salman Khan was sitting with his laptop. There was a PC on the table, which he used to store data from the laptop. He was instructed by the secret service department to change passwords frequently. On that day, he had altered his password and mentioned to Ashiq Khan, a conversation Razia overheard.

Turning her attention to him, she offered him a glass of whisky and a bottle along with a plate of kebabs. She settled herself on Salman's lap and handed him the glass, and he caressed her breasts. The alcohol began to take its effect. Accidentally, Razia switched off the power pack under the table with her leg, causing the laptop and PC to shut down. She apologized for her clumsiness and turned the power back on. She fed him a kebab, and he relished the moment. As Salman bent to restart the PC and laptop, she did the same while raising her gown, exposing her intentions. Salman enjoyed the view. As he carelessly typed in the passwords, she observed the keys closely, memorizing the passwords"Q@Salma2" and "Z@Saira3F." She then turned to him and kissed him, to which he responded, "Let me work for a few more minutes. You can assist Shama Didi in the kitchen for a while."

Razia was aware that in a village near Asadabad, a wedding had taken place between Afzal Khan's son Shahrukh and Ashiq Khan's daughter. Afzal had instructed Salman to visit the village frequently. Razia had quickly deduced that Salman's wife, Saira, and Shahrukh might be involved in an affair, but she had not disclosed this to anyone.

She was patiently waiting for an opportunity to extract data from Salman's computer, which she could then pass on to Nurse Rashida, with the ultimate goal of reaching the Mossad.

&&&&&

21.07.2032

Uttarakhand was still grappling with the aftermath of the devastation caused by the rains and a catastrophic cloud burst. In response to Sukesh Rawat's plea for assistance, the Prime Minister's Office (PMO) had swiftly allocated a contingency relief fund of Rs. 100 crores. The Prime Minister himself was scheduled to visit the disaster-stricken site.

On this particular day, heavy rainfall persisted in most of India and in Pakistan, except for Kashmir, where the rains had finally subsided.

The media had been reporting another 'Breaking News' story since the morning. A small Air Force aircraft was prepared at Safdarjung Airport, ready to transport Prime Minister Rajendra Kaul on a tour of Uttarakhand. The aircraft was planned to make a stopover at Jolly Grant Airstrip in Dehradun, where the Chief Minister of Uttarakhand, Rawat, would join the Prime Minister for an aerial survey of the cloud burst and flood-affected areas, in helicopter.

Around 9:30 a.m., there was news of a delay in the take-off, likely due to adverse weather conditions. Then, at 10:00 a.m., it was revealed that the Prime Minister's sister and President of BLP, Pratibha Kaul, would be accompanying him on the flight, causing further delay.

At 10:30 a.m., news channels reported that the flight had finally departed for Uttarakhand. However, by 11:00 a.m., a 'Breaking News' update shook the nation. The Prime Minister's aircraft had met with an accident, crashing near Devipura. The entire country was jolted awake, and both the Home Ministry and Defence Ministry immediately dispatched rescue helicopters. The nation held its collective breath, praying for the safety of the Prime Minister and his sister.

Uttarakhand CM Rawat was in shock. The Prime Minister had undertaken this visit upon his request. He mobilized the entire state machinery to locate the crashed plane and its passengers. News vans from various media outlets rushed to Devipura in the hope of being the first to report the "sensational coverage."

The President issued an appeal to the nation for calm and patience. He summoned the National Security Advisor (NSA), Trital, and held a meeting with the PrincipalSecretaryof PMO,Chief Secretaries of the Defence and Law ministries, alongwith the Deputy Secretary of the Home Ministry (as the Chief Secretary was on leave). The Solicitor General of India was to join the meeting via video conference.

In the BLP office, Vice-President Nagarjun Reddy conducted a small meeting where he suggested that Subhash Singh should assume the role of caretaker Prime Minister until the whereabouts of Rajendra Kaul were determined. Meanwhile, the crash site had been located, and it seemed highly unlikely that the Prime Minister and his sister had survived.

In the President's meeting, it was decided that Subhash Singh would be appointed as the interim or caretaker Prime Minister to manage the nation's affairs until a new leader was elected by the members of parliament in a special session. Subhash Singh and Nagarjuna were duly informed of this decision.

By 4:30 p.m., the wreckage of the crashed plane had been found in a valley. Some bodies lay scattered around, while others had been charred in the wreckage. The Prime Minister's body was identified by the gold chain he wore around his neck, along with a sapphire pendant and an imported belt with a distinctive buckle. Pratibha Kaul, the only female passenger, was easily identifiable. Among the other eight passengers, the bodies of six had been discovered.

Upon confirmation of the Prime Minister's death, Home Minister Avdhesh Singh expressed his condolences and informed his party members that, with their support, he was willing to assume the role of Prime Minister. Some members consented, while others deferred to the party's decision. Nagarjuna remained noncommittal. Avdhesh Singh sent a fax message to the President, expressing his readiness to take on the responsibility during these challenging times, with the backing of a majority of Members of Parliament.

However, at that very moment, news channels reported that the President had declared Subhash Singh as the interim or caretaker Prime Minister. Avdhesh Singh was visibly frustrated by this news.

Over the phone, Subhash Singh accepted the responsibility and sent faxes to all ministries and state governments, confirming his acceptance. He instructed the defence minister to bring the bodies of the late Prime Minister, Rajendra Kaul, and the Party President, Pratibha Kaul, to Delhi with full state honours, placing them in the BLP office for the public to pay their respects. He paid condolence visits to the Prime Minister's wife and Pratibha Kaul's husband, Javed Khan. Both families were overwhelmed with grief, and he stayed with them for an extended period. Other ministers and leaders were also present.

The Indian public was deeply shaken, and BLP workers demanded that those responsible for the crash be brought to justice. Protests began in Delhi and quickly spread to the capital cities of other states.

Rajnarain Singh, the son of Avdhesh Singh, began openly suggesting that the RVP had a hand in the Prime Minister's death, prompting protests in the state and demands for decisive action against wrongdoers.

Subhash Singh made television appearances, appealing to the masses to remain calm and composed. The President's office also called for maintaining law and order.

In response to the President's request, Subhash Singh established a high-level committee to investigate the crash. The committee included representatives from NIA, NSA, IB, RAW, CBI, the Head of Military Intelligence, and a retired judge from the Supreme Court. The committee was chaired by HaribandhuMahaptra, a retired Chief Justice of the Supreme Court. The committee's primary task was to determine whether the Taliban, ISIof Pakistan, Rohingyas, or any opposition leaders were involved in the air crash.

Late at night, the bodies were brought to Delhi. Uttarakhand CM Rawat, the Home Minister, the Foreign Affairs Minister, the defence minister, and other officials were all in attendance. The caskets were first taken to the home of Rajendra Kaul, where his French wife and nine-year-old son, as well as Pratibha Kaul's husband Javed Khan and their two children, awaited. The scene was one of grief, with tears flowing uncontrollably.

Following this, the bodies were laid in state with full honours at the BLP office. Party supporters arrived to pay their final respects to their beloved leaders. The entire nation was in mourning, and police units were deployed in sensitive areas while paramilitary forces remained on high alert to manage any potential unrest or disturbances.

22.07.2032

Suresh Dutt, a former Member of Parliament from Nasik, Maharashtra, affiliated with RVP, had been residing in Pune. Several months ago, he had made derogatory remarks about the Prime Minister and expressed a desire for his assassination. Subsequently, he was tried for these statements and released on bail.

At 4:00 AM, a large mob, predominantly comprised of members of the Socialist Samata Dal (SAASAD), wearing masks and carrying torches, gathered in front of Suresh Dutt's residence. They set his house on fire, and in the chaos, his wife and daughter attempted to flee. Dutt contacted the police and the fire brigade for assistance. Alerted by the neighbours, the fire brigade was summoned, but the absence of rain that day allowed the flames to spread rapidly. Dutt's efforts to rescue his wife and daughter were thwarted as the mob hurled torches at them. Bystanders dared not intervene, fearing the violent mob. The family remained trapped inside. The mob dispersed upon the police's arrival, but the officers were unable to enter the house due to the raging flames. By the time the fire brigade arrived and extinguished the fire, it was too late— the family had perished in the blaze. OB vans from television channels captured the burning house and the firefighting efforts on camera, shocking and terrifying the public. All political parties unequivocally condemned the heinous act. Members of the Hanuman Shakti Dal grew agitated and discussed the possibility of retaliation.

The situation became highly combustible. Party leaders implored their supporters to remain calm, but demonstrations against RVP by SAASAD workers erupted. Hanuman Dal activists engaged in acts of arson and stone pelting at the residences of BLP workers, necessitating the imposition of Section 144 in Pune. The military was deployed to restore order.

The funeral procession was scheduled to commence at 4:00 PM that evening. Mourners arrived in a continuous stream to pay their final respects to the late Prime Minister and the President of the BLP at the party's headquarters. At 1:00 PM, when the President and Vice President arrived to offer their condolences, Subhash Singh, Ravindra Prasad, and Avdhesh Singh were also present there.

The caskets were placed on open military vehicles. Despite occasional light showers, crowds gathered along the streets to bid their leaders a final farewell. The route leading to the Nigam Bodh Ghat (Funeral Ground) was cordoned off. Leaders from various political parties were in attendance, although Socialist Samata Dal (SAASAD) workers intermittently shouted slogans against RVP. Despite RVP's statement from the previous night disavowing any involvement in the tragic incident, resentment against the party was palpable. The procession reached the cremation grounds at 5:30 PM, and the pyre was lit at 6:00 PM, marking a tearful farewell to the departed. The entire ceremony was broadcast on all television channels.

The atmosphere was fraught with violence and unrest. Raj Narain Singh made malicious accusations against RVP, inciting riots that spread from Pune to encompass Maharashtra, even reaching the borders of Gujarat and Karnataka. SAASAD and Hanuman Dal activists clashed, beating each other mercilessly. Despite leaders' fervent pleas for peace, Raj Narain's provocative statements added fuel to the fire. Calls for retribution against Suresh Dutt intensified. Raj Narain vented his anger against RVP and continued to allege that the party was complicit in the air crash that claimed the Prime Minister's life. He encouraged people to attack RVP workers. RVP reiterated that it had no connection to the incident, attributing it to a foreign conspiracy, but these assertions fell on deaf ears. Suspicion and doubt loomed everywhere.

Late at night, the caretaker PM, Subhash Singh, conducted a meeting. Many ministers participated online. All state governments received orders to maintain strict law and order. Defence Minister Ravindra Prasad was directed to place the Army and Air Force on high alert. Avdhesh Singh asked the Minister of State for Home Affairs to represent him. The entire cabinet denounced the arson attack on Suresh Dutt in Pune, and this message was relayed to the news channels.

The BLP office buzzed with activity. Avdhesh Singh made repeated phone calls to Vice-President Nagarjuna Reddy, urging him to convene a meeting of the Members of Parliament. He wanted Nagarjuna to arrange a meeting of the Party Working Committee to seek their opinions on electing a new leader. Nagarjuna assured him that this would be a top priority.

Meanwhile, unrest and chaos gripped the nation. Hanuman Dal and SSD activists clashed violently. Incidents of arson occurred. Subhash Singh appealed to the chief ministers of states to swiftly restore order. He attempted to reach Avdhesh Singh, but the latter seethed with resentment and declined to take the PM's calls.

&&&&&

23.07.2032

At 4.30 a.m., Iliyas Zaibuddin, leader of the Azad Kashmir Party called up ISI officer Ozair Ahmed. Ozair did not answer at first, but when the calls persisted, he answered the call and asked irritable, "What is it?"

Ilyas said, "The PM of India is dead."

Ozair said, "I know that. What else do you have? Why have you called so early in the morning?"

"The situation in India is explosive. I think we should grab this chance to do something,"

"What do you mean? What are you hinting at?"

Ilyas said, "The situation in India is unstable, you can launch an attack now."

Ozair said, "We will talk about this in the evening. I have to consult my seniors and also have a word with Taliban." He cuts the call curtly.

Tritals had a prearranged meeting with the President at 8:00 AM. The President was aware of the purpose of their visit. The couple, Tritals, brought a box of decorations for the Sawan Jhoola, a festive swing during the monsoon season. They underwent the routine security checks before the servants escorted them to the Darbar Hall, where the President's wife, Vinaya, awaited their arrival. Vinaya was delighted to receive them and the box of decorations. She led them to the drawing room on the second floor. Vijaya waited there, while Vinaya accompanied Trital to the President's chamber.

The President was engrossed in his *Pranayam*(breathing) exercises and gestured for Trital to take a seat. Trital initially rose to greet the

President, but the President motioned for him to remain seated and joined him on the sofa.

"Pranam, Sir," greeted Trital.

"Is there something urgent today?" inquired the President.

"Yes, Sir. The situation is extremely dire."

"I'm well aware of it. It's a highly explosive situation. Is it solely my responsibility to address this?"

"If the RVP and BLP don't halt their violent clashes and acts of arson immediately, we're heading towards anarchy, chaos, and widespread destruction in the nation."

"What if they refuse to reconcile?"

"You can suggest to the PM that an Emergency be declared."

"Yes, that appears to be the only solution under the current circumstances. I intend to speak with Subhash Singh. In fact, he mentioned that he would brief me at 10 AM today."

"I'm concerned that Pakistan and the Taliban may exploit the situation here."

"Yes, we must investigate that angle."

Following their discussion, they moved to the drawing room for a light breakfast. Afterward, Trital left the room, and Vijaya stayed with Vinaya.

From 9:00 AM onwards, incidents of arson and violence erupted across the country. In regions where BLP and its allies held sway, they apprehended, assaulted, stabbed, and even set Hanuman Dal activists on fire. The police stood idly by in some areas, while in others, they detained a few wrongdoers. In yet other places, Hanuman Dal activists assaulted SSD or SAASAD supporters, leading to mayhem.

By 12:00 PM, news broke that the Vice-President of BLP in Uttar Pradesh, Sajid Khan, had been immolated in Agra. An announcement declared this as retaliation for the killing of Suresh Dutt. This further fuelled tensions, with clear divisions between RVP and BLP supporters. Clashes broke out between RVP's allies, Hanuman Dal, and their rivals, SSD, who supported BLP.

Uttar Pradesh's Chief Minister, Mahant Surajnath, issued orders for the arrest of those responsible for the murder of BLP's Vice-President. Law enforcement agencies, including the CID and Crime Branch, sprang into action, resulting in the apprehension of five culprits by 4:00 PM.

The Socialist Samata Dal sought to avenge their members and demanded the surrender of the five individuals arrested. In an attempt to immolate these individuals, they set fire to the Lohamandi police station in Agra, where the detainees were held. The police responded by opening fire on them. This initial act spiralled into widespread violence in Agra and subsequently across Uttar Pradesh. By evening, this conflict took on a communal tone in some districts likeRampur, Muzaffarnagar, Azamgarh, Agra and Kanpurin lateleading to clashes between Hindus and Muslims.

These incidents were widely covered by TV channels, triggering riots in most of northern India. Madhya Pradesh, Rajasthan, Uttarakhand, Bihar, Punjab, Himachal Pradesh, Haryana, and Chhattisgarh all experienced violence and chaos. In some places, the clashes were between SAASAD and Hanuman Shakti Dal workers, while in others, Hindu-Muslim riots erupted due to the death of Sajid Khan.

Caretaker PM Subhash Singh convened a cabinet meeting,in late evening which Home Minister Avdhesh Singh attended along with his group of ministers, including Arvind Kumar, Bhavna Shinde, Venkatappaiya, and S. Subramaniyam. Other ministers, such as Ravindra Prasad, Kalavati, Manohar Reddy, Basavraj Patil, Kamlesh Yadav, and Rakesh Pilot, were also present. Some ministers, like Riyaz Mehmood, Shamrao Patil, Joginder Kaur, Nambudripad, and Tribhuvan Singh, participated via a Zoom meeting.

A heated argument erupted between Defence Minister Ravindra Prasad and Home Minister Avdhesh Singh over the law-and-order situation in the country. Ravindra Prasad accused Avdhesh Singh of failing to control his son, Rajnarain Singh. The cabinet became divided into two factions: one supporting Ravindra Prasad's allegations, and the other defending Avdhesh Singh. Initially, nobody paid heed to the PM's pleas for order. Eventually, when calm was restored, the PM declared the need to impose an Emergency. Avdhesh Singh opposed this decision, leading to further chaos. The meeting was adjourned before the PM could explain that the suggestion for an Emergency had originated from the President. Rakesh Pilot was instructed to document that the President's suggestion had not been deliberated and brought to its logical conclusion. Additionally, it was recorded that the defence minister was directed to involve the military as a precautionary measure. The defence minister subsequently conveyed this order to the Chief of Defence Staff, Ashok Bhat, to issue appropriate instructions to all three-armedwings.

It was imperative for everyone to adhere to the directives of the Home Ministry, as instructed by the PMO.

At 10:30 PM that night, Subhash Singh againhad a brief conversation with President Shivkalyan Singhji. Earlier in the morningalso He had talkedand got suggestions.He expressed his helplessness and sorrow. The President recommended that the PMO implement stringent measures to maintain law and order and instruct the state governments accordingly.

At 11.00 p.m., Iliyas, Ozair and Majid Khan have a Zoom meeting. Iliyas asks Majid Khan about the line of action, to which Majid Khan replies that his seniors had given the go ahead.

Ozair said, "There is a consensus at all levels, that is, the Prime Minister, ISI and Military, that we must take advantage of the delicate situation in India.

Iliyas asked, "When will the donkeys arrive?"

Majid Khan said, "It will take at least two days to prepare for it."

Iliyas said, "That's alright. I have confirmed news from Delhi that the military in Kashmir is being deployed elsewhere in the country, we won't have much resistance in Kashmir."

"You too make internal preparations, it will help us," said Ozair.

Iliyas nodded.

All this talk was being overheard and recorded by Soshe Dayan's agents. This tape was to be delivered to the higher ups but the method of delivery was a different one.

&&&&&

24.07.2032

At 4 a.m., the Home Ministry's call centre received a distressing message regarding riots in Hyderabad. The message was promptly relayed to the relevant officials. Home Secretary Sandesh Vora was already awake at that early hour due to a strong gut feeling that the riots might escalate across the nation.

It was revealed that clashes had broken out in Hyderabad between the BLP and RVP activists, with support from the Deccan-e-Majlis party for the BLP. Two RVP party members had sustained head injuries during a stone-pelting attack by the BLP at 11 p.m. the previous night. They were admitted to Osmania Hospital and remained unconscious.

In a retaliatory attack at 2 a.m., a BLP activist was stabbed in the stomach and rushed to the hospital in critical condition. By 3 a.m., this incident had further fuelled tensions, resulting in a full-scale confrontation between the two parties. Initially, the RVP activists found themselves at a disadvantage, facing the combined forces of the BLP and

Deccan-e-Majlis. They rallied their members in the old city of Hyderabad, escalating the violence.

Reports indicated that more Hindu victims than Muslims were affected in Hyderabad. These distressing updates reached Delhi. The Hyderabad police attempted to control the riots, but the involved political parties refused to cooperate. By the afternoon, the riots had extended to Secunderabad and nearby districts of Telangana, including Karimnagar, Warangal, Rangareddy, and Khammam. Both RVP and BLP activists clashed, and the police had to deploy forces everywhere. Hospitals were inundated with injured individuals, prompting the Chief Minister of Telangana to impose a curfew in the evening.

The temporary break in rainfall made it easier for people to take to the streets, leading to an increase in incidents of arson, riots, and looting.

Soon, the repercussions were felt in Maharashtra, as the longstanding conflict between RVP and BLP, compounded by the violence in Telangana, incited anti-Muslim sentiments. Communal riots began in Nanded, Aurangabad, and Parbhani before spreading to Akola, Paratwada, Malegaon, and Bhiwandi. Even Mumbai faced unrest, with clashes erupting in Bhindi Bazar, Kurla, Behrampada, and other areas. Although Pune was already under curfew, BLP and SSD activists targeted RVP activists and their offices. In some instances, the police merely stood by as the riots were instigated by the ruling party.

Karnataka and Gujarat followed in the footsteps of Maharashtra and Telangana. Despite RVP being in power in both states, hooligan elements within the BLP wreaked havoc on the streets, forcing the governments to arrest and detain both RVP and BLP activists.Uttar Pradesh, Madhya Pradesh, Bihar, and Chhattisgarh faced similar situations, with widespread clashes between the BLP and RVP.

In Delhi, interim Prime Minister Subhash Singh and the President were deeply concerned. Subhash Singh had briefed the President on the cabinet meeting's failure the previous night. With the assistance of the Home and Defence ministries, he did everything in his power to control the situation. The army in Ladakh, Kashmir, Punjab, and Uttarakhand were mobilized and sent to the riot-affected areas. Through various media outlets, he made heartfelt appeals to the nation to maintain peace.

RVP President Ashok Chaddha took to the media to appeal for peace to the nation, but it seemed to have little effect.

In Bengal, the longstanding enmity between RVP and the DeshbandhuSwabhiman Party (DESWAP) was widely known. RVP had employed various tactics to seize power in West Bengal, all of which had failed. DESWAP activists commonly targeted RVP members, but they took advantage of the situation to intensify their attacks. Violence erupted swiftly. The death of Prime Minister Rajendra Kaul brought joy to DESWAP, as they held him responsible for their loss of power at the centre. They unleashed violence on RVP workerstaking advantage of situation in the country, while the police department in Bengal, aligned with the ruling party, remained unresponsive. DESWAP workers disregarded Chief Minister Ashutosh Chatterjee's pleas for peace. In retaliation, RVP volunteers attacked DESWAP, only to be arrested by the police and sent to jail. By evening, the entire state of Bengal was engulfed in riots.

&&&&&

25.07.2032

In the early hours of the morning, Punjab CM Ranbir Singh was roused from sleep by a call from his secretary. His head was heavy from a night of heavy drinking, but upon hearing his wife inform him that it was an urgent matter, he mustered the will to answer the phone.

Secretary Gurmit Singh apologized for the early wake-up call and conveyed that there was a call of CMfrom Andhra Pradesh. Ranbir Singh requested to be connected to the call. It was the Chief Minister of Andhra, Dr. Shekhar Reddy, speaking from the other end. After exchanging the usual pleasantries, Dr. Reddy expressed his desire to discuss party affairs.

Ranbir Singh responded, "Of course, that's a good reason. Our party thrives thanks to well-wishers like you."

Dr. Reddy waved off the compliments. "Let's put the pleasantries aside. We need to address the impending party crisis."

"I'm not entirely clear on this," Ranbir Singh replied.

Dr. Reddy explained, "Things aren't going smoothly within our party in Delhi. Power politics is at play, and we need to find a solution."

Ranbir Singh pondered, "But the solution should come from those in power at the centre. Should we jump into the fray?"

Dr. Reddy insisted that there was a need for action, at least for the party's sake.

Ranbir Singh concurred, "ThatAvdhesh Singh donot agree at all."

Dr. Reddy continued, "We must promptly convene a meeting of the parliamentary committee and members to elect the next Prime Minister. Until then, the nation will remain in turmoil."

Ranbir Singh added, "I believe Ganeshraman from Kerala wants to join this conversation. (Addressing his secretary, he said, 'Let Ganeshraman join the meeting.')"

Dr. Reddy informed them, "He was practicing yoga when I called."

Ganeshraman greeted them, saying, "Good morning, my friends, good morning."

"Welcome, welcome," responded Ranbir Singh and Dr. Reddy.

Ganeshraman shared, "The Home Minister reached out to me yesterday. He discussed the law-and-order situation first and then delivered a lengthy sermon."

Ranbir Singh inquired, "Did he seek your support?"

Dr. Reddy mentioned that he had also received a call from the Home Minister.

Ganeshraman opined, "I think we should start by electing the Party President. Nagarjuna Reddy is a suitable candidate; let's vote for him."

Ranbir asked, "After that, can we proceed to convene a meeting of the members of parliament?"

"Yes," said Reddy, "that's the correct procedure. Everything will happen with the Party President's approval, which is Nagarjuna's consent."

Ganeshraman posed a question, "To maintain party unity, is it necessary to remove Subhash Singh from the position of Prime Minister?"

Ranbir Singh remarked, "He's a decent man, albeit on the older side."

Dr. Reddy suggested, "Then let's stick with this strategy."

Ganeshraman recommended, "At this stage, there's no need to inform the Home Minister."

Ranbir Singh concurred and asked for permission to leave the call, as he needed to attend to a nature's call.

The meeting concluded with this understanding.

Meanwhile, media channels showed that riots were still happening everywhere and the situation was deteriorating, with Telangana and Karnataka being the hardest-hit states. Clashes were escalating in Telangana, and as a consequence, Karnataka was also suffering from the consequences, being a neighbour state. Riots had erupted in Hosur, Bellary, Belgaum, and Bengaluru. The governments in both states had deployed police teams to control the riots, while caretaker PM Subhash Singh had arranged for military assistance. In contrast, Tamil Nadu, Andhra Pradesh, and Kerala remained relatively peaceful due to the imposition of Section 144 and the pre-emptive arrests of potential troublemakers, but the situation remained volatile.

In Maharashtra, Bihar, Chhattisgarh, and Uttarakhand, RVP and Hanuman Dal activists were increasingly targeted, prompting them to retaliate against BLP and SSD activists. Urban areas were more affected than rural ones, and military personnel were airdropped in various cities by army airplanes and helicopters.

The situation in Uttar Pradesh, Madhya Pradesh, Rajasthan, and Gujarat was equally dire. SSD activists were being subjected to violence, as they were associated with the BLP. Many BLP workers were injured and hospitalized. Despite the imposition of Section 144, activists took to the streets, leading to widespread anarchy, baton charges, and street firing.The buses and trains were burned.

Even capital cities were engulfed by these riots. Starting from Bhindi Bazar in Mumbai, the unrest spread to Girggaon, Dadar, Worli, and the suburbs. Local taxi, bus, train services, and metro lines were suspended in Mumbai. A similar scenario unfolded in Pune, Nagpur, Hyderabad, Aurangabad, Bengaluru, Ahmedabad, Surat, Vadodara, Bharuch, Bilaspur, Raipur, Bhopal, Indore, Jabalpur, Sihor, Jaipur, Jodhpur, and Udaipur. Railway coaches were set ablaze in several places. Cars on the road wereon fire.

In Uttar Pradesh, Jharkhand, and Bihar, the situation was dire. In cities like Lucknow, Kanpur, Varanasi, Prayagraj, Saharanpur, Muzaffarnagar, Ayodhya, Agra, Patna, Ranchi, Saharsa, Ara, Ballia, Chhapra, and Tatanagar, life had ground to a halt. Due to widespread riots across India, airlines had suspended their services for the safety of passengers and crew.

At 8 p.m., Buddhadev Trital arrived at Rashtrapati Bhavan to meet the President with a prior appointment. After adhering to the usual security protocols, he proceeded to the upstairs drawing room, where he was welcomed by Vinaya. The President joined them a few minutes later.

The President inquired whether Trital had met the Prime Minister.

Trital replied, "Yes, at 4 o'clock in the evening."

"Has he devised any concrete plans?" the President asked.

Trital responded, "Yes, he has, but Avdhesh Singh isn't cooperating. Perhaps he doesn't want the PM to succeed in restoring order so that he can stake his own claim to the position of PM."

The President remarked, "I wouldn't want Avdhesh in that position."

Trital silently agreed but refrained from expressing this openly to the President. What if Avdhesh did become the PM? He would then have to work under him, and Avdhesh might prefer someone else in his place.

Seeing Trital lost in thought, the President asked, "What's on your mind?"

Trital replied, "I was thinking about Kashmir, Sir."

The President questioned, "At a time when the rest of the country is in turmoil?"

Trital explained, "Sir, nearly 75% of the states are in the midst of riots. Except for the northeastern states, Punjab, and three states in the south, law and order have collapsed everywhere. Some state governments are acting irresponsibly. Imposing Section 144 won't be of much help. Total curfew is necessary. We are relocating the army from Punjab and Kashmir to the affected states, which might help restore peace there. But I don't recommend withdrawing the army from Kashmir. Even Arunachal Pradesh could face trouble if the army is moved from the northeast. China might take advantage. I've conveyed this to the PM, but he insists that we have no choice but to withdraw the army from Kashmir and the northeast."

The President acknowledged, "Your concerns are valid. Please convey to Subhash Singh that even if the army is withdrawn from Kashmir, he must maintain vigilant oversight there."

Trital nodded, and their conversation paused when snacks were brought in by the butler. The President was served coffee without sugar but with a dash of sugar-free granules, which Trital also requested due to their shared diabetes. They had a few biscuits with their coffee.

Once the butler cleared the table and left, Trital shared, "Currently, there's peace in Kashmir, but it's unsettling. There have been one or two riots in Jammu."

The President pondered, "Yes, I'm wondering about that as well. Let's wait and observe."

Trital concurred, "Yes, Sir, but I've received some feedback indicating that the Taliban and Pakistan might be planning something regarding Kashmir. I'm awaiting confirmation of the news."

"Keep me updated," the President requested.

Trital assured him, "Yes, Sir."

Following this, there were moments of silence as both men immersed themselves in their thoughts. Vinaya entered and invited Buddhadev Trital to join them for dinner. However, he declined, stating that his wife Vijaya would be waiting for him at home.

Trital turned to the President and said, "I'm working on various strategies to address different scenarios. I'll keep you informed in a couple of days."

"Okay," the President agreed.

After some time, Trital left for his home.

In Kabul, Salman Khan had become remarkably active, constantly shuttling between his office and home. Razia wondered what might be going on. She knew that nurse Rashida was scheduled to visit the next day with a supply of birth control pills, and Razia had hoped to discreetly gather some information from her about what Salman and his brothers knew. She was aware of a major operation planned for Kashmir but was unsure about when it would be put into action. Razia had tried to eavesdrop on the brothers but couldn't obtain any information. She was eager to access Salman's computer, but one of the three brothers was always present at home. She patiently waited for the right opportunity.

&&&&&

26.07.2032

The Taliban forces, who had been waiting on the border between Pakistan and Kashmir, were now fully prepared for action. Those Taliban members serving as conduits for terrorists from Kashmir and Pakistan were eagerly awaiting further orders, knowing they could be activated at any moment. Taliban soldiers were transported from Kabul and air-dropped into strategic locations in Pakistan, with the Pakistani army deploying armoured tanks and rocket launchers, as well as readying their Pak F16s, war planes. As a precaution, Karachi port had bolstered its security, while the entirety of Pakistan-occupied Kashmir (POK) was teeming with army troops.

Balakot, Jhelum, Mirpur, Muzaffarabad, Gujrat, Gujranwala buzzed with troop movements, with army camps established in Gehlan, Muri, and Bhimber. Meanwhile, terrorists lurked in the jungles of Uri, poised to cross the border into Kashmir at a moment's notice. The Indian army was well aware of these developments and had received orders from top brass to maintain maximum readiness, facilitated by receding rains in Pakistan that eased troop movements.

Soshe Dayan received this intelligence and strived to convey it to Trital. Although there were some delays, the intelligence eventually reached Trital, who was deeply concerned about the gravity of the situation. He promptly informed senior officers in the Defence Ministry, who then alerted the Defence Minister, Ravindra Prasad. Prasad immediately ordered the army to repel the attack on Kashmir. However, most of the Indian troops and Air Force jets had been relocated from Kashmir to other parts of India.

Trital attempted to secure an appointment with the Prime Minister, but was informed that the PM was occupied with pressing matters. Trital emphasized the urgency of the matter concerning Kashmir, and the Principal Secretary to the PM assured him that it would be relayed to the PM. Trital's efforts to meet the defence minister also proved fruitless, as he was told that the Minister was in a meeting with the PM. Trital relayed all this information to the President.

Riots had broken out in various cities, including Kolkata, Asansol, Birbhum, Bankura, Chandigarh, Noida, Gurugram, and Panipat. The army was deployed across New Delhi, keeping riots under control there, but Old Delhi witnessed several violent incidents. RVP leaders took to the streets of Delhi to protest the attacks on RVP and Hanuman Shakti Dal activists, leading to the imposition of Section 144 in Delhi. Riots had also erupted in Uttarakhand and Himachal Pradesh, garnering extensive coverage on news channels.

Over the course of two days, Avdhesh Singh reached out to all Lok Sabha members, seeking their support for his bid for the PM's post. He attempted to convince them that Subhash Singh was too old and that he, as a younger candidate, was more suitable for the position. While many members were swayed, others remained neutral.

Ravindra Prasad also harboured aspirations of becoming the PM but hoped that Subhash Singh would propose his name, facilitating his election without impediments. Given the dire state of the country, he refrained from discussing his bid for the PM's post with Subhash Singh. However, when he learned that Avdhesh Singh had entered the race and was actively seeking support, he rallied in favour of Subhash Singh and campaigned against Avdhesh Singh.

In the cabinet, Avdhesh Singh managed to garner support from Venkatapaiyya, Arvind Kumar, Bhavna Shinde, and S. Subramaniyam. He also vied for the position of party president.

In the evening, the BLP party's central working committee meeting was convened. Subhash Singh, Avdhesh Singh, and other senior leaders were present, with some state chief ministers joining via Zoom. Initially, they discussed the grave situation in the country and unanimously recommended stringent measures.

Nagarjuna, the Vice President of the party, had assumed the role of acting President as per constitutional procedure. However, during the meeting, he proposed holding a fresh election for the President's post. Subhash Singh and Ravindra Prasad endorsed Nagarjuna's nomination, while Avdhesh Singh attempted to veto it and declared his own candidacy. A heated debate ensued, and under Subhash Singh's chairmanship, an election was conducted. Some members voted via Zoom. Ultimately, Nagarjuna secured 19 votes, while Avdhesh Singh received only 7 votes. In a fit of anger, Avdhesh Singh stormed out of the meeting, realizing that he would likely lose the race for the PM's post as well.

A decision was made at the party meeting to convene a meeting of MPs within a week, contingent on the law-and-order situation in the country. Two camps emerged: one believed Subhash Singh was too old for the PM post, favouring Avdhesh Singh as a better choice, while the other camp argued that since Avdhesh's son, Raj Narain Singh, had incited riots nationwide and was beyond his father's control, Subhash Singh should continue as PM with Ravindra Prasad's cooperation.

Unfortunately, many members of parliament were unable to travel to Delhi, as air, rail, and bus services had been suspended due to the riots. Holding a Zoom meeting with over 200 participants was impractical. Subhash Singh, being the most experienced leader at the time, was considered the best choice as caretaker PM until all members could meet and elect a new leader.

Upon returning to his residence, the Prime Minister was informed that Trital was waiting for him, leading him to suspect it was related to the Kashmir situation. He immediately headed to his office within his bungalow and asked Trital what he had to report.

"Sir, the situation in Kashmir is extremely dire, and I recommend that you provide relevant instructions to Ravindra Prasad," Trital stated.

"Alright," the Prime Minister replied, "I'll take care of it. Right now, I'm feeling quite exhausted and need to rest." Trital noted the time, which was 10:30 p.m., and too late to contact the President, so he decided to return to his office.

&&&&&

27.07.2032

According to their plan, local terrorists in Baramulla and the Taliban had sprung into action. A significant contingent of the Pakistani army and Taliban soldiers infiltrated Baramulla under the cover of darkness. Taliban members who had sought refuge in the Burhari Masjid on the outskirts of Baramulla, posing as devout Muslims, ambushed Indian army outposts, inflicting heavy casualties. They made their way into Baramulla via Gujrial, and Taliban and Pakistani soldiers were infiltrating Baramulla from various cities, including Gehlan, Daryari, Muri, and Bhimber. Some crossed the Kaman Aman Bridge in Uri, while others used the Titwal bridge, and some managed to cross the Hajipir canal.

The Taliban forces outnumbered the Pakistani army, but the Pakistani forces possessed a substantial arsenal, including armoured tanks like 90-2M, Al-Khalid, VT-4, VT-85, Al Zarar, and T-80UD. They had also brought in A-100 rocket launchers. Supported by artillery and armoured divisions, the Taliban believed themselves to be invincible. They were armed with German-made Heckler and Koch rifles. Meanwhile, the Pakistani army was equipped with assault and sniper rifles, such as the PSR-90, Rangemaster, and Barrett rifles, as well as RPD and MG-3 machine guns. They also had a Spain-manufactured anti-tank rocket launcher called Alcotan-100 and an LLR 81 mortar launcher.

The pause in the rains favoured Pakistan and the Taliban, facilitating their mobilization. The Taliban had an array of weapons, including those supplied by the USA such as M-16, M-24, machine guns, M-203 grenade launchers, and S-2 heavy machine guns. They also possessed Russian-made AK-47 and AK-74 rifles, Dragunov sniper rifles, RPD machine guns, KPV heavy machine guns, a GP-25 grenade launcher, and a B-10 rocket launcher. In essence, they were well-prepared for this attack. In contrast, while the Indian army had an ample supply of weapons, they needed time to respond to this surprise assault.

The combined Pakistani and Taliban forces initially seized Gikote and Banali posts as planned. They then advanced into Baramulla, where they overwhelmed the Indian army, breaching Indian territory. Indian armoured tanks initially inflicted heavy losses on the Pakistani-Taliban troops, but they used trenches to shield themselves. Subsequently, they targeted Indian armoured tanks with rocket launchers and continued to push deeper into Indian territory. Pakistani F-16 warplanes carried out an aerial assault that Indian fighter jets struggled to repel. The F-16s bombed the Srinagar Military Depot, leading to the destruction of stockpiled Brahmos missiles, ATGS, WHP, Prahar missiles, QRSAM, and medium-range surface-to-air missiles. Some of these missiles stored in small depots in Baramulla fell into the hands of the Taliban.

Iliyas Zaibuddin's men were holed up in the Masjid Sharif at Chhoti Pranthi near Baramulla. They emerged from the mosque and joined the Taliban units. At 2:00 a.m., the terrorist unit from Gujriyal reached Baramulla, and by 3:00 a.m., while it was still dark, the sounds of clashing armies and the chants of "Taliban Zindabad, Pakistan Zindabad" filled the air. Citizens watched from their homes as Pakistani tanks rolled in from Uri and, rumbling through the streets, laid siege to the DC office.

The news was swiftly relayed to military sub-headquarters in Srinagar and then to headquarters in Delhi. By 4:00 a.m., the defence minister was informed that Baramulla had fallen to the enemy. Caretaker PM Subhash Singh directed him to take appropriate action.

At 8:00 a.m., Trital held a pre-scheduled meeting with the President. The previous night, Trital had briefed the President on the potential combined attack by Pakistan and the Taliban. However, when the President learned that Baramulla had been captured, he was deeply distressed.

In the meantime, Samajik Samata Dal SAASAD had unleashed havoc across the country. They initiated a series of violent attacks against Hanuman Dal and RVP activists, seemingly driven by the agenda of avenging the death of former PM Rajendra Kaul. BLP party supporters also passionately rallied around this issue and took to the streets. Anarchy prevailed everywhere, with violent clashes erupting. By the time the police arrived, incidents of arson, immolation, stabbing, and stone pelting had already occurred.

Violence escalated in Uttar Pradesh, with Section 144 imposed in Lucknow and curfews enforced in Muzaffarnagar, Agra, Jhansi, Bareilly, Varanasi, Prayagraj, Kanpur, Mainpuri, Rampur, and other areas. While Gomatinagar in Lucknow had remained peaceful until now, the old part of the city witnessed violent incidents from the morning. At 10:00 a.m., a large mob gathered at the UP-Chief Minister's residence, hurling petrol bombs. The police used tear gas to disperse the crowd. Simultaneously, another mob attacked the CM's office with stones and petrol bombs. The CM alerted the police, leading to a series of arrests. While efforts were made to avoid firing on the mob, the police had to resort to firing at the CM's office to regain control. Five SSD party workers fell victim to police bullets, and several were injured. News channels extensively covered these events, plunging the entire state of Uttar Pradesh into turmoil. SSD and BLP supporters clashed against Hanuman Shakti Dal and RVP activists. The situation was comparable throughout the country.

Union Home Minister Avdhesh Singh urged the nation to maintain law and order but struggled to control his own son, Rajnarain Singh, who was causing havoc. Military personnel were air-dropped in various states to restore control. Transport and communication networks came to a standstill, and curfews were imposed everywhere. People anxiously awaited curfew relaxations to secure their essential needs. The situation in Bihar, Jharkhand, Madhya Pradesh, Rajasthan, Haryana, Chhattisgarh, Maharashtra, Telangana, Gujarat, Karnataka, and various other states was more or less the same.

In Kashmir, the Taliban had seized full control of Baramulla and detained the District Collector and other bureaucrats, confining them. Two officers who had opposed the Taliban were silenced permanently. Some local separatists had welcomed the Taliban, boosted their morale and justified their actions. The Baramulla police proved ineffective against the Taliban and their armoured tanks, eventually surrendering. Two Indian Air Force aircraft had been downed, resulting in the loss of 380 Indian army soldiers and officers and significant damage to the Indian army. About 140 Pak-Taliban soldiers also lost their lives.

Back at the military headquarters in Delhi, a flurry of activity was underway to devise a counter-strategy against the Pak-Taliban attack in Kashmir. The atmosphere was fraught with tension. Caretaker PM Subhash Singh and Defence Minister Ravindra Prasad were collaborating to find ways to halt the enemy's advance in Kashmir. The PM expressed the need to deploy more army and air force units in Kashmir, but he was informed that they had already been dispatched to other riot-afflicted states in India.

Trital provided regular updates on the Kashmir situation to the President. The President had phoned the PM at 7:30 p.m. to obtain a status report on Kashmir and other states, urging swift action. The PM assured him that he was addressing the situation, though the President remained concerned.

In addition to the dire state of affairs in Kashmir, the President worried about the situation in Kolkata also. The city was engulfed in violence, with DESWAP activists assaulting RVP and Hanuman Dal workers, even subjecting TV channel reporters to beatings. Since the police were reduced to mere bystanders, the DESWAP cadre had a free hand to wreak havoc.

At 8:30 p.m., Trital visited the retired former Chief Security Advisor, Radhakrishnan. Trital had previously informed Radhakrishnan, upon his retirement, that he would seek his advice when necessary. Trital was aware that Radhakrishnan's experience would be invaluable in the current situation. After inquiring about Mrs. Radhakrishnan's health, Trital delved directly into the main issue. Their meeting lasted for an hour and a half, during which Radhakrishnan expressed his satisfaction at being contacted. Trital had maintained contact with him since his retirement, seeking his guidance. Radhakhrinan mentioned that he had a flight booked to his hometown, Kochi, on the 16th of August, but it now seemed impossible to make the journey.

&&&&&

28.07.2032

At dawn today, the situation in Kashmir deteriorated significantly. The Indian army struggled to respond to Pakistan's aggressive attacks. Iliyas and his associates remained in contact with Ozair, who provided them with information on where to air drop weapons and arms in Kashmir. In places like Sopore, Kupwara, Shopian, and Poonch, people were chanting slogans in support of Pakistan and the Taliban. Iliyas's group led uprisings in various parts of Kashmir, waiting for the arrival of Pak-Taliban troops. Pakistani helicopters landed soldiers in these areas. Indian Air Defence guns managed to bring down some Pakistani planes, but in other instances, Pakistan had the upper hand. Pakistan lost two planes and three drones, while India lost three planes. Dogfights occurred in the air as well, and there was a continuous stream of infiltration into Kashmir by Pak-Taliban forces.

The rain had subsided in Kashmir and most parts of India, as if even nature was working against India. Meanwhile, heavy rainfall was reported in Pakistan.

Rather than facing the situation, the Chief Minister of Kashmir and his cabinet ministers discreetly relocated from Srinagar to Jammu. This had a detrimental impact on the morale of Indian troops and the general public in Kashmir. The pro-Pakistan and anti-Pakistan divide in Kashmir became increasingly apparent.

With Baramulla under their control, the Taliban advanced into Badgam, Poonch, and Kupwara, proudly displaying the flags of Pakistan and the Taliban. The commander in Baramulla was a Taliban officer who began to threaten the public, warning them to cooperate with the Taliban, or face torture or being handed over to the military, with women sometimes being forcibly taken. Panic spread as more and more Taliban infiltrators emerged from the jungles of Uri, taking control of military camps in Baramulla and establishing their offices there.

Avdhesh Singh had one all-consuming aspiration: to become the Prime Minister. He was willing to go to any lengths to achieve this goal. He reserved two five-star hotels, the Grand and the Pride in Connaught Place, and invited all the Members of Parliament who supported his bid for the PM's post to stay at the hotels, with all expenses covered. Due to the closure of air and rail travel, the hotels had very few guests. He instructed Bhavna Shinde, Venkatapaiyya, Arvind Kumar, and S. Subramaniyam to persuade as many MPs as possible to support him. He emphasized his belief that Subhash Singh was too old and unfit for the office of Prime Minister, lacking the ability to unite all the members. The Home Ministry staff was also tasked with assisting the ministers in bringing as many MPs as possible to Delhi in support of Avdhesh Singh.

Trital was deeply troubled by the developments in Kashmir. Adding to his mental distress was the news of MPs gathering at the five-star hotels, which led his intuition to warn him of an impending disaster. He felt a profound sadness that when the country was facing internal and external challenges, the person responsible for maintaining law and order and national security was preoccupied with such activities.

Trital had requested an appointment with the Prime Minister at noon, but he had to wait until 4 p.m. to finally meet the PM in his office. As Trital entered the PM's office, the Principal Secretary, who was present, initially stood up to leave. However, the PM signalled for him to stay, and the secretary looked at Trital. Trital nodded, indicating his agreement, and the principal secretary gladly resumed his seat.

The PM inquired, "Yes, Mr. Trital, what brings you here?"

Trital explained, "Sir, the situation is extremely critical, which is why I've come."

The PM reassured, "Yes, I am aware of the seriousness of the situation, but I'm confident there is a solution."

Trital continued, "We need to urgently advise state governments to restore law and order."

The PM asked, "I share your concerns; have you met with the Home Minister?"

"No, he's quite occupied. I spoke with the Home Secretary, who assured me he would consult with the Home Minister and prepare an advisory."

The PM turned to his Principal Secretary, Brajraj Mishra, and directed, "Please make a note of what he's saying and follow through. Also, send a message to the Chief Secretary of the Cabinet and issue an official advisoryto all states, bearing my signature."

Trital added, "Sir, concerning Kashmir, you've given instructions to the Defence Minister. However, the ground reality is different. Pakistan and Taliban forces are making rapid gains in Kashmir. I fear we might lose Kashmir for good."

The PM turned to his Principal Secretary, saying, "Summon the CDS (Chief of Defence Services) to meet with me immediately. I'll be available until 8 p.m."

"Understood, Sir."

"Is there anything else troubling you, Mr. Trital?"

"Yes, Sir."

"What is it?"

"There are 60 Lok Sabha members who have been kept in confinement at Hotel Grand and Hotel Pride in Connaught Circle."

"I know. I have discussed this with the honourable President. What is the solution to this?"

Trital contemplated for a moment, knowing that the President had advised the PM to declare a state of emergency and remove the Home Minister from office. However, as a caretaker PM, he hesitated to take such a step.

Trital replied knowingly, "Sir, I don't mean to be presumptuous, but you're aware of the solutions."

The PM chuckled and said, "Let's see."

Trital understood it was time to depart. He stood up, leaving the PM and Brajraj Mishra to devise a plan to address the situation.

Later that evening, at 5:30 p.m., another meeting took place in the PM's office, attended by Nagarjuna Reddy, President of the BLP party, the defence minister, and the Foreign Affairs Minister.

Following the meeting, Foreign Affairs Minister Basavraj Patil left the PM's office and went to his own office. All the offices in the Central Vista were conveniently located near each other. Before meeting with the PM, he had already instructed all his secretaries and the staff to assemble in his office, as he had anticipated significant communication from the PM.

He instructed his team, "We need to express our grievances regarding Afghanistan and Pakistan at the UNSC (United Nations Security Council). Arrange a Zoom call with our ambassador in Washington. It will be daytime in the U.S. during our nighttime. Prepare a draft for presentation at the UNSC. The General Assembly meeting must be convened without delay. We might need to work through the entire night."

At 7 p.m. that evening, an alert swept through the area as the Prime Minister's convoy headed towards the Rashtrapati Bhavan. The three VIP vehicles were allowed to pass without undergoing any security checks. The PM and the President were scheduled to meet in the Darbar Hall, accompanied by their personal secretaries. As the President stepped out of the lift and entered the Darbar Hall, the PM greeted him with a simple rose, knowing the President's preference for modest bouquets. The press was granted permission to take photographs and report on the PM and President's discussion about the grave situation in the country.

Subsequently, they engaged in a private meeting in the State Drawing Room. The President said, "Subhash Singh ji, you can speak openly now."

The PM responded, "Your Excellency, it's challenging to express the dire situation I find myself in."

The President dismissed the formalities, saying, "Drop the 'Excellency' and all the pomp. We are old friends; you can call me Shiv Kalyanji. I would appreciate being addressed by my name for old times' sake."

The PM hesitated, replying, "No, Sir, I can't do that. After all, you are our respected President."

"Very well."

The PM provided an oral summary of all the events and decisions that had transpired, starting from his meeting with Trital and the two other ministers up to this moment.

The President remarked, "The situation is indeed grave, and you'll agree that Rajnarain Singh bears significant responsibility for this. He must be placed under arrest, without any special privileges just because he is the Home Minister's son."

The PM raised a concern, saying, "That's the crux of the problem, Sir. He's the Home Minister's son, and taking action against him is a complex matter."

The President insisted, "Show no leniency. If your party's state governments can't handle it, then involve opposition party state governments. I am sure you have a good rapport with Ashok Chaddha, the RVP President. This must be executed in complete secrecy."

"Do you not think that Raj Narain's arrest will further deteriorate the situation?"

"Perhaps temporarily, but eventually things will calm down."

"Yes, Sir, I will attempt it, but it will need to be done discreetly," the PM responded.

The President inquired, "What about Kashmir? We must act swiftly."

"Indeed, Sir."

"How will you handle the matter of Hotel Grand and Hotel Pride?"

The PM explained, "I've assigned Nagarjuna to handle it. He is gathering support against Avdhesh Singh."

The President asserted firmly, "Listen, it's crucial to redeploy the air force and military to Kashmir. I saw your order instructing Ravindra Prasad to transfer control of military and air force deployment to Avdhesh Singh."

The PM replied, "That was influenced by Avdhesh himself. I was deeply troubled by the country's grim situation, and now we have to address the Kashmir crisis as well."

"You need to rescind that order or amend it to regain control of military and air force deployment. I have faith in your ability to handle it."

The PM wondered whether this was an order from the President or a subtle criticism.

Both men looked sombre.

The President suggested, "You see, in extraordinary circumstances, you must make extraordinary decisions. I need not provide advice."

"Understood, Sir."

The President said, "Please organize a meeting with all the Members of Parliament as soon as possible, in your favour. It's primarily your party's affair, but I suggest this for the sake of our old friendship."

The PM acknowledged, saying, "Thank you, Sir."

The President concluded, "Alright, let's meet again at the Ashoka Hall ceremony." This referred to the prime ministerial oath-taking ceremony, though the PM appeared less confident.

The PM remarked, "As of today, I am only a caretaker PM."Internally he thought that I am a accidental prime minister.

The President smiled and offered his best wishes, saying, "Subhash ji, I can only extend my best wishes to you. The rest is in your hands."

The PM clasped his hands together in a namaste gesture to the President, who shook hands with him and provided a reassuring pat, as if boosting his confidence. Both the PM and the President's hands displayed a slight tremor.

The PM left, and the President sat quietly in a despondent mood. His wife, Vinaya, entered but he remained seated. After years of living with a man deeply entrenched in politics, she had the experience to gauge his mood and the situation. Now as the President's wife, holding the highest post in the country, she was well-versed in the politics and politicians of the nation. Television channels were broadcasting all the developments — curfews, violence, and the suspension of rail, bus, air, and road services. Her husband's restlessness and growing anxiety did not escape her notice. Several classified calls came in for her husband, and she understood how distressed he was about the state of affairs.

She knew it was pointless to suggest dinner at this time. She was aware that the PM and her husband had shared some coffee and biscuits during their meeting, but the samosas and kachori remained untouched. Her husband was not in the mood for dinner, so she decided to inquire about it later.

&&&&&

29.07.2032

In the early hours of the morning, there were urgent news reports detailing a surge in violence and arson across the country. The workers of the RVP (Rastriya Vicharmanch Party) were being ruthlessly targeted, with their homes set ablaze. Unfortunately, security measures proved to be woefully inadequate. Troubling reports were pouring in from various states, including Bihar, Telangana, Chhattisgarh, Gujarat, and Uttar Pradesh, where the situation was deteriorating rapidly. Street clashes were on the rise in Bengal, and the military's presence was insufficient, leading to constant pleas for reinforcements from the central government.

Grim updates continued to come in from Kashmir. Following the incidents in Baramulla, the Taliban and Pakistani forces had made incursions into neighbouring regions. Armoured tank battles erupted, with Pakistan gaining an advantage over India. Indian military helicopters were deployed to transport troops to the affected areas in Kashmir. However, the Indian forces were grappling with a shortage of troops to counter the enemy, and they were not yet fully prepared for this sudden incursion. Most of India's fleet of aircraft was deployed throughout the country to drop off armed forces, leaving the region vulnerable. As a result, Kupwara, Sopore, Badgam, Bandipora, Farhim, and Naushera had fallen into the hands of the combined Taliban-Pakistani forces, who were now advancing toward Srinagar.

In Kargil, a portion of the Pakistani army had descended via Gilgit and Skardu. However, they encountered strong resistance from the Indian army, resulting in heavy casualties. They urgently requested more reinforcements. Meanwhile, Afghanistan had airdropped Taliban soldiers, along with arms and ammunition, into Kashmir.

In the afternoon, a cabinet meeting was convened to address the dire situation in the country and Kashmir. Some ministers participated in the meeting via Zoom, and four ministers from Avdhesh Singh's faction were present. Ravi Prasad attended, but Avdhesh Singh abstained from the meeting. The primary agenda was the deteriorating security situation in the country and in Kashmir. States were demanding additional troops and air force planes to safeguard their regions. Each minister expressed concerns about the security of their respective states, but no decision could be reached regarding transferring control of aircraft deployment from the Home Ministry's authority.

On the international front, at the Security Council meeting in the United Nations, India raised the issue of attacks on Kashmir by Pakistan and Afghanistan. China exercised its veto power to obstruct any resolution in favour of India. Representatives from Pakistan and Afghanistan argued that the people of Kashmir sought independence, and the joint Pak-Afghan forces had acted at the behest of the Kashmiri people. Some nations expressed support for India, but their influence was limited. Many nations maintained a neutral stance, which played into China's favour, allowing them to use their veto. Several countries emphasized India's earlier stance that Kashmir was a bilateral issue between India and Pakistan, and no external intervention should occur. They urged the resolution of the Kashmir issue through bilateral means. The Secretary-General of the UNSC advised all nations in conflict to refrain from using nuclear weapons for the sake of humanity. The Indian ambassador cautioned that if India launched a full-scale attack on Pakistan and Pakistan sought UNSC intervention, the issue must remain bilateral, with no outside interference. China raised objections to this warning, leaving India's concerns pending before the Security Council.

&&&&&

30.07.2032

The domestic situation in India and Kashmir was a cause for grave concern. Throughout the day, the news had been deeply unsettling. State capitals across the country were under a bandh, and in cities like Mumbai, Kolkata, Chennai, Bengaluru, Hyderabad, Gandhinagar, Jaipur, Bhopal, Raipur, Lucknow, Patna, and others, business and industry had come to a grinding halt. The common people were enduring great hardship. The curfew was only briefly relaxed to allow the supply of essential goods such as milk and vegetables. The situation in districts and towns was no different, with riots erupting everywhere, and troublemakers taking advantage of the chaos, engaging in looting and pillaging. The state government machinery had failed miserably in restoring law and order, constantly appealing for urgent military reinforcements from the Home Ministry.

While heavy showers soaked Pakistan, the rains had nearly ceased in India, making protests and agitations more feasible. Only the bordering states of Punjab, Rajasthan, and Gujarat received some rainfall.

In Delhi, a gathering of 92 members of parliamentwas assembled at Hotel Grand and Hotel Pride. Some of them were genuine supporters of Avdhesh Singh, while others had been coerced into attendance. Avdhesh Singh had directed his circle of ministers to secure the support of at least 130-140 members of the Lok Sabha. Kamlesh Yadav of the Bihar Jan Shakti Party had offered substantial support to Avdhesh Singh.

Subhash Singh was not particularly ambitious, and Ravindra Prasad harboured aspirations of becoming the Prime Minister but could not openly declare his intentions. He was keen on preventing Avdhesh from becoming a contender for the post. Ravindra Prasad advised many members of parliament against coming to Delhi and voting in favour of Avdhesh. He put in significant effort to garner support for Subhash Singh to retain his position as Prime Minister. Already, Shamrao Patil, Manohar Reddy, Joginder Kaur, Kalavati, Nambudripad, and Tribhuvan Singh were aligned with Subhash Singh. Chief ministers of Punjab, Kerala, and Andhra Pradesh supported Subhash Singh. Some other chief ministers and MPs remained neutral, uncertain of the direction events would take.

By that time, Kargil had fallen into the hands of Pakistan. The Pakistani army was mobilizing from Jhelum, Gujranwala, Rawalpindi, and Sialkot military cantonments. Aerial clashes were occurring between Indian fighter jets and Pakistani F-16s, as well as Afghan C-130 aircraft. Some Pakistani aircraft were forced to retreat, while others dropped Pakistani soldiers at the Baramulla air strip. Pakistan's launchers had taken down two Indian helicopters, and the Indian army had similarly downed two Pakistani helicopters. The Indian 'Prachanda' helicopter caused the Pakistani soldiers to scatter in disarray. Pakistan and Taliban forces had advanced close to Srinagar but faced fierce resistance from the Indian side. Nevertheless, the armoured tanks and launchers of the Taliban continued their march toward Srinagar, receiving food supplies from Sialkot.

&&&&&

31.07.2032

Trital arrived at Rashtrapati Bhavan at 8 a.m. He had scheduled an appointment with the President. The First Lady kindly offered him a seat in the second-floor hall and inquired if he desired a cup of coffee. He declined, indicating that he might have it with the President later.

As Trital awaited the President's arrival, he watched the news on TV. The President, who had a sleepless night and was feeling troubled, started his morning routine a bit later than usual. Upon his arrival, Vinaya once again asked about coffee, to which the President suggested they have it along with breakfast at the dining table. Once Vinaya had left the room, the President inquired, "What is the news?"

Trital responded, "Sir, it's nothing but bad news everywhere."

The President sighed, acknowledging, "Yes, I'm aware of the situation. But what's the solution?"

Trital replied, "Sir, you've already proposed a solution to the Prime Minister, but it didn't gain the Cabinet's approval for declaring a state of emergency or removing Avdhesh Singh from office."

The President pondered, "What should be our next step?"

Trital hesitated but then ventured, "I wonder if I should dare to suggest this solution..."

The President encouraged him, saying, "Please, go ahead."

Trital proposed, "Sir, the situation is exceedingly critical, and the solution lies within your authority."

"In my hands?" the President queried.

"Yes, I beg your pardon ,Sir. I suggest suspending the central cabinet, dissolving the Lok Sabha, and implementing President's Rule," Trital suggested.

The President was taken aback, "What are you saying? It's a formidable task."

Trital emphasized, "It's the only viable solution, Sir."

The President was visibly concerned, "Don't you realize the consequences of such a move? All political parties will take to the streets, and the ruling party will create chaos."

Trital pointed out, "The streets are already in chaos. The nation is in turmoil due to the actions of Rajnarain Singh. Srinagar is almost under the control of the Taliban and Pakistan."

The President remained doubtful, "Is this constitutionally sound? What if the Supreme Court deems it unlawful?"

Trital asserted, "Sir, let the Supreme Court decide later. Right now, the priority is to save the country and Kashmir."

The President contemplated, "Mr. Trital, typically, a recommendation for President's Rule comes to me from the Cabinet."

Trital reminded him, "Sir, you've often mentioned that exceptional situations call for extraordinary decisions."

The President inquired, "Even if I proceed as you suggest, who will run the country?"

Trital replied, "You will have to manage it, Sir. With your extensive administrative experience, having served as the chief minister of a major state like Uttar Pradesh and held various key positions in the Cabinet, like home,finance,defence, agriculture and foreign affairsyou're more than capable. We can assemble a team of competent advisors from retired government officers to ensure smooth governance."

"Until this crisis is resolved, then we can hold fresh elections, is this is what you are suggesting?I assume?" the President sought clarification.

"Yes, Sir."

The President contemplated, "Let me think about it," and fell into deep thought. Trital observed his contemplative expression for a while.

"I believe we need to take Subhash Singh into confidence, or he might raise objections," the President suggested.

Trital responded, "I doubt he'll object. The Home Minister is already striving to gain support for the position of Prime Minister. Subhash Singh is in a precarious situation."

The President acknowledged, "This is a very bold and risky step."

Trital asserted, "To save the country, it's necessary, and it must be carried out discreetly tonight. I propose you inform Subhash Singh late at night and caution him not to disclose this information. He's already quite anxious. I request thatyou invite your friend, retired Chief Justice Anil Gajendragadkar, and his family to dinner at Rashtrapati Bhavan tonight to discuss how to fit this within the constitutional procedure or present it in a way that preserves face. In the meantime, I'll discreetly consult an acquaintance in the Home Ministry and the Law Department to draft the necessary documents. Please grant me permission to stay at Rashtrapati Bhavan tonight. Around 10:30 p.m., you can summon the Chief Secretary, Home Secretary, and CDS and instruct them to have the army prepared by dawn. Not a word of this should reach Avdhesh Singh."

The President remained hesitant and scrutinized Trital closely. Trital exuded confidence. "You're exceptionally confident, Trital."

"Yes, Sir."

"Very well, let's proceed, but with utmost secrecy and propriety."

"Thank you, Sir," Trital expressed his relief at receiving approval.

The two of them moved towards the dining table for breakfast and engaged in a discussion about the national situation state by state.

Avdhesh Singh was tense all day. Chief ministers of some states refused to be coerced. On the advice of the caretaker PM, some MPs also were not responding to his telephone calls. He doubted about Ravindra Prasad also. The military also did not give him full cooperation. Although some pilots had been placed under the Home Ministry and he was using them to ferry MPs to the capital, they had shifted their allegiance and were more involved in transporting military personnel. Avdhesh Singh had achieved only one political gain. He had now got the support of the chief minister of West Bengal. West Bengal was also in a dire situation. Avdhesh Singh had managed to win the support of 110 MPs out of the requisite 221. He needed the support of 25 more because there was every likelihood of some of these 110 changing sides at the last moment. The Party President was also not in favour of Avdhesh Singh for the post of PM.

&&&&&

01.08.2032

At 2 a.m. in the early hours of the morning, a proclamation was issued from the President's office, declaring a state of Emergency in the nation. The President had assumed control of the country's affairs to address a foreign invasion and the severe breakdown of law and order. The lower house of Parliament, Lok Sabha, was dissolved, while the upper house, Rajya Sabha, was suspended. This action was taken under the authority of sections 352, 356, and 360 of the Constitution, in conjunction with the President's duty as defined in Article 60.

The Central government was dismissed as per the provisions of the Constitution, and an Emergency was declared. The proclamation stated that the President had assumed all executive powers under Article 53 and had taken command of the military, being the supreme commander of the armed forces. Furthermore, the Prime Minister's office was now aligned with the President's office. News agencies were henceforth required to seek government approval before broadcasting any news, with censorship imposed on all news channels and newspapers. The National Security Act (NSA) was enforced nationwide, including within the state machinery. Anyone facing action under the NSA would be held in custody for three months without the possibility of bail.

During the night, the military had established guard posts at the residences of all ministers, including the Prime Minister and his associates. The Defence Minister, Ravi Prasad, was taken aback by these developments. His attempts to contact prime minister andmilitary headquarters were thwarted as his communication lines had been severed. He found himself unable to reach other ministers, and a senior military officer explained the situation to himat his residence. He was forbidden from leaving his home, even to meet with the Prime Minister.

In the early morning, Avdhesh Singh was awakened by his personal secretary, who resided in the guesthouse on his bungalow. Avdhesh Singh had been alone since the passing of his wife, and his son, Rajnarain Singh, was away. When he awoke, he was still groggy from the drugs he had taken the previous night. He repeatedly asked his aides the same question until an old and trusted family servant guided him to the bathroom and splashed water on his face, despite his resistance. He gradually snapped out of his stupor and returned to his bedroom, where he once again posed the same question. His aide then informed him about the declaration of the Emergency. He attempted to call the Prime Minister, but his aide conveyed that all communication had been severed. The military officer at the gate had confiscated the security guards' weapons at the Home Ministry and warned them against any ill-advised actions, mentioning the possibility of imprisonment.

Avdhesh Singh switched on the television in his room, where the news announced the dismissal of the central government and the President's assumption of power with military assistance. He began to express his frustration and anger towards the Prime Minister and the President.

The communication networks of all ministers were disabled with the cooperation of mobile companies. Internet connections were severed, and signal jammers were positioned outside their residences. All telecom companies were ordered to shut down internet services throughout India, with the exception of government-owned Bharat Sanchar Nigam Ltd, which was allowed to maintain internet services at government offices in select locations. A review of resuming internet services was planned on a case-by-case basis for each state and city, post-Emergency.

An order was issued to block all social media platforms, including Google, Twitter, Facebook, WhatsApp, YouTube, Instagram, and others for a duration of fifteen days. These platforms were treated as completely inaccessible. After fifteen days, a review would be conducted to determine their resumption based on the law-and-order situation in the country, state wiseand city wise,along with internet services. Even after resumption, content would be subject to censorship, and any objectionable political or religious material would result in actions under the NSA.

The President also mandated that each state government must restore law and order within three days. The National Security Act (NSA) had been enacted, prohibiting any antisocial activities. Those engaged in such activities would be incarcerated, with reports sent to the President's office. Failure to restore law and order within the specified timeframe would lead to the dismissal of the state government.

A wave of panic swept across the nation that morning. The police now had the authority to deal with troublemakers, with the added support of the military. However,nationwide, the BLP and SAASAD initiated protests against the Emergency. Under Rajnarain Singh's influence, BLP activists resorted to arson, but this time they were apprehended and sent to jail.

In themorning,members of parliament who had been staying at the Grand Hotel and Pride Hotel had planned a protest march against the Emergency, heading towards the Rajghat, the Gandhi Memorial Site. However, they were intercepted by military guards. Though the Home Ministry guards were still stationed at the hotels, military supervision had taken over. It was effectively a form of house arrest for the parliamentarians.

The second tier of RVP leaders welcomed the Emergency and the dissolution of Parliament, while the primary leaders were placed under house arrest. Signal jammers were positioned outside their residences.

In states where the RVP held power, SSD party workers were being apprehended. However, in states where the BLP was in control, party workers initiated protest marches and demonstrations against the Emergency, further fuelling the preexisting chaos in the country. These Chief Ministers had not taken the President's ultimatum seriously, as they understood that contacting central ministers was impossible, and their phones were under surveillance. While political uprisings were unfeasible, they aimed to take their protests to the streets. The police brandished the NSA, urging them to abandon their protests.

An important high-level gathering was convened in the President's office during the afternoon. Attendees included the Vice-President, Secretaries of key departments such as PMO, Home, Finance, Defence, International Affairs, Information Technology, as well as the Chief of Defence Staff (CDS), the heads of the Army, Navy, and Air Force, and the leaders of the Border Security Force (BSF) and the Central Reserve Police Force (CRPF). Representatives from intelligence agencies like the Intelligence Bureau (IB), Research and Analysis Wing (RAW), Central Bureau of Investigation (CBI), National Investigation Agency (NIA), and National Security Advisor (NSA) were also in attendance. As per instructions, they all brought written blueprints outlining their strategies to address the current situation.

A continuous 24/7 monitoring system would be established at Rashtrapati Bhavan to closely track the law-and-order situation, which was accorded top priority. Another monitoring cell would oversee the operations of the round-the-clock system, ensuring that it functioned effectively and maintaining a structured reporting system directly to the President. Additionally, this cell would work on resolving the Kashmir issue. An advisory committee, comprising retired high-ranking officials and retired supreme court Justices, would supervise this system and provide appropriate guidelines for the overall administration of the country, reporting directly to the President.

During the meeting, the President issued a stern warning that each department must promptly execute the given orders while maintaining responsibility and confidentiality. Chief Secretaries and Police Chiefs of various states had been directed to efficiently handle the law-and-order situation, with the understanding that any failure in this regard would lead to them being placed on leave, and official actions would be taken against them. State interference would not be tolerated, with the Cabinet Secretary conveying this directive.

The meeting, lasting for three hours, concluded with the announcement that similar daily meetings would be convened in the future.

&&&&&

02.08.2032

Mulla Ashfaq, the leader of the Taliban in Kabul, had been dispatched to Baramulla to assume command over the joint Taliban and Pakistani forces that had infiltrated into Kashmir. This bolstered the strength of the Taliban troops significantly. While this was a coordinated act of aggression by Pakistan and Afghanistan, the Taliban were the driving force behind this long-planned attack. Leaders like Iliyas, who sought an independent Kashmir, had been in contact with the Taliban for an extended period. Pakistan wisely recognized that having Afghanistan as an ally was more advantageous than attempting to seize Kashmir on its own.

Mulla Ashfaq conducted a swift assessment of the progress made by the platoons thus far. He devised a strategy for taking control of Srinagar. Their plan involved securing the areas surrounding Srinagar, effectively cordoning it off, before assuming full control of the city. Afghan and Pakistani aircraft provided air cover for the advancing army. Utilizing rocket launchers and armoured tanks, they moved forward, inflicting as much damage on the Indian army as possible. In the districts of Shopian, Kulgam, Pulwama, Gandharwal, and Anantnag, armoured tanks were employed to push forward. Additional forces from Afghanistan were being readied to enter Kashmir. Pakistani and Indian aircraft engaged in aerial combat, resulting in losses on both sides. Indian planes targeted the Taliban forces on the ground, while the Pakistan army remained vigilant against Indian drone attacks.

The Taliban had inflicted significant suffering on the public in Kashmir. Kashmiri women had been kidnapped, and anyone attempting to intervene was met with deadly force. This had enraged the people of Kashmir. Upon Mulla Ashfaq's arrival, the policy shifted. He advised that in order to maintain a presence in Kashmir, they needed the support of the local population. Incidents of women being kidnapped ceased.

In India, riots had taken on a religious dimension, with Hindu-Muslim conflicts escalating. Trital suspected that these conflicts had been incited by elements affiliated with Pakistan and the Taliban. He took precautionary measures to address these elements, assuming the role of a dedicated National Security Advisor and proceeding with extreme caution, relying on credible feedback. The Prime Minister's Office now reported to the President, and all information reached the monitoring cell established by the President. State Chief Secretaries and Police Chiefs were instructed to reinforce their monitoring cells and provide hourly reports on measures taken to control violence and the number of arrests. Anti-social elements were promptly apprehended and incarcerated, making it difficult for them to secure bail. Political parties in the state grew restless as their activists were being detained, potentially leading to the diffusion of violence.

The monsoon season had returned, making it challenging for protests to continue in the streets. Although achieving peace and restoring law and order remained a distant goal, the Emergency had instilled some fear in party cadres and activists.

The President had also issued an order to expedite the investigation into the death of former Prime Minister Rajendra Kaul. The committee responsible for presenting a report had faced delays due to the tumultuous state of the country. However, the Committee assured the President that it would expedite its report.

Avdhesh Singh grew increasingly irate when he received news through his trusted sources that Subhash Singh had been informed of the Emergency declaration beforehand. His aides managed to convey these messages through inconspicuous channels like milkmen, vegetable vendors, or newspaper vendors. At this point, creating a mutiny within the party seemed futile. Avdhesh Singh needed to prepare for future elections to ensure that only his name would be eligible for the Prime Minister's post. His son, Rajnarain Singh, had been arrested by the Haryana police, and it was evident to the public that his son was beyond his control. It appeared that the father would be held accountable for his son's transgressions.

Iliyas Zaibuddin, the leader from Kashmir, supplied detailed information about the movements of Indian troops to the Taliban officer, Mohammed Majid Khan, who, in turn, relayed this information to Salman Khan in Kabul. Salman Khan was tasked with diligently updating this information in his laptop and forwarding it in the required computer format to higher-ranking officers.

Before taking control of Srinagar, the strategy had to be communicated to leaders in Afghanistan. Over the years, they had already gathered intelligence on India's military capabilities, tanks, and launchers from Iliyas. However, the ongoing civil conflict in India had led to changes in troop formations, which were factored into the plan to minimize losses for the Taliban while causing maximum damage to the Indian army.

Raziya possessed both the laptop and PC passwords of Salman Khan. With the utmost care, she commenced gathering the data input by Salman, when men folk was not present. She learned from television news channels that India was currently under attack. Nurse Rashida, the one who provided her with birth control pills, only visited twice a month. However, it was crucial to send information regularly to the Mossad. Hence, she had to frequently contact Rashida, using the excuse of needing medication for various women's ailments.

Soshe Dayan of the Mossad had transmitted all the information regarding the aggression in Kashmir to Trital. Unfortunately, Trital couldn't take substantial action due to the accidental death of the former Prime Minister and the country's chaotic state. Nevertheless, Trital attempted to alert Defence Minister Ravindra Prasad and the Chief of Defence Staff (CDS). Regrettably, they were preoccupied with the prevailing anarchy and vandalism in the nation.

On that particular evening, the security committee submitted its report to the President. The report stated that there were several concerns in certain states, accompanied by fewer instances of violence. In some other states, there were ongoing protests against the President's rule, along with petitions directed to the Governor. States where agitations and acts of vandalism were carried out by the BLP and SSD party members were facing rigorous measures against the wrongdoers. It was anticipated that there might be a temporary surge in violence due to the strict measures, although not on the same scale as before. Party members were well aware that being apprehended under the National Security Act (NSA) would make it arduous to secure bail, leading to extended stays in jail. This realization had significantly restrained their activities.

&&&&&

03.08.2032

The MPs who had been confined to the Grand and Pride Hotels were now insisting on their release. They had grown bored and had come to realize that Avdhesh Singh had used them to his advantage. Some were content with this arrangement because they expected to be appointed as ministers if Avdhesh Singh became the Prime Minister. Others were opportunists who were merely waiting for the right moment to switch sides, and a few had been forcibly brought there against their will to support Avdhesh Singh.

Statutory orders were issued for the withdrawal of all the privileges and perks that these Lok Sabha and other parliament members had enjoyed, including their government residential quarters. Failure to vacate their residences would result in hefty fines. These former MPs submitted an application to the President, seeking permission to return to their constituencies. By this time, some air and rail services had been restored, allowing those who had been away from Delhi to return. They also received notices to vacate their governmenthouses.

Riots in Maharashtra, Bengal, Gujarat, Telangana, and Chhattisgarh remained uncontrolled. Public transport services had partially resumed in some other states, with metro cities gradually returning to normal. Curfews had been lifted in many states, and bus services had resumed. In those states ,the public, having endured enough hardship during the curfew, welcomed President's Rule. There were marches by the general public in support of President's Rule. Although live news coverage was prohibited, there was some freedom to report news with prior approval from the authorities. Any tough actions taken by the military and police against rioters were kept away from the public. Previously, party leaders would come to have their arrested workers released, but now, if any leader tried to protect a wrongdoer, there was a risk of the leader being arrested. This had created panic among party workers and leaders.

Despite this, there was still limited movement of the general public as rail, air, and road transportation had only partially resumed in some states.

In Kashmir, the conflict intensified as the Taliban army, along with Pakistani troops, had infiltrated in large numbers. Indian Air Force planes had begun returning to their bases in Pathankot, Hindon, Chandigarh, and Ambala from some states. Fighter jets in Sarwasa, Udhampur, and Kargil remained on duty in Kashmir.

A security committee meeting was held in the afternoon on this day. The President, Vice President, and those who had attended the meeting on August 1 were all present. Reports at both state and national levels were presented, and there was a preliminary discussion on the Kashmir issue. Subsequently, another meeting was held to address the Kashmir problem exclusively. The President had made critical decisions and desired utmost secrecy. Therefore, the attendance at the second meeting was minimal. The decision was to intensify the battle in Kashmir and adopt a different strategy regarding Pakistan and Afghanistan. Only the chiefs of staff of the army, navy, air force, and select high-ranking officials from RAW, IB, and the Defence Ministry were invited to this meeting.

While the upper house of parliament (Rajya Sabha) remained suspended, its members retained their membership. They were eager to be active, so along with some Lok Sabha members and a few supporters of Avdhesh Singh, they attempted to organize a peace march toward Gandhi Memorial grounds (Rajghat) in New Delhito protest against the Emergency. They were subsequently arrested and fined, with news of their arrest intentionally disseminated to TV channels. The channel that was going to cover the peace march could not broadcast the complete news as the purpose of the march was to shout slogans against the President, which the administration could not allow.

In the evening, a brief meeting was held with a handful of RVP members. They had obtained prior permission from the President officeto arrange this meeting. Party president Ashok Chadda, former leader Namrata Rupani, Member of Rajya Sabha Rameshwar Singh, and four other office bearers were in attendance.

Another meeting took place at the residence of PM Subhash Singh with prior approval from the President office. Party president Nagarjuna, VP Charan Singh, Ravindra Prasad, Manohar Reddy, Basavraj Patil, Nambudripad, and three other office bearers were present. Avdhesh Singh was the only one not allowed to meet anyone, and all his communication lines had been jammed.

The leaders of RVP and BLP appealed to the nation to maintain peace and expressed their concerns about the situation in Kashmir. The text of their appeal had been censored before its release to the press and the media.

That Evening,a festive atmosphere enveloped Afzal Khan's residence in Kabul as they revelled in the news that Kashmir was nearly under the control of the Taliban and Pakistan. Razia, dressed in provocative attire, entertained the gathering with her dance and supplied copious amounts of liquor. Shama and Nadira expertly handled the cooking and serving duties. The brothers requested a dance and song from Nadira, and she willingly obliged.

As the evening progressed, Afzal Khan, in his inebriated state, asked Nadira to perform another song. At that moment, Razia was busy bringing out delectable dishes such as *YakhniPulav* (a rice dish), *Korama-e-nadru* (a chicken dish), and *Nan* (bread).

Later on, Afzal Khan invited the three women to join them for dinner. Razia expressed her desire to serve some pulav(rice dish) to the guards stationed outside, and the brothers did not object. She served *Yakhnipulav* and generous amounts of alcohol to the guards, with a purpose in mind.

The three brothers insisted that the women partake in the drinking. While Shama and Nadira indulged in their drinks, Razia skilfully managed to discreetly pour her glass's contents into the nearby flower pots. Following dinner, the brothers would have likely slumbered in their inebriated state right there, but the women escorted them to their bedrooms on the first floor. Before retiring to their rooms, the brothers embraced each other and exchanged congratulatory remarks about their perceived victory in Kashmir. Razia observed the scene with a hint of sympathy on her face. It was already 11:30 p.m. by then.

&&&&&

04.08.2032

Anant Joshi

At 2 a.m. during the late hours of the night, an announcement emanated from the Rashtrapati Bhavan, declaring the dissolution of five state governments. Alongside, their legislative assemblies were also disbanded. The Chief Ministers of Maharashtra, Telangana, West Bengal, Chhattisgarh, and Gujarat received an unexpected jolt as they were rudely awakened from their slumber to be informed of their immediate dismissal. The governors of these states had been apprised just an hour earlier and were tasked with taking control of the state's administration. The military, Chief Secretaries of each state, and the Directors General of Police (DGGs) were all issued explicit instructions to prioritize the restoration of law and order. They were directed to show no leniency toward any party activists. The National Security Act (NSA) would be enforced across all sections of society, and in cases where the prisons were insufficient to accommodate the apprehended individuals, schools and colleges would be temporarily repurposed as detention centres. All newspapers were mandated to publish these directives, and all television channels were instructed to broadcast them.

Of these five states now under the rule of the President, three were governed by the BharatiyaLokshakti Party (BLP), Gujarat was under the rule of the RashtriyaVicharmanch Party (RVP), and Bengal was being governed by the DeshbandhuSwabhimanParty (DESWAP). Furthermore, it was specified that elections were already scheduled in Gujarat for December. This course of action was limited to these five states, with the intention of instilling fear and encouraging other states to promptly take measures to restore law and order.

At dawn in Kabul, something strange was happening at 3.00 AM. Razia had already plied the men folk, the women and guardswith liquor. At about 2.a.m., she started the preparation. First, she disentangled herself from Salman's embrace. He had tried making love to her last night; she had let him kiss her and press her breast in his inebriated state, but he had not consummated their love making.

She had got the news from one guard, that Rashida nurse has been arrested by Afghan police for spying, on that day.She knew this is a alarm bell for her. She was sure that Rashida will be subjected to rigorous interrogation before death and Taliban police will be successful in knowing her accomplices. The fate of her contacts hangs in air.

Razia goes down to the basement to get some bombs and explosives. She also brought up some opium and marijuana to the ground floor. There on the ground floor, she spread these drugs and placed the bombs and explosives at different places, including kitchen, near gas cylinders. The three brothers slept in the bedrooms upstairs. She managed to find some kerosene in the basement and made a torch using the bathroom mop, cloth, and handle. She also placed balls of cloth and cotton soaked in kerosene and placed them all over the floor. Then she drenched the torch with kerosene.

At 3 a.m., she lit the torch and set the whole house on fire. Within seconds, there was a roaring blaze. She was going to different corners of house and igniting the fire. In that process, she was also burning herself, but she was not bothered about it.

Razia knelt on the ground and asked for mercy from Allah. She remembered her little son, just 5 years old, who had been brutally killed when he was pleading with the murderers to spare his father's life. She had tried to stop her son from rushing out of home at that time, but he had fled from her grip towards his father and lost his life. Her family had taken part in the movement against the Taliban and they had retaliated. Her family was of Tazik tribe and were rebellion against Pakhtun tribe, who were part of Talibanis. She was spared because she had hidden herself in the house. Afzal Khan was the leader of the group of killers that had killed her husband and child. Her two brothers-in-law, one nephew and one servant were also killed at thattime.

She had earlier served as a receptionist in a hospital and was computer savvy. When the Taliban took over Afghanistan, she lost her job. She and some beautiful girls like her had been caught and sold at an auction. Her co-sisters were also auctioned. Ashiq Khan had bought her at the auction, because of her beauty. From the time he had brought her to the house of Afjal Khan, she had vowed vendetta. Her only purpose in life was to seek revenge, revenge and revenge and she was fulfilling her life's purpose today. She was only remembering the face of her child in the closed eyes. Before the three brothers realised what was happening, they were engulfed in flames. Afzal Khan tried to come down the stairs to save himself, with the gun, shouting. Before breathing her last, Razia had the satisfaction of seeing him collapse in a bundle of flames. The neighbours called in the fire brigade but the explosives were doing their work and there were blasts after blasts. The guards were too sozzled to notice the flames in time but afterwards screamed and yelled for someone to save the masters and fled away. When the news about Salman Khan and Afzal Khan spread, the military arrived, but found only their ashes.

n India, at 4 a.m., the military arrived at the residences of the chief ministers and ministers of five states. Their phone and internet connections had been disrupted. Some of the ministers only realized at that moment that the state governments had been dismissed. They were in a state of shock.

Suresh Yadav, the Chief Minister of Bihar, had worked diligently to maintain stability in his state. He had even taken strict actions against his own party members when necessary. Those party workers who were protesting against the RVP on the streets of Bihar were also arrested and detained. He understood the seriousness of the warning from Rashtrapati Bhavan and decided not to exacerbate the situation. Given the long-standing antagonism between his father and the President, he believed it was best to avoid further conflict. When his personal secretary woke him up at 5 a.m. and informed him that five states were under President's rule and Bihar had been spared, he breathed a sigh of relief.

At 8 a.m., a meeting was convened at the BLP office. They had simply informed the President's office about the meeting without waiting for formal permission. Only the party president, Nagarjuna Reddy, and a few members were physically present. Ravindra Prasad, Basavraj Patil, Bhavana Shinde, Venkatappaiyya, Nambudripad, and some former MPs joined the meeting via Zoom. Ravindra Prasad took the initiative to invite Subhash Singh to join the meeting via Zoom. They discussed the President's handling of the situation, condemned the dissolution of the five state governments, and requested select media outlets to report the news. However, the media did not broadcast their call to start a mass movement.

At 10 a.m., the Taliban and Pakistani armies launched an attack on Srinagar, the capital of Kashmir state, from all four sides. The attack came from Baramulla, Bandipura, Badgam, Gandharwal, and Pulwama. The Indian troops stationed in Srinagar, along with some policemen, attempted to confront the Pakistani-Taliban forces. Indian Air Force planes repeatedly targeted Pakistani armoured tanks and troops, but despite the losses, the Pakistani-Taliban forces continued to advance. Meanwhile, Pakistani planes patrolled the skies to deter Indian bomber aircraft. The weather favored the Pakistani-Taliban forces, as it remained sunny throughout the day with no rainfall. In Pakistan, it was cloudy with light showers.

Pakistani and Taliban troops advanced from Haji Masjid, Bujpura, and Hafizbaug. From the north, they marched through Arbaan Mohalla,

Naseembaug, Kakatbaug, and penetrated Dangarpura, Khagabaug Colony, Lal Bazar, and Saidpura. Fierce battles raged throughout the day, resulting in heavy casualties on both sides. However, the Taliban gained the upper hand, and by evening, they had captured the entire Srinagar, including areas like Badami Baug, Aramwadi, Ram Munshi Baug, and Maharajpur. The Taliban spared the army cantonment, intending to use it for themselves, as the Ammunition Depot had been burned down long ago.

Mullah Ashfaq, a Taliban leader, appeared on international media channels and declared that they had taken control of Kashmir. Iliyas was with him during the video shoot. Pakistani and Afghan TV channels repeatedly broadcast the video, and even the BBC aired it. China, Indonesia, and Turkey welcomed the declaration, while some countries, including a few Arab nations, protested against it. In India, there was deep concern, and some European countries predicted that India would eventually regain control of that part of Kashmir.

In India, protests erupted in the five states under President's rule, with party workersdemonstrating against the imposition of President's rule. In Bengal and Maharashtra, the protests turned violent, leading to the imposition of curfews in Kolkata, Hubli, Asansol, Birbhum, Raipur, Bilaspur, Vadodara, Surat, Hyderabad, and Khammam. Curfews extended to Mumbai, Pune, Nagpur, Aurangabad, Nasik, Solapur, Bhiwandi, Malegaon, and Amravati in Maharashtra.

The Chief of Defence Staff received instructions from the President's office to withdraw the military from Assam and Madhya Pradesh and deploy it to Bengal and Maharashtra, respectively. The army was to be moved from Orissa to Chhattisgarh, and from Karnataka to Telangana. In states with relative peace, the armies were to be redirected to Kashmir. Trital, the NSA, the Defence Ministry and other agencies had received instructions from the President to get the military from Uttar Pradesh, Bihar , Rajasthan, Tamil Nadu, Kerala, Andhra Pradesh, Haryana, Punjab, Uttarakhand and Himachal Pradesh focussed on getting back Kashmir. The agencies were to draw up a coordinated plan to achieve this goal. The Defence Ministry and Military Headquarters had already started working on the plan, and Trital's deputy, Kushal Ram, was tasked with focusing on this effort.

In Bengal, Ashutosh Chatterjee was upset and disappointed that his government had been dismissed. His party workers had initiated a violent protest against the suspension, exacerbating the situation.

Ashutosh Chatterjee was unable to find the courage to tell his mother about the dismissal, but Lalita Chatterjee learned of it through TV news channels and was shocked. She asked her nurse to confirm the news, and although it took some time for Ashutosh to reach her, the doctors had already arrived. He couldn't hold back his tears and wept bitterly. Lalita Chatterjee couldn't bear to see her son cry, and her ability to speak was impaired, making strange gestures. It was decided that she should be taken to a hospital, so an ambulance was called, and she was admitted to the ICU of a top-tier private hospital.

&&&&&

05.08.2032

In Kashmir, the flags of Kashmir and Afghanistan were observed, placing the Indian tricolor. A grand celebration took place in Srinagar, attended by Mullah Ashfaq and Brigadier Mansoor Khan from Pakistan. The Prime Minister of Pakistan and the President of Afghanistan participated via Zoom, along with many other senior leaders and officers, including Iliyas Zaibuddin and his colleagues. Iliyas Zaibuddin was responsible for presenting bouquets to honour Mullah Ashfaq and the other dignitaries. Most of them delivered speeches and expressed how their long-held aspirations had finally been realized.

The leaders of Azad Kashmir, in conjunction with Iliyas Zaibuddin, declared the restoration of their autonomy, which had been lost on date August 52019 due to the abrogation of Article 370. They emphasized that their dream had now become a reality, urging the people of Kashmir to embrace the birth of this new nation. They also called upon the people of Kashmir to be prepared to defend this newfound freedom, which garnered mixed reactions from the Kashmiri populace.

International news channels broadcasted these celebrations and the declaration of a sovereign Kashmir. The Taliban leaders had initially wanted to name the new nation "Kashmir-e-Taliban," but this faced opposition from some Pakistani leaders. The Prime Minister of Pakistan suggested retaining the old name, "Azad Kashmir," for a year and adopting a new name on August 5, 2033. By then, he hoped that Azad Kashmir would be under their control, and they would inform international organizations that they had liberated Kashmir temporarily, with governance entrusted to Azad Kashmir leaders. This information was shared by Pakistan and Afghan TV channels with international organizations.

In India, strong reactions emerged in response to these developments. RVP leaders squarely blamed the BLP for the violence and arson, which led to the imposition of curfews across the country and the military being redeployed to quell the disturbances, thus enabling the entry of the Taliban and Pakistani forces into Kashmir. The BLP leaders made claims that all of this was a result of escalated violence by RVP, and one BLP leader even alleged that a leader from RVP had killed the former PM, Rajendra Kaul. These claims were circulated through pamphlets and flyers due to media censorship.

Pakistan, not content with taking control of Kashmir alone, expressed a desire to advance into Jammu as well. However, the Afghan /Taliban disagreed, asserting that their plan only involved gaining control of Kashmir and they were not willing to take on the risk of encroaching deeper into India. They had a different strategy aimed at unsettling the Indian psyche.

Afghan leader Najib Khan publicly disparaged former PM Rajendra Kaul, depicting him as a worthless individual who contributed nothing to the welfare of the country. Khan released a video featuring Rajendra Kaul in compromising situations with two Thai girls, alleging that Kaul had indulged in sexual escapades during trips to Thailand. While the video did not circulate within India due to censorship, it triggered strong reactions internationally. Some foreign journalists suspected that the video might have been manipulated or was very old based on the outdated quality of the footage. The video was secretly sent to opposition parties in India, and some BLP leaders received it as well.

RVP faced a dilemma regarding whether to oppose the imposition of President's rule in Gujarat, as doing so would mean opposing it in other states as well. They left it to the leaders in Gujarat to determine their stance on the matter.

The committee tasked with investigating the air crash that resulted in the death of the former PM submitted their report to the President, albeit with delays. The report was not comprehensive, but it revealed astonishing findings. The aircraft carrying the former PM and the BLP president had a time bomb on board, placed on the roof of the plane using a drone. While the inside of the aircraft had been thoroughly examined for suspicious devices at Safdarjung Airport, the top of the aircraft had only been inspected in a hangar. A drone was detected on one of the CCTV cameras, suggesting that it was a specialized drone capable of evading radar tracking, a technology typically used by the

DRDO (Defence Research and Development Organization) and under military control. Investigating how the drone fell into unauthorized hands became a critical matter.Near Safdarjung Airport, the Park Hotel, a 5-star establishment, was utilizing small drones for food delivery and other services like bringing groceries, fresh chicken, and vegetables. These drones were usually visible on the airport radar, but this particular drone managed to avoid detection. Despite numerous CCTV cameras, inadequate monitoring occurred by the air traffic control and security agency, a significant lapse on their part. Investigations into this drone were ongoing.

In Delhi, six Supreme Court lawyers residing in the Lutyens Garden area submitted a petition questioning the legitimacy of the President's Rule. The Supreme Court accepted the petition but deferred the hearing. The lawyers had requested an urgent hearing, but the Advocate General argued that given the situation in Kashmir and the country's ongoing violence, the Court should postpone the hearing. Consequently, the Court decided to hold the hearing after three months.

The President had issued orders to the military to restore law and order and control the situation. In states where the governments had been dismissed, law and order had deteriorated. Chief Ministers Ashutosh Chatterjee and Manik Rao Shinde of Bengal and Maharashtra, along with their cabinet ministers, took to the streets to voice their protests. Normal life was disrupted in cities such as Mumbai, Pune, Aurangabad, Nagpur, Kolkata, Asansol, Birbhum, Bankura, and Siliguri. With the ministers violating the curfew and protesting on the streets, the police were left as mere bystanders. Following orders from Rashtrapati Bhavan, the military took action, arresting the chief ministers, their ministers, and detaining them in military facilities under the National Security Act. Ajay Patil of the Chhatrapati Sena and Dilip Deshmukh of the Maharashtravadi Party were also apprehended for participating in the protests. It was hoped that their detention would deter rioters and restore normalcy in these two states.

In the rest of the country, the situation was gradually returning to normal. Military and paramilitary forces from these peaceful regions were being redeployed to Kashmir and Punjab. In the northeast, the military remained on alert to address any potential threats from China.

That evening, a high-level meeting took place at Rashtrapati Bhavan. It was attended by the Chief of Defence Staff, the Chiefs of Staff of the Army, Navy, and Air Force, and senior officials from the Home

Department, Defence Ministry, Foreign Affairs Ministry, Telecommunication Ministry, NIA, R&AW, MI, and NSA. During the meeting, several policy decisions were made regarding Kashmir.

&&&&&

06.08.2032

At 6 o'clock in the morning, the Indian military had deployed twenty battalions in Kashmir. Four of these battalions were stationed in Rajouri near Jammu, two in Kishtwar, and four battalions launched an offensive from Jammu into Pakistan. Additionally, five battalions moved from Kargil to attack the Gilgit-Baltistan area of Pakistan. Another five battalions arrived from Amritsar, and in Leh and Pathankot, five more battalions each were preparing for battle.

The battalions that had moved from Rajouri had their sights set on Bhimbar, Kotli, and Mirpur in Azad Kashmir or POK (Pakistan Occupied Kashmir). These cities were located within a mere fifty kilometres. The troops from Kishtwar were positioned at the Jammu and Kashmir border in a defensive stance, ready to respond to any potential Pakistani or Taliban attacks in Jammu. The troops from Amritsar were given orders to cross the Wagah-Attari border and advance towards Narowal, Gujarat, Iminabad, and Gujranwala, which were all within a hundred kilometres. The battalion from Jammu was tasked with moving towards Sialkot and Jhelum. Sialkot was a mere forty kilometres away, while Jhelum was a hundred kilometres distant. The battalion from Kargil, destined for Skardu a hundred kilometres away, would require helicopters due to the challenging terrain. They were to be para-dropped there with aerial support from our air force.

The weather in Pakistan was favourable for an attack, with clear skies and no rain. The roads were suitable for troop movement, except for the trenches dug by enemy forces, which impeded the rapid advance of Indian troops initially. The Indian forces were equipped with rocket launchers. Arjun, Ajay (T-72), and Bhishma (T-90) armoured tanks advanced from Punjab. Special artillery equipment from various military bases was also being transferred to the border. Although the equipment at the Kashmir border had been damaged in previous enemy attacks, Vajra, the self-propelled Howitzer with precise targeting capabilities, and some towed guns were repositioned in suitable directions from the borders of Punjab and Rajasthan. Sharang 155/45 calibre cannons and Dhanush cannons had been deployed. The advanced Pinaka, a multi-barrel rocket launcher with a firing range of 125 kilometres, had been positioned at various locations. Most importantly, the strategically placed Russian-made S-400 missile system, along with the Israeli-made Spider, was set to counter and neutralize Pakistan's ground-to-air and air-to-ground missiles. In addition, India's anti-ballistic missile system Prithvi had been deployed at various locations. A comprehensive plan had been devised to employ all this equipment and decisively defeat the enemy once and for all. The objective was to swiftly capture the designated areas.

Rafale, Tejas, Mirage, and Sukhoi aircraft, previously used for troop transport within the country, were stationed at military airfields. The newly introduced warplane, Vayu Putra, was also part of the fleet. Military transport planes, including the Dornier 228, Antonov A-32, and EADS-C 295, supported the fighter craft fleet. Indian helicopters such as Prachanda, Dhruv, Chetak, Rudra, and Cheetah proved highly useful in various locations. As the situation returned to normalcy, these airplanes and helicopters could focus on their primary mission. Some of them had already commenced strafing targets in occupied Kashmir.

The former MPs who had been confined to two hotels in Delhi were now released on the condition that they would not participate in any protests. They had to sign affidavits confirming this. They were required to vacate their official residences in Delhi within fifteen days and return to their Lok Sabha (Parliamentary) constituencies. If they violated any of these conditions, they would be subject to arrest under the NSA and imprisonment in military jails. Other ex-MPs from all political parties who wanted to come to Delhi and were willing to relinquish their official residences were granted a month and a half to vacate. Only five senior ministers, Subhash Singh, Avdhesh Singh, Ravindra Prasad, Basavaraj Patil, and Venkatappaiyya, were given four months to vacate their residences.

Avdhesh Singh grew restless and irritable. He expressed his frustration to the military and police sentries stationed outside his house, even threatening them with dire consequences once he assumed the role of Prime Minister.

In Gujarat, protests had mostly ceased, with a few scattered skirmishes. Senior leaders of the RVP in Delhi advised former state cabinet ministers not to prolong the demonstrations. The military had issued shoot-at-sight orders for any protestors, which seemed to effectively control the rioters.

Telangana, Chhattisgarh, and several other states remained relatively peaceful. Minor incidents occurred in Uttar Pradesh and Bihar, but Maharashtra and West Bengal were still in turmoil. Restoring peace in these two states was proving to be time-consuming. In most other states, traffic had returned to normal, factories resumed operations, and "Work from home" had become the standard. Air, rail, and road transport had been restored, but schools and colleges were yet to reopen. The general public was growing weary of curfews so continued to support the administration. In Delhi, strict action was taken against some state government police officers who had failed to act promptly during the violent riots, serving as an example to other officers to perform better.

It was 8 p.m. in Hyderabad, and siblings Ojas and Swapna were having a conversation.

"You've come home quite late," Ojas remarked.

Swapna inquired, "What's the matter?" "

I got so worried," Ojas admitted. "S

illy boy, our housing complex is very secure. We have security guards, CCTV cameras, and intercoms everywhere. Why would you be scared?"

Ojas replied, "I worry about all of you when you don't return home on time. I fear something might have happened to you. Mom and dad haven't returned yet."

"We hadn't left the house for almost fifteen days. There were some pending tasks," Swapna explained.

Ojas remained silent. "Is something bothering you, Ojas?" "Nothing." Swapna moved closer to him, gently taking his hand. He put his arms around her and began to cry. She comforted him with affectionate pats. "I couldn't bear seeing so much violence on the streets, Akka. I couldn't sleep. It's raining heavily today, and the power and internet keep going on and off."

"Don't be so scared, Ojas. Mom and dad will be home soon; they've texted me."

"I received their message too, but I get very anxious about your safety until you're back home," Ojas confessed.

She consoled him, saying, "Don't worry." She got up and retrieved the pastries and chocolates she had bought for him. She offered them to him, but he wasn't as enthusiastic as usual. He seemed disinterested. "What's the matter?"

Ojas replied, "I feel very sad. The Taliban has taken control of Kashmir. It has become a separate nation."

Swapna burst into laughter but quickly composed herself when she saw it had upset him.

She spoke seriously, "Why are you so concerned about Kashmir? There are leaders and powerful people addressing the issue." Ojas gazed at her in silence.

She said, "You know Buddhadev Trital, right? He'll sort things out." Quickly,

he asked, "How do you know about Trital?"

"You told me about him, so I looked him up on YouTube."

"Are you sure he'll fix things?"

"Yes, I'm absolutely certain." Ojas's face brightened a bit.

She offered the plate of pastries again, saying, "You can have one now; you must be hungry."

He looked at her with affection and said, "You're a wonderful sister," as he started to enjoy the pastry.

&&&&&

07.08.2032 to 10.08.2032

On 7th August , in the midnight at 2.00 am at Kahuta in Pakistan, It was peaceful and quiet. It had rained until midnight and there was a kind of heaviness in the weather. At 2.a.m., two unmanned Indian robotic planes, ESvidyut-3flew into Kahuta from Amritsar. They flew at a speed of 100 kms. per minute and had covered a distance of 260 kms. in just three minutes. These solar-electric powered planes were remotely controlled from Amritsar and had been equipped with comprehensive data about Pakistan and, more specifically, Kahuta, enabling them to execute their predetermined flight path.

Kahuta was home to Pakistan's nuclear research laboratory, responsible for the production and storage of long-range missiles and highly enriched uranium (HEU). As the Indian planes breached Pakistani airspace, they triggered an immediate response from Pakistan's radar system, preparing to intercept the intruders. However, the sudden attack caught Pakistan off guard, causing a brief delay in the missile system activation. During this crucial interval, the Indian planes circled over Kahuta and released two drones from each.

These drones, developed by DRDO (Defence Researchand Development Organisation), were constructed using an innovative carbon polymerization technique, incorporating PEEK and PAI polymers with minimal molybdenum for added strength. Titanium was employed as a catalyst in their construction, and they featured electronic components made from polymer materials. Each drone had a solar battery with a twelve-hour capacity and was designed to be self-destructive. Furthermore, they were equipped with a variety of bombs and possessed the capability to elude radar detection, making them a formidable threat.

Following the drone deployment, the ESvidyut-3 planes retreated but were soon detected and subsequently destroyed by the Pakistani missile system. Although Pakistan's radar system identified objects resembling drones being released, it failed to track them effectively, offering some consolation to the Pakistani defence forces, who believed they had thwarted an aerial bomb attack. Regrettably, their recently acquired radar system from China proved inadequate in detecting those advanced drones.

The first drone targeted the electric generator supplying power to the Kahuta radar, causing a blackout and damaging the power cables. The drone fulfilled its mission and self-destructed. The second drone sabotaged the communication facility and severed communication lines, disrupting contact with the radar and missile systems. The third drone eliminated the radar system's equipment, including the discs and dishes. The fourth drone demolished the anti-missile site, responsible for intercepting incoming enemy missiles, inadvertently causing collateral damage to the missile command system situated at the same location.

All four drones were obliterated in the operation. Their explosive devices were crafted using an advanced chemical process of RDX, shielded from radar detection by a rotating magnetic field. Polymers played a crucial role in the composition of these explosives. What set these drones apart was their dual-control system, first from the IS-Vidyut-3 platform and subsequently shifting control to Amritsar. Cameras fitted on the drones facilitated the identification of the radar and anti-missile systems in Kahuta. Indian intelligence had simplified this task by providing detailed maps of the area to the military, which were integrated into the drones. The extensive investment in a state-of-the-art satellite system had ultimately paid off by providing access to these maps. It took only a matter of minutes to neutralize Kahuta's radar and anti-missile systems, leaving the security of the facility in a precarious state.

This triggered panic within Pakistan. In the middle of the night, the army and air force were alerted, but by then, eight missiles had been launched from the Pathankot air base towards Kahuta. The drones had already incapacitated Kahuta's radar system. These eight missiles struck multiple locations in Kahuta, resulting in the devastation of the missile and nuclear production facility. The entire Kahuta region was engulfed in flames, and 225 lives were lost, with hundreds more injured. By the time the Pakistan government responded, the damage had been done.

Nangarhar, the Afghan military and air base, suffered a similar fate. Nangarhar was approximately 500 kilometres from Amritsar. Two IS-Vidyut-3 unmanned robotic planes, traveling at a speed of 100 kilometres per minute, covered the distance in five minutes and released four drones while hovering over Nangarhar. Afghan radar detected these planes and destroyed them, but the drones successfully damaged the radar and anti-missile system. Shortly thereafter, ten missiles were launched on Nangarhar base from the Indian base in Jaisalmer. This resulted in the deaths of 330 Afghan soldiers and injuries to hundreds more. Afghanistan was shaken by this unexpected invasion from India, and the Taliban government was caught off guard. They had wrongly assumed that the conflict would be limited to Kashmir due to internal strife in India.

Early the following morning, India's External Affairs Ministry spokesperson declared that the two nations were at war. Pakistan and Afghanistan were given a 24-hour ultimatum: vacate Kashmir or face the consequences. The External Affairs department also informed the United Nations Security Council that this action had been taken solely to defend Kashmir.

Leaders of Afghanistan and Pakistan held bilateral discussions and reached a mutual agreement not to yield to India's demands and refused to leave Kashmir. They had tacit support from China, though it was unlikely that China would actively engage in the war due to international pressure. Both Afghanistan and Pakistan declared their lack of interest in a ceasefire and their determination to hold Kashmir at any cost. They began launching missiles on Indian air bases.

All major air bases in Pakistan became operational, launching missiles towards India. From airbases like Masrur and Faizal in Karachi, MM Alam in Mianwali, Shahbaz in Jacobabad, Noor Khan in Rawalpindi, and Mushaf in Sargodha, Pakistan launched 34 missiles at targets in Amritsar, Adampur, Bhatinda, Jaisalmer, and Jodhpurair bases.

However, all these missiles were effectively neutralized by India's anti-missile defence system. States in India, including Delhi, Rajasthan, Himachal Pradesh, Uttarakhand, Gujarat, Maharashtra, Goa, and Haryana, were placed on high alert.

There was a shift in the Indian public mindset. Patriotic fervour replaced the earlier agitation. It became evident that Pakistan and the Taliban had exploited India's domestic instability to seize Kashmir. The realization that Kashmir was an integral part of India and must be reclaimed took hold. To achieve this goal, peace had to prevail in India, and violence needed to be curbed. People stepped forward to establish peace, forming peace committees that received a positive response from the general public.

Pakistan had received intelligence from its sources that the hidden underground nuclear missiles andoriginal uranium lab in Kahuta remained undamaged. This information provided Pakistan with enough confidence to persist in its conflict with India rather than consider surrender. They were eager to engage in war. The leadership in Pakistan, both politically and militarily, was divided on the matter of war. Some believed that the war should go on, and Kashmir should remain under Pakistan's control. Others believed that prolonging the war was futile, that defeat by India was imminent, and that pursuing a peace treaty was the better option. Opposition parties in Pakistan demanded to be informed about the government's actions. Overall, Pakistan found itself in a situation of internal division.

Afghanistan had suffered losses but was a resilient and combative nation, determined to avenge these losses. They had Pakistan's full support.

Brigadier Mansur Khan, stationed in Kashmir, inquired with Pakistan's military headquarters about whether his troops should return to Pakistan. However, he was instructed to remain in Kashmir. The Taliban soldiers also were denied permission to retreat.

The Indian army made advances into Azad Kashmir, also known as POK (Pakistan-occupied Kashmir). The following day, they entered Poonch through Rajouri. The Taliban had underestimated the Indian advance in Poonch, initially believing that they were heading towards the Poonch area in Indian Kashmir. They observed only a limited number of troops and tanks, appearing to be in a defensive posture. They were in for a harsh awakening when they witnessed the intensity of the Indian assault in POK. Pakistan retaliated with a counterattack, during which

Pakistan's VT-4, Al-Zarar, and Al-Khalid tanks unleashed a series of artillery shells. India's Arjun, T-90, and Bhishma (Improved T-90) tanks responded with a barrage of artillery shells on Pakistan.There were casualtieson both sides.

Both sides were engaged in aerial combat as well, either downing each other's aircraft or forcing them to retreat. India's Dhruv, Chetak, Rudra, and Cheetah helicopters airdropped troops into Pakistan, with air support from Rafale and Sukhoi fighter jets. Pakistan retaliated with their fighter jets, including Thunder (JF-17), Mirage-135, and F-7 PC, pursuing Indian jets and downing three Rafale jets. In turn, India had taken down six Thunder and five F-7 PC jets. The paratroopers advanced at a brisk pace in support of the Indian assault.

By this point, India had gained control over Mirpur. Battalions from Jammu advanced southward into Jhelum and Gujarat.

Throughout this operation, India ensured that the 150-kilometer-long Line of Control (LOC) bordering Kashmir was sealed, preventing the Taliban and the Pakistani army in Kashmir from retreating into Pakistan. They were effectively trapped in Kashmir.

The Indian military now put into action all the weaponry stored in various depots, such as Pathankot, Udhampur, Amritsar, and other locations. With the aid of Brahmos missiles, Advanced Artillery Gun Systems (ATAGS), Wheeled Armoured Platforms (WHP), Prahar missiles, Rudram missiles, Quick Reaction Surface-to-Air missiles (QRSAM), and Medium-Range Surface-to-Air missiles (MRSAS), Indian troops penetrated Pakistan's territory with remarkable speed.

Pakistan found its troops and equipment insufficient to confront the advancing Indian forces. They were continuously subjected to intense aerial bombardment, and their numbers were dwindling. It appeared as thoughtheir Kashmir (POK) was slipping from their grasp.

In Kashmir, the Taliban leaders were puzzled about why Indian forces were attempting to breach Pakistan's borders instead of trying to reclaim control of Kashmir.

While some Indian troops from Kargil were stationed near the Kashmir border, the main battalions began advancing toward Skardu and Gilgit, after regaining Kargil. When India's T-90 (Bhishma) tanks entered Gilgit with air support from Rafale and Mig-29, Pakistan realized that India aimed to take control of this region in addition to POK. Both Pakistan and Afghanistan had assumed that India would initially focus on liberating Indian Kashmir; they had never anticipated that India would initiate an attack on Pakistan. Once this became clear, the Pakistan army started moving its forces from Peshawar and Baluchistan in the west, as well as from the cantonments in Faisal, Karangi Creek, Manura, Jacobabad, Peshawar, and Risalpur towards POK. They requested assistance from Afghanistan, and in response, Afghan troops from Sherpur and Kandahar cantonments were airlifted in 14CI130J transport planes and deployed into POK. In 2021, when the Americans withdrew from Afghanistan, they left behind these transport planes, which had been seized by the Taliban.

Typically, Pakistan experiences heavy rains in August, but this year, it rained in July, and August saw a scarcity of rain. India's plan was to capture as many Pakistani cities as possible in the shortest time.

Intense battles were waged on multiple fronts, with Indian aircraft bombing Pakistani cities. Pakistani planes attempted to enter Indian territory but were repelled. India managed to destroy five of their AF-16 and seven J-10C jets, while Pakistan succeeded in bringing down three Mirage 2000 and two Jaguar jets belonging to India.

Out of the five states placed under President's Rule in India, peace had almost been restored in Gujrat, Telangana, and Chhattisgarh. Many Telangana leaders were incarcerated, and in Maharashtra and West Bengal, most of the ministers were in military detention. Protests and riots had ceased. A few party workers continued to protest against the President's Rule and willingly allowed themselves to be arrested. These protests were conducted peacefully, putting an end to violence. The detained ministers were permitted to use a phone only in cases of deteriorating health. They received decent food but were denied alcohol, which frustrated the ministers accustomed to a luxurious lifestyle. They were desperate to be released and were concerned about the upcoming elections. They also feared that the President could initiate a CBI and ED inquiry into corruption allegations if he wished. The ministers from Maharashtra, in particular, were anxious, having previously been under the ED's scrutiny and having barely escaped. They eagerly awaited the end of this phase and advised their party workers to maintain a low profile for the time being.

In Bengal, DESWAP party workers were deeply disheartened. The imposition of President's Rule, and more significantly, the military discipline they encountered, had a negative impact on their morale. Many of them were serving three-month jail terms, weakening the spirits of other workers. Furthermore, their practices of receiving cuts and commissions had come to a halt. People had become more aware and were directly approaching government departments for their needs instead of going through party workers who acted as intermediaries. Government staff had become more punctual and focused on their work. Twenty employees were dismissed for neglecting their duties, and two corrupt employees were imprisoned. The general public was grateful for the imposition of the President's Rule. The military personnel from Telangana, Gujrat, and Chhattisgarh states were withdrawn and deployed to the borders.

Trital, acting through the president's office, issued orders to retrieve the phone records of former MPs dating back to the period before the former PM's tragic plane crash. The focus was primarily on Avdhesh Singh and his group of ministers. This operation was carried out in complete secrecy to avoid sparking further controversy.

On the following day, August 8th, an operation was launched from Udhampur. India's robotic aircraft caused significant damage to Pakistan's nuclear reactor in Khusab, which was approximately 270 kilometres away from Udhampur. The operation closely followed the same system used in the destruction of Kahuta. The robotic plane reached Khusab from Udhampur in a mere five minutes, deploying four drones that disabled the radar, communication, anti-missile, and missile command systems. This paved the way for ten missiles launched from Udhampur, causing substantial damage to the nuclear reactor in Khusab and igniting a fire in the nearby cantonment, resulting in significant damage to an ammunition depot.

In Afghanistan, missiles originating from Jamnagar followed a sea route to reach Bagram, located 1400 kilometers away. The radar and anti-missile systems in Bagram had already been compromised by Mossad agents, with Soshe Dayan playing a role in this mission, whoreallocated himself to Afghanistan from Pakistan. Salman Khan's computer data had raised suspicions about Soshe Dayan, but before this information could reach the relevant parties via email, Razia managed to ignite a fire, destroying the computer and leading to Salman Khan's demise.

Throughout the day, the Indian military made rapid advances in Pakistan, utilizing state-of-the-art technology to overpower Pakistani tanks attempting to impede their progress. The objective was to secure as much Pakistani territory as possible before any intervention from the United Nations Security Council.

India had finally decided to teach Pakistan a lesson and initiated a "Clean-up" (*Safaai*)mission on the same night. This mission targeted forty-one sites, with two robotic planes and four drones deployed at each site, following the same procedure used to destroy nuclear facilities, radar, and anti-missile systems in Kahuta, Khusab, Nangarhar, and Bagram. Primarily, twenty-three cantonments were attacked, including Attock, Bhawalpur, Chaklala, Gujranwala, Jhelum, Sherkot, Sialkot, Walton, Khariyan, Rawalpindi, Sargodha, Clifton, Faizal, Hyderabad, Karachi, Karangi, Malir, Manura, Jacobabad, Abotabad, Skardu, Kharmag, and Gilgit. The plan to destroy radar and anti-missile systems in these cantonments saw an 87% success rate. However, Rawalpindi, Sherkot, and Abotabad could not be destroyed, as the missile systems there shot down the Indian robotic planes before they could release the drones. The other twenty cantonments were successfully "cleaned up," allowing the Indian army to rapidly invade Pakistani territory.

Similarly, eighteen Pakistani airbases were targeted for "clean-up."(*Safaai*) These airbases included Kotali, Rawalpindi, Mushaf of Sargodha, Bholari of Jamshora, Rafiki of Sherkot, Masrur, and Faisal of Karachi, Murid of Chokwal, MM Alam of Minawali, Minhas of Kamara, Jakobabad, Risalpur, Dadu, Skardu, Gilgit, Karimabad, Manshera, and Mujaffarabad. However, Rawalpindi and Jakobabad survived the attack, as their radar and missile systems destroyed the ES-Vidyut-3 robotic planes before they could release drones. Nonetheless, sixteen airbases became non-operational due to the lack of radar and missile systems.

A radar system can detect enemy fighter jets, guide its own fighter jets, and prepare the missile system for defence. Any base lacking a radar system is akin to a blind wrestler in a wrestling ring. Despite their size, strength, and powerful grip, a blind wrestler is at a disadvantage as their sighted opponent can easily evade their grasp. Pakistan found itself in a similar vulnerable position, much like the blind wrestler in the ring.

Subsequently, missile attacks were carried out on these twenty cantonments and sixteen airbases in a coordinated manner, with most of the Indian airbases assigned specific targets in Pakistan. The resulting destruction in Pakistan was extensive. There were casualties in thousandsand more injured.The basic infrastructures were damaged to the extent of getting repaired within two months.The loss of so many airplanesand artillery was a rude shockto Pakistan. This action served as a nearly final warning to Pakistan to surrender its claims in Kashmir, but the lack of proper coordination between the military, politicians, and ISI hindered their ability to make a sound decision.

Both Pakistan and Afghanistan were severely rattled by the Indian assault on the crucial cities of Khusab and Bagram. Pakistan was moreinfuriated by the attack on its air bases and military facilities. In retaliation, Pakistan launched a volley of approximately fifty-six missiles aimed at important Indian cities in the north, including Amritsar, Pathankot, Chandigarh, Ambala, Jaisalmer, Bhatinda, Ahmedabad, Jaipur, Jodhpur, and Jammu. However, all these attacks were successfully thwarted by India's anti-missile system. In response, India launched forty-five missiles targeting Karachi, Lahore, Risalpur, Muzaffarabad, Rawalpindi, and Sialkot. All of these strikes were successful, except the one on Rawalpindi, where the anti-missile system remained intact. India took great care to ensure that its missiles primarily hit military installations, minimizing civilian casualties and property damage in Pakistan.

Now it wasvery easy for the movementof Indian warplanes to moveinto Pakistan anddamage the Pakistaniairplanes andArtillery like tanks, and rocket launchers,as they remained undetected by radar system and not susceptible to missile attack. Thishas helped the movement of Indian troopsto capturethe maximum area.

Swift troop movements were observed in Ladakh and the surrounding regions. Transport planes, including U.S.-made Boeing C-17s and C-130 JS, Ukraine-made Antonov A-32s, and Dornier 228S developed with German technology by HAL India, were deployed to paradrop a significant number of troops into Ladakh and further areas. These troops first secured control of Ghanche, Kharmang, and Shigar in the Gilgit-Baltistan area and then advanced towards Diamer, Ghizer, Astore, and Karimabad. Artillery guns such as Sharang, Dhanush, and Pinaka had already reached the area via Kargil. The Prithvi air defence system and Russia's missile defence system, S-400, were put into action. The Indian army aimed to capture the entire 70,000 square kilometresof territory with armoured tanks supporting their advance. Rafale and Vayu Putra jets provided vital aerial cover, and Pakistani resistance gradually weakened.

Indian forces gained control of Skardu airport, with Indian planes landing there. A team of Indian technicians commenced radar system repairs at the airport. Helicopters were employed to paradrop army units in the vicinity of Ratti-Gali Lake in Neelam Valley. This operation continued throughout the day without resistance from Pakistan since, by then, Muzaffarabad airport was also under India's control. Spain-made EADS-CASA 295 and Dornier 228 transport planes airdropped food supplies to the troops.

The helicopter operations persisted throughout the night, and Indian jets began patrolling over Kashmir. They faced some resistance in Pakistan Occupied Kashmir (POK) but continued their efforts to target military depots and airports. Pakistani launchers managed to down five MIG-29 aircraft, but in response, India destroyed seven Pakistani Mirage-5 aircraft that attempted to enter Indian territory.

In Kashmir, Iliyas Zaibuddin was in contact with leaders from Pakistan and the Taliban. He expressed his concern that these leaders were no longer discussing Kashmir but were more focused on Pakistan-occupied Kashmir (POK). It was evident to Iliyas that these leaders believed India would likely reclaim its portion of Kashmir but might find it challenging to retain control over POK. These leaders were aware of the change in India's political administration. Under the President's Rule, the military administration was swift and decisive in planning strategies against Pakistan and the Taliban. With many ministers in jail or under house arrest, the military faced no political interference. However, Pakistan and Afghanistan were still indecisive, with political intervention preventing autonomous military decision-making.

On the fourth day, which was August 10th, the entire Indian army had crossed into Pakistan. The three divisions of Azad Kashmir, specifically Mirpur, Muzaffarabad, and Poonch, were nearly under India's control. India had taken full control of ten districts in these areas. In 1948, Pakistan had sent an army contingent disguised as *Kabilies* (tribals from the North-West Frontier Province) to capture the districts of Muzaffarabad, Hattian Bala, Neelam Valley, Mirpur, Bhimber, Kotli, Poonch (Rawalakot), Bagh, Haveli, Sudhnuti (Pallandari). This time, the Indian military successfully reclaimed these ten districts, covering an area of approximately 13,300 square kilometres. This was a significant setback for Pakistan.

Indian armoured tanks rapidly advanced into Pakistan, leading to close-quarters combat between Indian and Pakistani soldiers in Gujranwala, Gujarat, Sialkot, and Jhelum. The infantry and armoured divisions received air support from the Indian Air Force (IAF), which first neutralized Pakistan's fighter aircraft and then targeted Pakistan's artillery. As the Pakistani army began to withdraw, the Indian assault grew increasingly potent.There were continuous missile attacks on Pakistan,which couldnot be detected by non-functioning radar system and replied by ineffective missile launching system.Only a couplewere working and that was not sufficient tocounter fast onslaught of India.

On the fourth day, fresh battalions from India reached the Indian soldiers in Pakistan. Some units of the Indian army from Amritsar launched an attack on Lahore, further shocking Pakistan. It became increasingly difficult for Pakistan to fight on multiple fronts. Pakistani leaders feared either an all-out takeover by India or the complete destruction of Pakistan.

After capturing Gilgit and Skardu, Indian forces turned their attention towards Karimabad. Pakistan attempted to halt the Indian advance with Chinese-made AF7 PC and J-10C bomber aircraft. India, on the other hand, possessed Brazilian-made EMB-145 (Airborne Warning & Control System), which effectively detected early warning signals in the sky and destroyed Pakistani jets. Pakistan had sought military assistance from China in this region, but China declined under international pressure. Instead, China provided equipment in the form of armoured tanks such as Type-59, Type-69, and 8 H-15 Howitzers. Many of these had already been sent to Kashmir but were now trapped there due to border closures. Pakistani tanks faced stiff competition from Indian Ajay T-72 and Bhishma T-90 tanks. Rafale and Tejas bomber aircraft strafed Pakistani tanks and destroyed them, resulting in heavy casualties among Pakistani and Taliban soldiers. Gilgit and Baltistan were now effectively under India's control.

Taliban soldiers in Kashmir were becoming increasingly restless and insecure, wondering if they had made the right decision in accepting Pakistan's invitation to infiltrate into Kashmir. Initially welcomed by the people of Kashmir, the public's opinion began to shift as they fell victim to Taliban atrocities. The Indian public was fed up with the looting, plundering, rape, and murder, and they longed for the Indian government to free them from the Taliban's grip.

A platoon of Taliban soldiers attempted to escape to Balakot through the jungles of Uri, but the highly alert Indian army regiment stationed in Uri foiled their escape plan, inflicting significant losses on the Afghan platoon. Many Afghan soldiers were killed in direct combat or while trying to flee. The soldiers who remained in Kashmir heard about this and grew increasingly fearful. They reached out to Pakistani headquarters for rescue, but Pakistan was occupied with multiple fronts and did not respond to their call. This further disheartened the soldiers, and with dwindling food supplies, they faced near starvation. The food supplies from Sialkot cantonment were not reaching them.They contemplated confronting Indian soldiers to secure their escape but lacked the courage to do so, given their deteriorating mental and physical condition. They chose to remain silent and wait for a better opportunity.

In India, aside from Maharashtra and West Bengal, peace prevailed across the country, and the army and paramilitary forces had withdrawn from the cities to reinforce the borders.

&&&&&

11.08.2032

The Indian army had nearly taken control of the entire Pakistan-occupied Kashmir (POK). After capturing cities and districts like Muzaffarabad, Patan, Neelam Valley, Hattian Bala, Bhimber, Bagh, Poonch, Haveli, Kotli, Jhelum, Kartarpur, Narowal, Gujranwala, Gujarat, Sheikhpura, Sialkot, Nankana Sahib, Mandi Bahauddin, and Hafizabad, a fierce battle was underway for control of Lahore between the Pakistan Air Force (PAF) and the Indian Air Force (IAF). Risalpur, Karachi, Mianwali, and Jacobabad were under missile attack, and Pakistan's radar and anti-missile systems had been rendered ineffective. Pakistan was in a dire state.

The Indian side had also suffered significant losses. So many army men and pilots were martyred. Advanced weaponry such as Electric-3 robotic crafts and drones had incurred immeasurable damage. So many tanks, warplanes were lost. Orders for fresh equipment had been placed with ordnance factories and private manufacturers, but production would take time. The human casualties were high on both sides. Pakistan had suffered more significant losses, but the Indian army had also paid a heavy price in terms of personnel and equipment in the war against the Taliban and Pakistan in Kashmir.

In Afghanistan, Indian air strikes were targeting Kandahar, Asadabad, Jalalabad, and Kabul. Pakistan attempted to send missiles towards Indian cities like Amritsar, Mumbai, Ahmedabad, Surat, Jaipur, and Chandigarh. In the Arabian Sea, Indian naval carriers INS Rana, INS Ranveer, INS Ran Vijay, and INS Vikrant-6 were working tirelessly to thwart Pakistan's missile attacks on Mumbai, Ahmedabad, and Surat. Jaipur and Jaisalmer were protected by the anti-missile system in

Jodhpur, while the system in Pathankot safeguarded Chandigarh and Amritsar in Punjab.

Within India, various committees convened daily. On this particular day, the President had called for a confidential meeting in the afternoon, and only top officials from the Home, Finance, Defence, Prime Minister's Office (PMO), and Foreign Affairs departments were invited. In a move to ensure confidentiality, a couple of high-ranking officers suspected of leaking sensitive information had been placed on forced leave. It was clear that the President took a stern approach and was ready to take disciplinary action against those who breached confidentiality.

It was well-known among bureaucrats, government departments, and the defense establishment that the President had the utmost trust in his co-brother, Buddhadeva Trital. It was evident that Trital was the mastermind behind 'Operation Save India.' Therefore, any information provided to the President's chief secretary was also shared with Buddhadev Trital. While there was a coordination system in place, Trital oversaw it, and the committee members recognized his competence in managing the domestic situation in India and dealing with Pakistan and the Taliban.

During the meeting, the domestic situation was the first topic of discussion. Various agencies and organizations submitted their reports on the law-and-order situation across the country. Most states reported positive results, except for West Bengal and Maharashtra. Arunachal Pradesh's report indicated concerns about potential Chinese intervention in the region, prompting the army there to be on high alert.

Chief of Defence Staff (CDS) Ashok Bhat was also impressed by Trital's efficiency and capability. When a team of defense officers led by Brigadier Balwinder Singh Saluja suggested that India should launch an attack on Pakistan before reclaiming Kashmir, Ashok Bhat expressed reservations. Brigadier Saluja, who had experience from the Kargil war, felt differently. However, Ashok Bhat believed that such a strategy would result in substantial losses, both in terms of personnel and equipment, and attract international criticism. During a special meeting with the President, Trital supported the proposal, and it proved to be the right decision as Pakistan was now in a desperate situation, considering approaching the United Nations Security Council (UNSC) or threatening a nuclear response.

All these matters were discussed in the meeting on that day. Trital emphasized the need to be prepared for the worst when going to war and urged that once the decision was made, there should be no turning back.

The meeting also reviewed the on-ground situation, assessing the captured territory and potential areas for further advancement. An estimation of India's losses in terms of personnel, equipment, weapons, aircraft, tanks, and drones was made, highlighting the greater losses incurred by Pakistan. The proposal to demand the surrender of Pakistan and Afghanistan in Kashmir was unanimously approved, with the External Affairs ministry tasked with making a declaration to the international community and the UNSC.

Another special meeting was scheduled to determine which territories in Pakistan should be retained and which should be released in the event of international pressure on India to declare a ceasefire. Only six officials were authorized to attend this meeting.

The leaders of the RVP party found themselves in a state of uncertainty. They were unsure about the direction of political events in India. They had a strong feeling that the BLP party was on the verge of splitting into two or even three factions. All political parties had to obtain permission from the President's office to conduct their online Zoom meetings. Even Nagarjuna Reddy, the president of the BLP, needed clearance from the President's office to host any Zoom meeting. However, when it was revealed that Subhash Singh would be attending the meeting, the permission was granted without any hassle.

Later in the evening, Trital returned home for dinner. He had to head back to the military HQ after the meal. His wife, Vijaya, subtly hinted that having meals so late wasn't ideal. Trital explained that they had organized a working lunch at the President's office after the meeting, and because the meeting had dragged on, they were served snacks with the evening tea.

Following dinner, Trital picked up some papers from his desk and departed for work at the military HQ. Once Trital had left the house, Vijaya entered his office and noticed that the key to his office desk was hanging from the drawer. For some inexplicable reason, she felt tempted to peek into the desk drawer.

Upon opening the drawer, she found a stack of files at the top. Four of them were labeled as 'Top Secret' and contained information about various leaders and some official correspondence related to China, Pakistan, and Afghanistan. Beneath these files were three marked

'Personal.' As she skimmed through these files, she discovered information about Trital's different postings and appointments since he joined the government. In the middle of the last file, she found an envelope, and she guessed that it might contain photographs.

Indeed, there were three photos inside. In the first photo, there was a young lady posing with Trital, both of them looking young. The second photo featured the same young lady, alone, and she seemed to be dressed as if she worked in a beauty parlour or salon. The third photo showed the same lady with a little girl in her arms. Vijaya flipped the photos and noticed that there were no names on the first photo with Trital and the lady. The lady's single photo had 'My Dear Reshma' written on the back, and the third one with the little girl had 'Reshma and Madhubala' along with a date from seventeen years ago. Vijaya deduced that this must have been from the time Trital was an undercover agent or spy in Pakistan. The lady appeared very fair, while the little girl had a darker complexion, suggesting that the lady's husband might also be dark-skinned. Vijaya closely examined the girl's photograph and was shocked to see that her features matched those of her husband. As she regained control of her emotions, she realized that Buddhadeva Saheb sang those soulful songs in Reshma's memory.

She contemplated asking Trital about this that night but decided to wait for a better moment. On a few occasions in the past, she had noticed that whenever Trital held a young child in his arms, his eyes welled up with tears. The mystery was now unveiled to her, and she neatly returned the files and papers to the drawer.

She couldn't sleep that night, as numerous thoughts raced through her mind. She felt that her husband should have confided in her, and she wouldn't have been offended. Then she considered that this might be the case with many couples who had pre-marital affairs, keeping their secrets from their spouses. These thoughts kept her awake, and when Trital returned home at midnight, he was surprised to find her still awake.

On that day itself , in fateful evening, the Indian Navy hadlaunched a powerful assault on Karachi's harbour. The warships Vikrant-S-6 and S-5 unleashed rockets and missiles over Karachi. These naval vessels, along with others in the fleet, had previously thwarted Pakistan's missile attacks on Mumbai and Ahmedabad. Pakistan had assumed that these fleets were solely in a defensive posture, but they were prepared and promptly retaliated by firing missiles at Vikrant. However, Indian anti-missile systems successfully intercepted and neutralized these incoming threats. Karachi's naval base bore the brunt of the attack, causing significant damage to both the city and the military establishment.

Pakistan was profoundly shaken, realizing that India had launched a full-scale military operation. The Pakistani Ministry of External Affairs declared their intent to launch a nuclear attack on Ayodhya and Varanasi, vowing to reduce these cities to ashes. India responded with a bold challenge, warning Pakistan that they would make any such attack unsuccessful and, in retaliation, annihilate Islamabad. Initially, Pakistan maintained a hardline stance.

Their Army Chief issued orders to activate the nuclear missile system, with launch pads located in five different places: Karachi, Isakhel, Rawalpindi, Kahuta, and Khusab. The central control point was in Karachi, where all the necessary codes and computers were stored. The Prime Minister's Office had the responsibility of generating the launch codes and transmitting them to the military headquarters, which, in turn, would send them to the central control point in Karachi. However, this process was disrupted because the underground base in Karachi was inaccessible, and the approach road had been destroyed by Indian missiles. Many engineers stationed there had tragically perished due to suffocation, and the underground cables leading to the base point were severely damaged. These cables carried both electricity and internet services, leading to a significant problem for Pakistan. Repairingand reactivating thewhole system wouldtake considerabletime. They were left with no alternative but to heed India's warning about the consequences for Islamabad.

Pakistan's External Affairs Minister sought advice from the Chinese Foreign Minister, who recommended approaching the United Nations Security Council (UNSC). That very night, in the early hours in the USA, Pakistan instructed its ambassador to the United States to file an urgent appeal and call for a session of the Security Council. The Indian ambassador in the USA promptly filed a counter-appeal, highlighting that when India had brought the matter to the UNSC on July 29th, all nations had unanimously agreed that it was a bilateral issue to be resolved through mutual negotiations. India emphasized that it was now Pakistan and Afghanistan refusing to surrender control of Kashmir.

China swiftly requested an urgent Zoom meeting and exercised its veto power against India's position. The Secretary-General of the UNSC announced that a decision would be made the following day, with all member nations duly informed.

&&&&&

12.08.2032

By this point, India had taken control of Lahore, Muzaffarabad, Gujranwala, Mirpur, Poonch, Skardu, Gilgit, Kotli, Bhimber, Jhelum, Gujarat, Karimabad, Narowal, and Sialkot. The road ahead indicated a fierce struggle because Pakistan had relocated its troops and artillery from other areas and positioned them on the borders of these regions. Pakistan had realized that if the advance wasn't halted, India would soon dominate all of Pakistan.

Afghanistan was also on edge, fearing that India might continue its advance and potentially enter Afghanistan. Despite Afghan assistance, Pakistan was fighting a losing battle to regain lost territory. Both Afghanistan and Pakistan were suffering heavy casualties on the battlefield. The Pakistani skyline was filled with Indian warplanes, and 90% of Pakistan's radar and anti-missile systems had been destroyed, rendering them unable to detect Indian aircraft. Pakistan was in a dire situation, seeking face-saving measures through the United Nations Security Council (UNSC) with support from China and seeking help from Arab nations. They made every effort to convene a Security Council meeting on this issue.

In Delhi, Habib Khan, the Rohingya leader, was attempting to contact DESWAP leaders in Kolkata. Indian Intelligence Bureau had received information about this three days ago and alerted the NIA. NIA arrested Habib Khan at dawn on that day and conducted a search of his house. During the search, they found incriminating documents, bank passbooks, three mobile phones, and two laptops. One of the laptops contained a document making unsubstantiated allegations against former PM Rajendra Kaul, suggesting that Kaul was responsible for preventing Rohingyas from gaining permanent citizenship in India. They also retrieved significant data from Habib Khan's mobile phone, leading to the arrest of some of his associates, including Kalpak Sanodia and Mustafizur Khan. When Sanodia was taken into custody, the Praja Dharma Party protested, threatening the NIA with a widespread agitation. However, the NIA disregarded this threat, as they knew that the party's president, Akshay Sabharwal, would be incarcerated for three months if he caused any trouble, making their threat essentially empty.

That afternoon, the President convened a general meeting of all departments to discuss the law-and-order situation. Different committees presented their reports, indicating that most states had returned to normalcy. The Governors, Chief Secretaries of states under President's Rule, and DGPs of those states were present at the meeting and gave genuine reports. Additionally, Chief Secretaries and DGPs from other states, not under the President's Rule, participated in the meeting via Zoom and faxed their reports in advance.

The President set the agenda for the next meeting, instructing the states to compile a list of the dead and injured individuals during the riots, categorized by state and party. States were also required to collect data on losses suffered by party offices and individuals, as well as the number of injured people admitted to hospitals. It was emphasized that any state refusing to provide compensation to the heirs of the deceased must be identified, and all states were tasked with creating an inventory of losses and disbursing due compensation. A helpline was established at the president's officeto facilitate applications for assistance.The same helplinewas available for wivesof martyrs inwar.The instructions to the military to take care of them were already in existence.

The issue of releasing jailed political leaders was also discussed, with a clear indication that this matter would be reviewed in the next meeting. The President approved the process of obtaining affidavits from ministers willing to pledge under oath that they would not incite further agitation. Most of these ministers were from West Bengal and Maharashtra. However, their release was contingent on further scrutiny. Ajay Patil of the Chhatrapati Sena and Dilip Deshmukh of the Maharashtrawadi Party were facing significant legal challenges. They were under investigation by the Enforcement Directorate (ED) and had been granted bail, but the Home Ministry reviewed their bail and successfully petitioned the high court to cancel it, extending their custodial terms. When they might receive relief remained uncertain.

The President issued an order outlining the guidelines for releasing or detaining political leaders. The cases of leaders from states under President's Rule were to be reviewed in Delhi, while the cases of leaders from other states would be addressed in the subsequent meeting. The leaders in jail were growing increasingly restless.

In relation to Kashmir, the President also announced that following the UNSC session, India might consider declaring a ceasefire, but under the condition that Pakistan and the Taliban forces in Kashmir would surrender to India. This move was aimed at preventing heavy losses to India. The President also emphasized that India should maintain pressure on both Pakistan and the Taliban in Kashmir.

That night, Kashmir came under attack from all sides. The morale of Pakistani and Taliban soldiers was severely low, and they showed little inclination to resist the Indian offensive. They anticipated that surrender was inevitable. Some units of the Indian army, having redirected from Uri, moved forward into Baramulla. Simultaneously, assaults were initiated from Rajouri, Ramban, and Kishtwar in the Jammu region. The skies over Kashmir were filled with Indian Air Force jets. Pakistani and Taliban troops received orders to prepare for surrender, and consequently, they made no attempts to combat the advancing Indian forces. Indian troops descended into Kashmir from Ladakh as well, effectively cornering Pakistani forces within India.

Taliban leader Mulla Ashfak had fled Kashmir, while some members of the Azad Kashmir Organization were determined to fight and save Kashmir. They were provided with weapons, although lacking formal training, which limited their effectiveness.

&&&&&

13.08.2032

At 3 a.m. IST that night, the UNSC requested that India halt the hostilities. India agreed to do so on the condition that the Taliban and Pakistani armies surrender and withdraw from Kashmir, with Pakistan and Afghanistan needing to concur with this.

Since the break of day, the Indian army began to concentrate in the vicinity of Srinagar. Local police units commenced merging with the military forces. Prior to this, the local police had been under the control of the Kashmir leadership. There was an extensive search for Azad Kashmir leaders like Iliyas Zaibuddin, who had gone into hiding. The residents of Kashmir warmly welcomed the Indian army as it arrived in Srinagar by evening.

The news of Pakistan and Afghanistan agreeing at the UNSC to surrender in Kashmir was broadcast on all Indian television channels. The arrival of the Indian army in Srinagar was also reported in the media, leading to widespread celebration throughout the country.

The defeated enemy soldiers were transported to various camps across the nation as Prisoners of War (POWs), and their weapons and tanks were confiscated.

An announcement from the Rashtrapati Bhavan declared the imposition of President's Rule in Kashmir. The legislative assembly was dissolved, the cabinet dismissed, and the ministers were placed under house arrest in Jammu due to indications that they might incite agitation. Consequently, the state would largely be under military control. The administration of both POK, Kashmir, and Jammu was entrusted to the Governor of Kashmir for a duration of six months, with administrative support from the military.

In the ongoing investigation by the NIA in Delhi, it was discovered that out of the five individuals arrested, namely Habib Khan, Sanodia, and Mustafizur Khan, were in contact with the Chief Minister of West Bengal. When questioned about the nature of this contact and whether they were involved in any way in the assassination of former PM Rajendra Kaul, they were evasive in their responses.

Trital was well-informed about the progress of the investigation. Through the President's Secretary, he conveyed to the NIA that the investigation must be thorough. Although the NSA did not directly control the NIA, all of the agency's activities reached Trital through the Home Ministry. The Home Ministry was aware that, even though the President had taken charge of the country's administration, the de facto decision-maker was Buddhadeva Trital, the Chief of the NSA, and the President made all administrative decisions based on Trital's advice.

Sanodia and the other suspects were transported to Kolkata for further questioning. There, they were confronted by the former Chief Minister of West Bengal, Ashutosh Chatterjee, who was still in jail, to verify their contacts. Ashutosh was genuinely fearful but reluctant to divulge additional information.

Before the NIA investigation, the four arrested individuals were collectively questioned about the nature, duration, and purpose of their contact with each other, but they could not provide satisfactory answers. When confronted with phone conversations and coded chats along with dates, they became more cooperative. At this point, a decision was made to interrogate them individually, with a warning that coercive methods would be used if they did not cooperate. Ashutosh Chatterjee vehemently objected to this line of questioning and warned of potential violence in Bengal if he was subjected to torture. NIA officers pointed out that his arrest had not yet provoked a public reaction, dispelling his misconceptions about his popularity.

Trital was aware that Avdhesh Singh was a drug addict, and his dwindling drug supply was causing restlessness. Trital closely monitored his behaviour and observed that Avdhesh Singh occasionally overdosed, depleting his drug stash faster than expected. Measures were taken to ensure that he could not obtain his usual drug supply, further increasing his restlessness. Additionally, Avdhesh Singh was cut off from the outside world and unable to contact his son Raj Narain, who was incarcerated in Bhiwani, Haryana. Avdhesh realized that his dream of becoming Prime Minister was slipping away.

On the 13th, peace prevailed in Pakistan, with no missile attacks or the sound of aircraft. Therewas only somesmoke or firewas seen. The people of Pakistan breathed a collective sigh of relief. The Pakistani government focused on assessing the human and material losses incurred during the conflict. They also calculated the territory lost to India. Opposition parties in Pakistan began raising their voices, urging Pakistan to make efforts to reclaim the lost territory from India. It became evident to Pakistan that while they had succeeded in halting the war by involving the UNSC, the evolving political landscape was daunting. Their troops and armoured tanks were trapped in Kashmir. Prime Minister Ijaz Khan was in a state of misery, feeling immense pressure from all sides. His military forces had not lived up to his expectations, and it was clear that Pakistan had brought disgrace upon itself. Despite stopping the war through the UNSC, the political situation in Pakistan was becoming increasingly worrisome. Discussions began with his ministers regarding diplomatic strategies to regain Pakistani territory from India.

&&&&&

14.08.2032

It was a Pakistan's Independence Day, but this year, it was a day of mourning.Flags were raised, but the atmosphere lacked the usual enthusiasm and patriotic fervour. Opposition parties directed their curses towards Prime Minister Ijaz Khan. Pakistan once again approached the UN Security Council, demanding that India evacuate Pakistani territory, including Lahore and all other cities. India's response was that it considered this matter a bilateral issue, paying no heed to China's objections. Pakistan, in turn, reached out to leaders of other nations to exert pressure on India and convene another Security Council meeting. India remained steadfast, as it was Pakistan that had provoked hostilities by attacking Kashmir with the assistance of the Taliban.

Pakistan's short-lived joy at fulfilling its dream of capturing Kashmir was now replaced by the bitter reality that they had not only lost it but also relinquished control of Azad Kashmir, or POK, with little hope of regaining it.

On that day, Trital sent a message to his old friend Sadaqat Khan, who was in Pakistan for Republic Day, and they engaged in a conversation on Messenger.

In Kolkata, during the NIA's questioning of the four detainees, whether individually or in pairs, they gradually began to divulge information under persistent interrogation. Sanaodia admitted to the meeting at the Digha resort. Each of them claimed no involvement in the plane crash that killed Rajendra Kaul, but the NIA harboured suspicions to the contrary and brought them back to Delhi for further questioning. Chatterjee tried to evade going to Delhi, citing his mother's illness and the need to remain in Kolkata.

During their discussions with the NIA, the topic of the video CD related to Rajendra Kaul came up. This CD, which had been obtained by international media, was now in the possession of the IB and R&AW. When Chatterjee was confronted with this CD, he confessed to using it to blackmail Rajendra Kaul and ensure his mother's appointment as Prime Minister. However, he denied involvement in Kaul's assassination. Despite their claims, the central investigative agencies were not convinced and gave them a five-day ultimatum to reveal the truth. They would be subject to a NARCO test and a lie detector test if they failed to cooperate. According to NIA rules, they could be held in custody for up to three months.

The previous night, the Governor arrived in Kashmir from Jammu and assumed control of the administration. He held a meeting with local police departments to confirm the restoration of law and order in the state. He cautioned the police to remain vigilant and ensure that captured Pakistani and Taliban soldiers were not engaged in any treacherous activities. He also instructed them to assess the extent of human and property losses, as well as damage to infrastructure, including roads, bridges, and buildings. The assessment of military losses was to be reported directly to the President's office.

The people of India were overjoyed. Kashmir was not only secure, but Azad Kashmir or POK was back under Indian control. They realized that, with pressure from the UNSC and other nations, India might eventually have to return some Pakistani territory. However, this did not dampen their high spirits. They were thrilled that peace had finally returned to the country, and the politicians had learned their place. Preparations were underway for a grand celebration of India's Independence Day. The Home Ministry proposed that the President hoist the flag, but the President insisted that the honour should go to the Vice-President. That night, the President addressed the nation.

For a change, Trital returned home early that evening. Vijaya was delighted to see him home at such an early hour. She considered asking him if he was going back to work, but refrained. She noticed that he wasn't in a rush to have dinner. He received a couple of calls during their evening tea but didn't make any himself. Vijaya contemplated discussing the photographs she had seen on his desk but wasn't sure how to broach the topic. They had a leisurely dinner, and Trital appeared relaxed and inclined to chat. He spoke with great admiration for the President's decision-making capacity and resolute nature, which had played a pivotal role in bringing this moment of glory to India. Vijaya decided that she would broach the subject of the photos when they retired to the bedroom for the night. However, upon entering the bedroom after completing her kitchen chores, she found husband fast asleep, something he had struggled to do for many days.

&&&&&

15.08.2032

Independence Day was celebrated across the nation with immense enthusiasm. In states still under President's Rule, it was the Governors who raised the national flag. This year, common citizens joined the festivities in unprecedented numbers.

A multitude of people flocked to the Red Fort to witness the Independence Day celebration, where the Vice-President Mr. Shamsuddin hoisted the flag. Former Prime Minister Subhash Singh and former Defence Minister Ravindra Prasad were invited to the event. Ravindra Prasad attended alongside the BLP President, Nagarjuna. However, all other former cabinet ministers were notably absent. Opposition leader in the Rajya Sabha, Rameshwar Singh, Lok Sabha leader Namrata Rupani, leaders from several other parties, and retired military officers were in attendance.

The weather was favourable with no sign of dark clouds, allowing people to gather outside their homes and witness the ceremony comfortably.

Kashmir-e-Taliban 2032

A grand Independence Day celebration took place in Kashmir. The Governor raised the national flag, and under military administration, the region enjoyed peace and contentment. The people had endured great suffering at the hands of the Taliban, with women being kidnapped and subjected to horrific experiences. Their yearning for Kashmir to return to Indian control had finally been fulfilled, bringing relief and assurance. The period of hardships experienced under Pakistan's subjugation, marked by shortages of essential goods and services, was now over. The people enthusiastically participated in the flag-raising ceremony, singing the national anthem with patriotic fervour.

The imprisoned ministers of Maharashtra and West Bengal were released, with the condition that they would not engage in public demonstrations for two months. While they were allowed to participate in flag-hoisting ceremonies, they were barred from hoisting the flag themselves, an honour reserved for government officials. Most ofthem skipped the ceremony. Other prominent leaders were also released from detention after providing written affidavits stating they would not participate in any agitation. Ajay Patil, of the Chhatrapati Sena, and Dilip Deshmukh of the Maharashtrawadi Party were in deep trouble of rotting in jail.

Ashutosh Chatterjee remained under arrest in Delhi, while his mother, Lalita, was receiving treatment at a Bengal hospital, and her health was improving. Chatterjee's associates, Sanodia, Habib Khan, and Mustafizur Khan, underwent daily questioning, and their bank accounts were scrutinized for potential involvement in terror funding. It was evident that they had intentions against the former Prime Minister Rajendra Kaul, but the means they had employed remained unclear. They admitted that Kaul had been a hindrance but denied any involvement in his demise. Orders were received for them to undergo lie detector and NARCO tests soon.

To honour those who lost their lives in riots and the martyred soldiers, a ban was imposed on government and private parties and extravagant celebrations on Independence Day.

Trital received Republic Day wishes from Sadakatkhan in Pakistan.

On that evening, Mr. and Mrs. Trital were invited to the President's residence for dinner. Former Chief Justice Anil Gajendragadkar and his wife were also in attendance. The meal was kept simple, as it was unanimously understood that this was not a joyous occasion. There were no sugary treats or desserts to embellish the dinner. Prior to the meal, the men on the first floor engaged in extensive discussions, while the ladies convened on the second floor.

The President expressed, "I am content with my decision to declare a state of Emergency in the country."

Chief Justice Gajendragadkar remarked, "That was a brilliant move, Sir!"

"Thank you, and it was gracious of you to be part of the process," acknowledged the President.

The Chief Justice responded, "I feel honoured, Sir, that you included me in the process. I am truly grateful."

The President smiled and said, "If gratitude is to be extended, direct it towards this gentleman here, Trital, who suggested that I should seek your advice."

Gajendragadkar chuckled and said, "I see. Thank you."

Trital replied, "Sir, it was evident. The situation in the country was dire. As the national security advisor, I was facing a dilemma. There was chaos both within and outside the country. I merely proposed seeking your counsel."

The President acknowledged, "That was within the scope of your duty, and you executed it admirably."

Trital responded, "Thank you, Sir. Now, the question remains: how much territory will Pakistan yield to us? They have the backing of China, making it difficult to predict the internal dynamics."

The President concurred.

At that moment, the waiter served tomato soup, and everyone began to savour it.

Justice Gajendragadkar revisited the topic, stating, "There is a distinct contrast between the Emergency declared in 1975 and the one in 2032."

"In what way?" inquired Trital.

Justice Gajendragadkar elucidated, "In 1975, the Emergency was imposed to safeguard one individual's hold on power. However, this time, it was enacted to protect our nation, primarily to safeguard Kashmir from foreign aggression."

The President added, "There is one more distinction. Buddhadeva, please tell us what it is."

"Last time, the proposal to impose President's Rule was ratified by the central cabinet. One can only imagine how it was endorsed. This time, however, the cabinet and parliament were dissolved concurrently while declaring President's Rule. It's the first occurrence of its kind in Indian history."

Justice Gajendragadkar remarked, "Yes, indeed. As they say, extraordinary situations call for extraordinary decisions."

Trital concurred, "Yes, you are absolutely right. What else can we do when the country's Home Minister himself disregards the law-and-order situation?"

The President declared, "We were compelled to make such a decision, and there's one more thing I'd like to share with you."

"What is it, Sir?" inquired the Chief Justice.

The President elaborated, "Look, the decision of our military to first strike Pakistan before gaining control of Kashmir was an incredibly proactive move."

The Chief Justice agreed.

Trital added, "Sir, this idea was conceived by Brigadier Balwinder Singh Saluja from Army Headquarters. He made a casual proposal, and all branches deliberated on its feasibility before implementing it. It has yielded significant returns."

The President promptly responded, "Bravo, he's a clever individual. I will commend him."

Just then, Vijaya descended from the second floor and asked, "Brother-in-law (*Jijaji*), are we ready for dinner?"

The President replied, "Yes, of course, we will join you as soon as we finish this soup."

At the dining table, the President suggested to his wife Vinaya, "Why don't you play something religious on Alexa for our Chief Justice?"

Vinaya glanced at Mrs. Gajendragadkar and inquired, "Would you like to listen to the *Ramraksha* (Hymn in praise of Lord Rama)?"

Mrs. Gajendragadkar expressed her approval.

Alexa played, "*Om sriganeshayanmaha, asyasriramraksha Stotra mantrasyaha, budh Kaushik rushihi, srisitaramchandra devata.*" Everyone listened with closed eyes and joined palms in reverence.

Sahasranaamtutulyau ram naam varanine, itisribudh Kaushik virachitsrisitaramrakshastrastrautamsampoornam, srisitaramchandrauarpanamastu... Sriram...Sriram."

All of them chanted "*Sriram, Sriram.*" Then, they each began to partake of the meal.

Mrs. Gajendragadkar remarked to her husband, "Sister-in-law had her cook prepare your favourite potato and poppy seeds curry (*Alooposhtu*) for you."

"Thank you, Sister-in-law (*Bhabhiji*)," Chief Justice Gajendragadkar expressed his gratitude. Vinaya added, "Thank you."

After the dinner, Chief Justice Gajendragadkar and Buddhadeva Trital departed from Rashtrapati Bhavan together.

Back at home, Buddhadeva listened to a melancholic Hindi song playing on his mobile, "*Jab wohyaadaaye, bohotyaadaaye...*" (When she crosses my mind, the memories flood in).

Vijaya inquired, "May I share something?"

"What do you wish to express that requires my permission?" Trital responded.

"Allow me to speak my mind," she requested.

Trital nodded in agreement.

"Do you often remember Reshma?" she asked.

Trital was taken aback. "How do you know?"

Vijaya admitted, "I'm sorry, I accidentally opened one of your office drawers and came across some photographs."

Trital expressed his disapproval, saying, "You shouldn't have done that." As he walked toward the bedroom, she inquired, "Are you planning to search for her in Pakistan?"

He became emotional and confided in Vijaya, "Reshma is no longer in this world; her husband had taken her life a long time ago."

"That's truly tragic. Then where is Madhubala?" she inquired.

Trital replied, "I need to find her. After seventeen years, I wonder if I can locate her."

"What name did you use in Pakistan?" she asked.

He responded, "Sher Khan."

She remarked, "Ah, so it's the story of Reshma and Shera..."

Trital said, "Yes, the heart-wrenching tale." He swiftly turned away from her, wiping his eyes. Climbing into bed, he allowed his tears to flow freely. Vijaya refrained from entering the bedroom for some time, allowing him to grieve in peace.

&&&&&

16.08.2032

It was a serene day, marked by the general sentiment of contentment following the peaceful celebration of Independence Day. The

158

patriotic fervour was running high, and the populace was brimming with joy. All the chief ministers were awe of President .all thepolitical leaders were tense and anxious because the Emergency had not been lifted. The welfare of the people remained the primary concern, and corruption had been effectively curbed. The beneficial impact of the Emergency was evident in various aspects of governance.

Meanwhile, it was a time of mourning in Pakistan, especially for those in regions that had been ceded to India. They were now subject to a different administration. The people who had properties and assets spanning both India and Pakistan faced even more challenging dilemmas. They had to decide in which country they wished to reside and subsequently had to dispose of their properties. On the other hand, individuals in Pakistan-occupied Kashmir (POK) seemed less concerned.

In Pakistan, ominous signs of heavy rains and impending floods loomed large. Dark clouds only deepened the despondency and the low morale among the public.

Avdhesh Singh had been grappling with intense loneliness since his wife's passing, and he had turned to drugs as a coping mechanism. Over time, this had developed into a full-blown addiction. Throughout these years, he had never encountered any difficulties in procuring drugs. However, with the declaration of the Emergency, all sources for procuring drugs had been cut off. He was under constant surveillance, and reaching out to drug peddlers was no longer an option. His behaviour had deteriorated to the point where he appeared deranged without his customary drug doses. Trital, getting proper information, didn't overlook Avdhesh Singh's deteriorating condition. Through the President's office, he issued orders for Avdhesh Singh to be sent to a military hospital in Hissar, a city in the state of Haryana, to be treated as an ordinary patient in need of drug treatment.

Within the confines of the hospital, Avdhesh couldn't help but ramble, "I will become the Prime Minister one day, and then I shall settle scores with each and every one of you."

&&&&&

17.08.2032

A meeting of high-ranking officials convened at the Rashtrapati Bhavan, with the President and Vice-President in attendance. The session encompassed a thorough review of the law-and-order situation and an in-depth discussion about India's policy on Kashmir. It was decided that if the United Nations Security Council (UNSC) were to propose such an arrangement, India would consider returning certain cities to Pakistan. The deliberations included considerations on which cities to retain and which to relinquish, with the understanding thatearlier Pakistan-occupied Kashmir (POK) would not be part of the return. Before any handover, it was crucial to ensure the safety and return of Indian army units, tanks, and other equipment. The bodies of our martyred soldiers had already been repatriated to their respective hometowns, and Pakistan's fallen soldiers would be handed over as well. Likewise, the bodies of Taliban soldiers would be transferred to the Afghan government. There was a mutual interest in repatriating some of our prisoners of war (POWs) held in Pakistan and releasing Pakistani and Taliban POWs in Kashmir and other locations.

That morning, the UNSC had convened to discuss the Indo-Pak situation. India reiterated its stance that it was a bilateral issue and strongly encouraged Pakistan to engage in one-on-one dialogue with India. Other nations joined in appealing to India to engage in bilateral talks. India had been resolute in making its position clear.

Pakistan had come to terms with its defeat and was formulating a new strategy. They had initially sought UNSC intervention to halt the war but had ended up with unfavourable outcomes. The political leadership and military officers realized belatedly that yielding to Taliban pressure and launching an attack on Kashmir had been unwise.

On that same day, Trital received an assignment to plan a two-day tour to Pakistan. His visit, scheduled for the 19th and 20th of August, would take him to Lahore and Gujranwala to assess the situation and offer advice to the administration. Similarly, Brig. Balwinder Singh Saluja from Army HQs was tasked with streamlining the administration in Muzaffarabad and Gilgit-Baltistan, with a three-day timeline for his mission. Both appointments were made by the President himself.

The Pakistani External Affairs Minister, Siraj Ahmed, and Defence Minister, Latif Khan, held a virtual meeting with the Secretaries of External Affairs and Defence from India, in the presence of the Chief of Defence Staff (CDS). Afghanistan's External Affairs Minister, Mulla Qader Khan, was invited to join the discussion. India firmly declined to cede control over POK and Gilgit-Baltistan, but Pakistan pressed for the return of the remaining territory. India expressedto hold control over the four sacred sites and retain the area from the border to Nankana Saheb and Gujranwala, which included the birthplace of Maharaja Ranjit Singh.

This meant that Narowal, Sialkot, Gujarat, and Sheikhupura districts would remain with India. The four religious sites - Darbar Saheb Gurudwara, Kartarpur, Shri Rori Sahib Gurudwara, Eminabad, and Nankana Sahib Gurudwara, along with Damdama Sahib Gurudwara in Gujranwala, would also be retained, as they held immense significance for the Sikh community. India was willing to return Lahore, Mandi Bahauddin, Hafizabad, Jhelum, Karimabad, Ghaizar, and Hunzanagar to Pakistan. Pakistan was disheartened to lose Gujranwala to India permanently, given its status as a significant industrial hub. Sialkot, Gujarat, and Narowal were also of importance. India, however, agreed to return the Tehsils of Ferozepur and Sharakpur in Shekhpura District, which bordered Lahore districts.

India outlined another condition stipulating that both Afghanistan and Pakistan must cease all terrorist activities within India. Both nations were required to submit written assurances of their commitment to this effect to the UN Secretary-General. If they were found involved in terrorist activities on Indian soil, they would risk losing their UN membership. While both nations were taken aback by this condition, they had little choice but to agree.

Pakistan and Afghanistan were repeatedly interrogated regarding their involvement in the demise of former PM Rajendra Kaul. Indian agencies suspected the Taliban's hand in it, and the Taliban leaders were questioned about their Indian connections. They responded that since they were not involved in the former PM's death, they had no access to inside help from India. They were warned that if any evidence implicated them, India would launch a vigorous attack on their country, even if the UN objected. The Taliban leaders assured India of their non-involvement in the former PM's demise and encouraged India to identify the culprits within its own borders.

The most significant blow to Pakistan in this conflict was the loss of Azad Kashmir and Gilgit-Baltistan. Over the past two decades, Pakistan has invested substantially in developing infrastructure in these areas, including highways, flyovers, bridges, factories, and educational institutions. Pakistan had erroneously assumed that India would not take action in Kashmir until domestic turmoil was resolved. However, India had once again displayed its might. Pakistan's loss in 1971 when it relinquished control over East Pakistan to become Bangladesh was still a painful memory. This time, the wound was deeper, with a larger portion of Pakistan slipping away. Pakistan was in shock and remained a passive observer, adhering to the line dictated to them. Pakistani leaders requested a day to contemplate and provide their decision.

That evening, Trital informed Vijaya that he would be traveling to Pakistan for two days. She inquired about the timing, and he responded that it would be during the same week. Curious about his destination, she learned that he would be visiting the areas won by India and retained. She expressed concern about the potential risks, given that he would be Pakistan's top adversary at that moment. Trital assured her that there was no cause for worry, as he would receive comprehensive security coverage, and Pakistan wouldn't dare harm him. He emphasized that, should any harm befall him, Lahore would not be handed over, and the conflict would persist. He reassured Vijaya that his tour had the President's approval.

Then, Vijaya asked if Trital would be on the lookout for Madhubala. He chuckled and remarked, "How is that possible? Where could I possibly find her after seventeen years?"

Vijaya responded, "If you do happen to find her, bring her back to India. I won't object."

Trital confirmed, "Are you certain?"

Vijaya nodded firmly, "Yes."

&&&&&

18.08.2032

A series of meetings took place in India, with the aim of dividing the administration of Kashmir into two sections. One part encompassed the original area of Kashmir under Indian control, while the other included the territories reclaimed from Pakistan, including POK and other areas. The former would be known as the Srinagar division, while the latter would be called the Muzaffarabad division. The Muzaffarabad division would further have Gujranwala sub-division and Gilgit-Baltistan sub-division for administrative purposes. This decision received unanimous approval, as the Muzaffarabad Divisional Office was conveniently situated close to Srinagar (125 kilometres), making it practical for maintaining contact and exchanging official documents. It was also agreed upon that in the future, Gujranwala would be handed over to Punjab (India), given its proximity to Amritsar. Additionally, it was anticipated that Gilgit-Baltistan would become the third administrative division in Kashmir, but this decision was to be made in the following year by the ruling party, in power, as would the decision regarding Gujranwala.

Major Ranbir Singh, the Chief Minister of Punjab, demanded the immediate inclusion of Gujranwala sub-division in Punjab, but he was informed that his request would be addressed at a later time.

The President called for a meeting between the two prominent political parties in India, the *Bharatiya Lok Shakti Party* (BLP) and the *RashtriyaVicharmanch Party* (RVP). Although the nation was currently under President's Rule, one of these two parties would soon be responsible for governing the nation. This meant that the administration of recently acquired territories from Pakistan would fall under their purview, so it was essential to gain the trust of both parties. The leaders of RVP agreed with the decisions that had been made, but Nagarjun Reddy, the President of BLP, raised objections. While the honourable President was somewhat vexed by this, he chose not to express his frustration. Nagarjuna, the BLP President, believed that his party should have been consulted before agreeing to return Lahore to Pakistan. Subhash Singh and Ravindra Prasad remained silent on the matter.

The party leaders found satisfaction in being informed about the decisions by the President, as they had assumed that President's Rule would persist for an extended period, silencing their voices. However, it was now evident that the President did not intend to prolong it.

In Delhi, individuals such as Ashutosh Chatterjee, Sanodia, Habib Khan, and Mustafizur Khan were subjected to NARCO and lie detector tests. Unfortunately, the investigative agencies could not extract any new information from them. It appeared that they were not involved in the former PM's assassination, despite having harboured such intentions previously. They were questioned regarding the acquisition of drones and the time bomb, but they could not provide answers. As per the NSA rules, they would now have to spend the mandatory three months in jail until the mystery of the case was resolved.

Many of the investigating officers present began to believe that the former PM's murder would remain unsolved. Pakistan and Afghan secret services also denied any involvement in the killing, admitting only to discussions about a potential assassination. Pakistan had to acknowledge all this before India agreed to halt the war.

On that day, Trital busied himself with preparations for his visit to Pakistan. He had contacted army officers in Gujranwala and Lahore, finalized security arrangements, and issued orders. Vijaya remained anxious about his safety, but Trital was resolute in making the visit.

In the evening, there was another Zoom meeting involving officials from the Foreign Ministries of Pakistan, Afghanistan, and India. The Prime Minister and President of Pakistan had consented to hand over control of Sikh religious sites, including Rori Sahib Gurudwara Eminabad, Damdama Sahib Gurudwara Gujranwala, Nankana Sahib, and Darbar Sahib Kartarpur, to India. In return, India would cede control of Lahore, Jhelum, Karimabad, and a few other cities to Pakistan. Muzaffarabad, Mirpur, and Poonch, along with ten districts, would be under India's administration. The part of Gilgit-Baltistan acquired by India would remain in its possession, except for Karimabad and the adjoining area, which would be returned to Pakistan. Sharadapeeth, a pilgrim site in Neelam Valley, would be in Indian hands; its restoration was a future commitment, as it currently lay in ruins. The farthest end of Gilgit-Baltistan, including Karimabad, Ghaizer, and Hunzanagar, would be handed over to Pakistan. Gujranwala, Sialkot, Eminabad, Gujarat, Sheikhpura, and Narowal, along with their respective districts, would remain under Indian jurisdiction. Pakistan's ministers felt uneasy attending the Zoom meeting and announced their intention to provide duly signed agreements and approvals for scanning and exchange.

&&&&&

19.08.2032

Chief National Security Advisor, Buddhadeva Trital, arrived in Lahore that morning aboard an IAF plane. His first stop was at the Dera Sahib Gurudwara in Lahore, where he paid his respects. During a three-hour meeting with Indian officials, he issued a series of directives.

First and foremost, Trital ordered that Lahore be returned to Pakistan. Prior to the formal handover of Lahore, India was instructed to release all individuals in its custody, but only after Pakistan had released all of the captured Indian soldiers. The captured Indian soldiers held in Islamabad and Multan were to be transported to Amritsar by Pakistan airplanes before India would release Pakistani prisoners. Trital emphasized the importance of receiving confirmation from Indian military officials that women, children, or elderly individuals had not been subjected to mistreatment.

Following his visit to Lahore, Trital and his entourage proceeded to Gujranwala, where they spent the night at the Pakistan Government

Guesthouse. They were scheduled to meet with Pakistani officials the following evening.He alsovisited oneplace,whereas a spy he lived there for 20 years.

&&&&&

20.08.2032

At 7 o'clock in the morning, Trital made a visit to the Damdama Sahib Gurudwara in Gujranwala, where he paid his respects.

By 8 a.m., he had moved on to the Mubarak Shah burial ground in Mohmadnagar, accompanied by his friend Sadaqat Khan. Sadaqat Khan had informed Trital that Reshma was interred there, as he had been present during her burial. In those days, Sadaqat Khan worked as a reporter, but he has since become the owner and editor of a small newspaper.

Trital had brought an umbrella, although it turned out to be unnecessary since the heavy downpour of the past five days had suddenly ceased. Trital and the accompanying soldiers were relieved that the weather was clear that day.

It so happened that August 20th was Reshma's death anniversary. Trital had brought a floral wreath with him. As he approached Reshma's grave, only two soldiers accompanied him, while the rest of the security team remained with the vehicles. He noticed a veiled girl sitting near the grave, and someone had left yellow roses, Reshma's favourite flowers, on it. Trital had a faint suspicion that the veiled girl might be Madhubala. She was gazing at him. Trital offered the wreath and sat down with a heavy heart, struggling to hold back the tears welling up in his eyes. The girl approached him, and he asked, "Are you Madhubala?"

Her astonished expression confirmed his suspicion, and she replied, "Who are you? (*Aapkaun hain?*)"

"I used to be known as Sher Khan," he said. (Mera naam Sher Khan hotatha)

Her eyes welled up with tears upon hearing his name, and she asked, "Do you know my mother?"

"Yes, I do," he replied.

Sadaqat Khan excused himself and said he would wait in the car while Trital talked with Madhubala.

Madhubala removed her veil, and Trital was surprised to see the striking resemblance between them. She seemed to sense the similarity as well, having learned the truth about her birth from her maternal grandmother (Reshma's mother) two years ago when she was sixteen.

Trital asked, "Who do you live with?"

"I live with my grandmother," Madhubala replied.

Trital inquired, "Can you take me to meet your grandmother?"

"Yes, of course," Madhubala agreed.

Trital and his entourage then proceeded to Gulshan Labour Colony, where Madhubala and her grandmother resided. When Madhubala announced Trital's visit, her grandmother stared at him in disbelief and said, "Better late than never."

The elderly woman put on her glasses and approached Trital with trembling hands, wanting to touch him but unable to summon the courage. She alternated her gaze between Madhubala and Trital. Their similarity was astonishingher.

With a bit more composure, she asked, "Why have you come now?"

Trital replied, "I had one wish, to see you once."

Tearfully, she asked, "To see me or to see your daughter?" Her tears began to flow. Madhubala consoled her and brought her a glass of water.

Then, the grandmother said, "I think my time is near the end." (*Mere intakal kasamaynajdikaayahai , aisalagatahai*)

At that moment, Madhubala opened a small box and showed Trital some photographs: Reshma, a child Madhubala, and Trital in his younger days.

Madhubala handed Trital his photograph and asked, "Is this your picture, right?"

Trital confirmed, "Yes."

Trital then inquired, "How do you sustain yourselves?"

The grandmother replied, "I wash dishes for people. My son has a small farm in the village, and he sends us food grains and vegetables. Madhubala does some tailoring work and pays for her own education."

Trital asked Madhubala, "What are you studying?"

Madhubala responded, "I'm pursuing an online computer course offered by the British Institute. I topped the preliminary test, so I have a scholarship."

The elderly woman added with pride, "She's a very bright girl," perhaps wanting to say, 'Bright like you,' but unable to express it.

Trital offered, "Is there any way I can assist you?"

The elderly lady replied, "If you genuinely want to help us, please take this girl away from here. That wretch will be out of jail in a year.

He's unpredictable and won't hesitate to sell her, maybe even to a brothel."

Trital questioned, "How could he do such a thing?"

"You see, hisname is in her records, as her father. He will take her away," the agitated grandmother explained.

Trital reasoned, "She's an adult now. How can he take her away without her consent?"

"You can't trust him. He'll beat both of us and forcibly take her with him," the grandmother responded anxiously.

Madhubala declared, "I will never go with that monster who killed my mother. I will never go with him."

The grandmother said, "If you don't want to go with that wicked man, you can go with this man to Hindustan, where he lives."

Trital questioned, "Is that even possible?"

The elderly woman replied, "If you can bring so many soldiers here, I'm sure you can take this poor girl with you. Don't worry about me; I'll go to my son in the village. He didn't want to take Madhubala into the house."

Trital agreed, "Alright. I'll speak to the officers here. You'll need to come to one of the offices, and the process may take two or three hours."

He asked Madhubala to provide her identification documents, collected her birth certificate, ration card, school leaving certificate, and photographs, and departed.

Trital then convened a meeting with government officials and expressed his desire to adopt Madhubala. He requested them to prepare the necessary documents, including stamp papers and such. When the officials saw Madhubala's photograph, the striking resemblance prompted them to speculate that Trital might be her father. They suggested that if he was her biological father, he should undergo a DNA test, which could provide results within two hours using new technology. Trital returned with Madhubala to have the DNA test conducted at the Government Medical College. The doctors informed them that the results would be available on their mobile phones within an hour. The medical team recognized the very senior-ranking Indian officer Trital, from the time when Gujranwala was under Indian occupation, and they had felt the pressure back then.

Subsequently, Trital, Sadaqat Khan, and Madhubala, along with their convoy, headed to the Registrar's office to initiate the adoption process. A joint photograph was required for which a photographer was summoned, and the affidavit was typed on stamp paper. By the time they completed these formalities, the DNA report had been received on Trital's mobile phone, confirming that Madhubala was indeed his daughter. Throughout this entire episode, Sadaqat Khan provided invaluable assistance to facilitate the proceedings.

Trital informed Vijaya of all that had transpired over the phone. She was delighted and immediately shared the news with her sister, Vinaya. When Vinaya discussed it with her husband, the President, he remarked, "I knew about Madhubala, but I am very happy that she is coming here."

Madhubala's grandmother also attended the Registrar's office and willingly provided her thumb impressions where required. All the formalities for adoption were smoothly completed by 3 p.m. Trital offered her fifty thousand rupees as a token of gratitude, but she declined to accept such a large amount. Eventually, at Madhubala's insistence, she accepted a sum of thirty thousand rupees. Trital assured the elderly woman that she would receive a fixed amount every month in her bank account, as she had been receiving a meagreone thousand rupees per month as an old-age pension from the Pakistan government.

It was time for Trital to take Madhubala to the guest house. As he rose to leave, Madhubala addressed him in her grandmother's presence, saying, "I have something to ask."

Trital replied, "Yes, go ahead."

Madhubala inquired, "I was born a Muslim. After adoption, you're giving me a Hindu surname. What will be my religion now?"

For a moment, Trital was perplexed. Then he said, "Look here, my child, from now on, your religion is Humanism. You can choose whether or not to pray the Namaz or visit the temple with us. There will be no coercion. We are human beings, bound by the ties of humanity (*Insaniyat*). There will be no religious issues between us. If you agree, we will proceed; otherwise, we can withdraw the papers from the Registrar's office, and you can stay here."

The grandmother was deeply moved and, with teary eyes, said, "No, Sir. She will go with you. You have set a beautiful example of humanity (*Khubsurat missal*)."

Madhubala added, "Yes, *Abbajaan*, or rather, I will say 'Dad.'"

The elderly lady remarked, "What a fortuitous occurrence it is. Today is Reshma's death anniversary, and you two have met today."

Trital respectfully touched the old lady's feet, though she kept insisting, "No, don't."

It was an emotional farewell for Madhubala and her grandmother as they embraced each other, both in tears. Madhubala promised, "I will definitely come to meet you during Ramzan."

Madhubala stayed at the guest house. Trital had an official meeting in the evening, attended by military and civil administrative officers from POK, along with Indian military officials. POK was to remain under military control, under the authority of the Governor. Arrangements were put in place for this administrative setup. While most of the POK population had welcomed India, the possibility of Pakistan attempting subversive actions had to be considered. Trital gave the relevant instructions on these matters and concluded the meeting.

A delegation of businessmen and industrialists from Gujranwala met with Trital. They were assured that there would be no interference in their businesses, but they would have to adhere to Indian rules and regulations from that point on.

That night, Trital arrived at Gujranwala airport, where he had asked Sadaqat Khan to meet him before departing. The two friends embraced warmly, and Trital expressed his deep gratitude to Sadaqat Khan for reuniting him with his daughter. Sadaqat Khan attributed it to the mercy of God (*Allah ki marji*).

As they sat on the IAF plane, Trital was lost in nostalgia. He remembered an incident with Reshma. When Madhubala was a toddler, she was asked to kiss her father (*Abbajan*), and she had planted her tiny, tender lips on Trital's cheek. He felt as though he had drawn sustenance from that precious, sweet moment(*lamha*) throughout his life. He was overwhelmed with emotions. While this was a moment of joy and happiness with Madhubala, the absence of Reshma brought immense sadness and sorrow, which had tormented him and would continue to do so for the rest of his life. Trital contemplated how this sorrow and sadness, though they hollowed out one's heart internally, also provided external toughstrength. They offered the energy and power to confront the world and its challenges if needed. It was a source of inspiration, spontaneity, and consciousness.

Trital landed in Delhi at 10 p.m. and arrived home at 10:30 p.m. Vijaya was waiting at the doorstep with an *aarti thali* (a plate with an ignited lamp used in Hindu rituals) to welcome them. Madhubala asked, "How should I address her?"

Vijaya replied, "*Chhoti Ammi*" (Second/younger mother), bringing a smile to Trital's face.

&&&&&

21.08.2032 to 25.08.203

India remained peaceful during this time, with only a few minor incidents of note. In regions where state governments held power, governance proceeded as usual, with a focus on maintaining law and order. However, the failure to maintain law and order in any region raised concerns about the imposition of President's Rule.

Upon the Indian army's withdrawal from Lahore, Pakistan did not create any issues. All soldiers, tanks, rocket launchers, and equipment arrived safely at the Indo-Pak border, sincerevised. India had also acted honourably in returning Indian prisoners of war. Furthermore, India released twelve thousand Taliban soldiers and ten thousand Pakistani soldiers from Kashmir, with the injured individuals receiving proper medical care, and the deceased soldiers' remains exchanged with due respect.

A retired military General assumed the role of Governor in Kashmir, entrusted with the responsibility of overseeing the administration of the former POK and Gilgit-Baltistan areas, as well as the management of Sikh religious sites. The administration of these religious places was to be later transferred to the state of Punjab in India, while Sharadapeeth would remain under the sovereign authority of Kashmir.

On August 23rd evening, Madhubala was warmly received at the Rashtrapati Bhavan. In the days leading up to the 23rd, Vijaya spent three days selecting dresses for Madhubala and assisting her with preparations for the occasion. Madhubala also visited a beauty parlour, during which she shared with Vijaya that her mother had worked in one. Vijaya told her that sheknows it. At the Rashtrapati Bhavan, Madhubala initially felt overwhelmed and confusedby the vast expanse and the beauty of the palace and large security. However, her anxiety eased when Vinaya seated her next to her and engaged her in conversation. Madhubala quickly learned traditional customs, including showing respect by bowing to her aunt (*Mousi*).

That evening, the President and Trital engaged in a serious discussion about the political situation, focusing on Avdhesh Singh, Ashutosh Chatterjee, and issues related to Kashmir. It was time to devise a strategic plan for the future.

The next day, the high-level committee investigating the air crash that claimed the former PM's life reconvened to explore all possible scenarios. This committee was led by retired Supreme Court Judge Haribandhu Mahapatra and included the heads of NIA, NSA, R&AW, and the leader of MI, Maj Gen Baidya. The statements of Ashutosh Chatterjee and the other three were recorded in the presence of Justice Haribandhu Mahapatra, who ruled that they should remain in custody until the investigation into the former PM's death was complete.

There was an inquiry in the drone case,and it was revealed that the drone used in throwing a time bombat plane was used withoutauthorisation from home ministry.Since the home ministry was headed by AvdeshSingh, the committee discussed over the report.

With Afghanistan and Pakistan vehemently denying any involvement in the demise of Rajendra Kaul, suspicions began to shift towards Avdhesh Singh. Before Avdhesh Singh faced the high-level committee, the Chief Minister of Uttarakhand, Sukesh Rawat, was summoned. Rawat disavowed any connection to the air crash, explaining that his state had been devastated by the cloudburst, and he had requested aid from various central ministers. He had informed Avdhesh Singh about the need for a substantial disaster relief fund, and Avdhesh Singh had suggested that Rawat approach Finance Minister Subhash Singh. Rawat had decided to reach out to the Prime Minister directly, urging him to witness the extent of the devastation in Uttarakhand. To this, Avdhesh Singh had responded positively, saying, "Good idea."

When Justice Mahapatra asked Rawat to repeat the words "Good idea," he made a startling remark that Avdhesh Singh's real "Good idea" might have been his plan to assassinate the former PM. This comment left everyone in shock. Consequently, it was determined that a hearing with the former Home Minister, Avdhesh Singh, was necessary. Although a difficult decision, Justice Mahapatra believed it was the right course of action.

&&&&&

26.08.2032 to 01.09.2032

The hearing occurred at the military hospital in Hissar, where Avdhesh Singh was presented before Justice Mahapatra for questioning. Maj Gen Baidya and other officers from central investigation agencies were also present. Avdhesh Singh was in a mentally unstable state due to the absence of his medication. Initially, he remained silent when asked about Rajendra Kaul. Subsequently, a decision was made to provide him with a two-day supply of drugs to encourage him to speak.

On the second day, under the influence of the drugs, Avdhesh Singh began to ramble and issued threats, claiming that he would take action if he didn't receive the drugs he desired. He boasted about having caused harm to numerous individuals.

From August 27th to 28th, Avdhesh Singh was administered drugs, but on August 29th and 30th, no drugs were given, leading to his irritability and continued threats.

On August 31st, Avdhesh Singh underwent a lie detector and NARCO test. When asked directly, "Have you ever been responsible for someone's death?" while under the influence of chemicals, he confessed, "I first killed that individual, Surendra Dhami, the former PM. I orchestrated an accident to eliminate him. Although Uday Patel and Manoj Mitkari had a notorious reputation, there was uncertainty about the next election."

When questioned about how he had engineered the accident, Avdhesh Singh explained, "I once served as the Chief Minister of Uttar Pradesh, and I held the home portfolio. I had significant control over state machinery and had loyal associates willing to execute my commands. The accident was planned in Uttar Pradesh under my instructions." He even divulged the names of party members and government officials involved in the accident.

He also bragged that as Home Minister, he could exploit the state machinery to his advantage and intended to do the same if he became the Prime Minister. He then confessed to having orchestrated the deaths of Ashutosh Chatterjee's wife and two sisters-in-law, explaining his motive as retribution for blackmailing Rajendra Kaul and facilitating his mother's appointment as the PM in 2029. He initially aimed to kill Ashutosh but decided to blow up the aircraft carrying all three of them, which he took pleasure in doing.

Committee members surmised that Avdhesh Singh was suffering from severe mental illness due to his sadistic enjoyment of killing people.

When asked about other victims, Avdhesh Singh admitted, " I killed Rajendra Kaul. I did not want to kill his sister, but she happened to be on the flight with him and got killed. They had all of a sudden decided to fly to Uttarakhand together. It turned out to be a good idea. If only Rajendra

Kaul had died, she would have got all the sympathy and as a party president, she would have been chosen as the PM.

He also disclosed that his men had placed a time bomb on the airplane carrying Rajendra Kaul with the help of a specialized drone developed by DRDO, which couldnot be tracked by radar systems. Two such drones had been requisitioned earlier for VVIP security, including the Prime Minister. He revealed the names of individuals within the Home Ministry who aided the operation.

Major General Baidya remarked, "It's ironic that drones intended for the Prime Minister's safety and security were employed to eliminate him."

When questioned about additional targets, Avdhesh Singh named Ravindraprasad, Mahant Surajnath, and Trital. He expressed his desire to eliminate them due to Ravindra Prasad obstructing his path, Surajnath expelling him from Uttar Pradesh, and Trital's constant surveillance.

The revelations were deeply shocking, and it was decided to keep this information confidential. Publicizing it could potentially incite riots. The committee agreed to convey this information to the President personally. Accordingly, only Gen Baidya and Justice Mahapatra met with the President. Trital was already present in the President's office, along with the Principal Secretary, Home Secretary, and Defence Secretary. The video evidence was shown to them. The President ordered a Court Martial with utmost secrecy. Under the authority of the President's Rule, he also sanctioned the arrest of all co-conspirators under the National Security Act.

&&&&&

05.09.2032

The Planning Commission convened a meeting that included the Finance Commission and the GST (Goods and Service Tax) Council. In attendance were Chief Ministers and state secretaries, Governors and Chief Secretaries from six states, including Kashmir, where President's Rule was in effect. Elected representatives from Union Territories also participated.

During the meeting, each state presented their plans, along with data concerning current and future expenditures, as well as new proposals. The President expressed disappointment with states that had lagged in implementing their plans without providing satisfactory explanations for the delay.

The Finance Commission presented statistics on state budgets, highlighting instances where expenditure exceeded revenue. The President sternly addressed these issues. It was made explicitly clear that funds allocated in the Union Budget or central allocations for specific projects could not be diverted elsewhere. Some state Chief Ministers were visibly uncomfortable upon hearing this warning.

The President emphasized that states needed to reduce unproductive spending and refrain from offering freebies to secure votes. Self-sufficiency was encouraged, with the understanding that the Centre would offer financial assistance periodically, but states should not over-rely on it. Those failing to adhere to financial discipline would face consequences.

A similar topic was discussed during the GST Council meeting, where the importance of boosting GST revenue was stressed. The secretaries and Chief Ministers from all states appeared disheartened by this announcement.

The meeting proved to be unpleasant for Chief Ministers and officials from all states, including those under President's Rule. They had to bear the consequences of past decisions by those in power.

Following the meeting's conclusion, some Chief Ministers requested a separate meeting with the President, which was scheduled for the evening. Many of these Chief Ministers belonged to the BLP and sought the President's intervention in lifting the Emergency restrictions, in the evening.

The President inquired about the specific restrictions that hindered their functioning, but none could provide a clear answer. The Chief Minister of Karnataka mentioned excessive interference by the Governor in the State's administrative matters. The President clarified that the Governor acted based on his instructions, leaving the Chief Minister without further comments.

The President delved deeper into their concerns. The Chief Minister of Bihar, Suresh Yadav, mentioned that many of his party activists were detained under the National Security Act. The President asked if each case had been forwarded to the central Home Ministry for review. The Chief Minister stated that most cases had been submitted. The President then requested statistics from Biharfrom his secretary, which revealed that out of 3205 arrests under NSA, 2450 were related to acts like violence against the imposition of President's Rule, scuffles with other party members, arson, and more. Most of these cases were under Home

Ministry review and were likely to receive bail on a case-by-case basis. There were 725 "Attempt to murder" cases, of which only 437 had been forwarded to the Home Ministry, while the rest remained with the state government. Additionally, there were 30 clear murder cases, backed by witness testimony or videos, which had not yet reached the Home Ministry. The data was provided by the state DGP and the Assistant DG of the CRPF. After this detailed information, the Chief Minister of Bihar had no further comments.

The President inquired whether other Chief Ministers wished to hear similar statistics about their respective states, but they confirmed they already possessed this information. The President then advised the Chief Ministers to approach these cases without a political lens, emphasizing that detaining these anti-social elements had contributed to restoring peace in the nation. These cases would receive a fair review, but serious crimes demanded gravity and sternness, a joint responsibility of the Central government and the state government, crucial for the future. Consent from all participants was sought for this declaration.

&&&&&

08.09.2032 to 10.09.2032

With the President's Secretariat's permission, the BLP held a meeting in their party office on September 8th, chaired by the party president, Nagarjuna Reddy. The Vice-President, General Secretary, and other office bearers participated, either in person or via Zoom. Former ministers, including Ravindra Prasad, Venkatappaiyya, Manohar Reddy, Bhavana Shinde, Joginder Kaur, Salma Heptulla, and Rakesh Pilot, were in attendance. Arvind Kumar, Shamrao Patil, and some Chief Ministers joined online through Zoom. Subhash Singh, the former Prime Minister, was also invited and participated via Zoom.

The meeting commenced with a tribute to the soldiers, officers, and civilians who had lost their lives in the war, with everyone praying for their eternal peace.

The next item on the agenda was a discussion on party affairs and functions. Nagarjuna proposed that all BLP party leaders should meet with the President and request the lifting or relaxation of the Emergency, followed by General Elections. This proposal was discussed.

Venkatappaiyya suggested"we should first discuss the reasons behind the President's declaration of the Emergency and the dissolution of the cabinet.Why and how ,President can declare the emergency and dissolve the parliament and elected government and cabinet"

Nagarjuna countered, "We have gathered here to discuss a different issue."

Venkatappaiyya found support from Bhavana Shinde, who stated, "Avdhesh Singh has been arrested and court-martialled solely because of the Emergency."

Ravindra Prasad responded, "Do you not know what Avdhesh Singh had done? He orchestrated the air crash of our former PM, Rajendra Kaul. Our party President also lost her life in that crash. Are you still supporting Avdhesh Singh? Are you not ashamed?"

Venkatappaiyya persisted, "I still don't believe that Avdhesh Singh is responsible. He has been framed. Trital must have implicated Avdhesh. I am certain that some foreign hand is behind the PM's death."

"Let's focus on the primary issue and hear Subhash Singhji's opinion," suggested Nagarjuna.

Subhash Singh remarked, "I agree with Nagarjuna about engaging in dialogue with the President. It's something we need to consider."

Ravindra Prasad concurred, "While it's the President's prerogative to lift the Emergency, he should at least consult with the former Cabinet and seek their input."

Everyone nodded in agreement.

As a result, it was decided that the party leaders would meet the President and submit a written request to schedule an appointment for September 10th. This request was duly made.

On September 10th, the BLP leaders met with the President as scheduled, urging the lifting of the Emergency and the holding of Elections. On behalfof all, onlyNagarjun Reddy and Ravindra Prasad spoke. The President patiently listened to their demands.

&&&&&

15.09.2032

The President convened an all-party meeting, which saw the attendance of leaders from mainstream parties such as BLP, RVP, Deswap, Tamil Munetra Party, Dalit Party, Deccan Awaam Party, Punjab Kisan Party, Praja Dharma Party, and Bihar Jan Shakti Party.

During the meeting, all the parties united in making a shared demand: the lifting of the Emergency and the organization of national elections.

In response, the President assured them that their demand would be carefully considered, taking into account all its implications and consequences. However, he simultaneously cautioned the parties against initiating any form of agitation or resorting to violent protests. He emphasized a policy of zero tolerance towards such disruptive actions. The parties readily agreed to this caution, remembering how five state governments had been dissolved as a result of their previous anti-Emergency protests and violent actions.

&&&&&

20.09.2032

A joint meeting was convened, consisting of the Chief Election Commissioner, the Home Secretary, and the National Advisor to the President. The Chief Election Commissioner expressed the view that it was imperative to ascertain whether the current state of peace in the country was genuine or merely superficial. Even a single act of violence could potentially incite widespread turmoil, drawing from their past experience in the Suresh Dutt case.

The Home Ministry responded by highlighting that a significant ninety-nine percent of individuals with anti-social inclinations were presently incarcerated. Maintaining them in custody was seen as a prerequisite for ensuring the peaceful conduct of elections.

The President's Advisor conveyed that this proposal would be submitted to the President for his approval, and any subsequent directives would be issued in accordance with his authorization. He also mentioned that there were requests from Chief Ministers to release individuals detained under the National Security Act (NSA) on bail. Ongoing deliberations on this matter were acknowledged. However, in light of the President's directive to hold elections and restore a democratically elected government in the country, including the five states under President's Rule, a decision to proceed with the elections was deemed necessary.

The Chief Election Commissioner indicated that, provisionally, he was inclined to say "Yes" to conducting the elections, contingent upon the maintenance of a peaceful atmosphere in the country.

It was unanimously agreed that elections in Kashmir required separate consideration due to the region's expanded territory. Establishing the necessary election infrastructure would take time, and a comprehensive census of the newly acquired territory from Pakistan was deemed essential to compile an electoral list. The responsibility for this task would be entrusted to the military authorities in the region. Consequently, it was deemed prudent to postpone the elections in Kashmir.

&&&&&

22.09.2032

Upon the President's directive, a joint meeting was convened at the Home Ministry to address the law-and-order situation in the country. In attendance were the Home Secretary, heads of R&AW, NIA, IB, Chief of Army Staff Ashok Bhat, Chief National Security Advisor Trital, and other senior officials.

The initial focus was on Kashmir, particularly the former POK region, to assess its prevailing tranquility. It was acknowledged that some pro-Pakistan loyalists may still exist in the area, necessitating vigilant monitoring. Additionally, efforts were deemed essential to identify and take appropriate action against any hidden conspirators. There was a prevailing sense of contentment regarding the gradual shift towards an India-centric administration inerstwhile POK.

It was decided to establish two trusts: one to oversee the restoration and maintenance of Sikh religious sites now under India's control, and another to oversee the restoration of Sharadapeeth in the Neelam Valley. Sharadapeeth held religious significance due to Adi Shankaracharya's historical presence there in very past. A proposal was suggested and approved, stating that the management and restoration of Gurudwaras would be carried out in collaboration with the Shiromani Gurudwara Committee in Amritsar. The renovation of Sharadapeeth, similar to the Ayodhya Ram Mandir, would involve the assistance of the Archaeological Survey of India (ASI). This proposal was slated for submission to the President of India.

Regarding individuals detained under the National Security Act (NSA), it was proposed that their release should only occur following the general elections. An exception would be made for those political prisoners who had not directly engaged in murder or significant criminal offenses and had previously contested elections; they could be considered for release on a case-by-case basis, provided they desired to contest the elections.

All political parties would receive new conduct guidelines to ensure the preservation of law and order during elections. State leaders of all parties, particularly those in Bengal, Maharashtra, Gujarat, Kerala, Bihar, the North-eastern states, and Telangana, would be required to provide a written undertaking to the Election Commission, pledging that their party members would refrain from engaging in any form of violence. Violations would be met with severe consequences.

Trital proposed a joint meeting for all State Directors General of Police (DGPs), despite the prevailing peace. This proposal received unanimous approval.

&&&&&

23.09.2032

The Home Secretary convened a meeting with all the Directors General of Police (DGPs) via Zoom. It was a well-understood fact that this year's elections would unfold in a different context. With no central government in power, the free use of helicopters and planes would be restricted. The former cabinet ministers would still require security, albeit not at the high-profile 'Z+' level they enjoyed during their time in office.

The President held a commanding influence that left everyone somewhat subdued. When it came to matters of national security, he had no qualms about suspending or transferring anyone. Even the interference of the chief ministers would not be tolerated. The administration was empowered to ensure national security and formulate policies accordingly. The President's office also issued a notice emphasizing that common citizens should not face any harassment. The responsibility for implementing the guidelines in the notice fell to the police department. In case a commoner encountered any issues, they had the right to file a complaint directly with the President, and orders were given to resolve these complaints. The general populace expressed their gratitude to the President for the welfare measures in place.

The Home Secretary informed the DGPs that the state of Emergency would only be partially relaxed, not entirely lifted. Consequently, the National Security Act would remain in effect. Police would have the authority to employ this act to quell violence and anarchy, as well as apprehend troublemakers. The DGPs were tasked with certifying that the situation in their respective states was calm and peaceful for the upcoming elections.

&&&&&

24.09.2032

The Chief Election Commissioner convened a Zoom meeting with all the State Election Commissioners. He commenced the meeting by delivering a briefing on the preparations for the Lok Sabha elections. The State Election Commissioners were tasked with identifying sensitive polling booths based on recent reports of violence within their respective states. They were instructed to pinpoint suspected troublemakers and implement measures to maintain control over them. The State Election Commissioners were further directed to liaise with the police department and furnish a report to the central authority. Comprehensive reviews were to be conducted for all aspects related to the elections, including voting machines,voter list, election personnel, vehicles, and law and order arrangements.

Subsequently, the Chief Election Commissioner conducted an evaluation of the five states currently under President's Rule. He requested district-wise data to assist in determining the election dates. The State Election Commissioners were informed that they would need to organize the elections with minimal support from the Border Security Force (BSF) and Central Reserve Police Force (CRPF), as several battalions of the CRPF and BSF were still deployed along the recently expanded borders. Leaders from every political party were to be cautioned regarding the continuation of the National Security Act (NSA) and the partial relaxation of the Emergency, ensuring that troublemakers were aware of the severe consequences. The elections were planned to be conducted in four or five phases, and preparations were to be made accordingly.

&&&&&

30.09.2032

In the morning, an announcement emanated from the Rashtrapati Bhavan, stating that the Emergency had been relaxed to ensure the smooth conduct of the polling process under normal circumstances. It was made abundantly clear that this relaxation should not be abused, and there would be a zero-tolerance policy for any form of violence. The authority to apprehend individuals under the National Security Act remained vested with the President, and no one was permitted to take the law into their own hands. A set of guidelines, comprising "Dos and Don'ts," was distributed.

Later in the evening, the Chief Election Commissioner (CEC) officially declared General Elections across the country, with varying dates specified for different states. The polling was scheduled to transpire throughout the month of December. The dates for Vidhan Sabha elections in the five states under President's Rule were also confirmed. Notably, both the Lok Sabha and Vidhan Sabha elections would be conducted concurrently in all five states.

The decision regarding elections in Kashmir was still pending, mainly due to the incomplete electoral list in the former POK, Gilgit-Baltistan, and Gujranwala division. Consequently, President's Rule would persist in these regions. The ongoing efforts to integrate the administration in the former POK under the Indian flag were gradually yielding positive results. In approximately a year, this endeavour would reach completion, coinciding with the assumption of power by a newly elected central government, which would then decide on the course of elections in Kashmir.

&&&&&

05.10.2032

The Bharatiya Lok Shakti Party (BLP) convened its Working Committee meeting to discuss potential candidates for the future Prime Minister position. The name of Subhash Singh was initially considered, but he withdrew his candidacy. Some members, particularly those who supported Avdhesh Singh, suggested Nagarjuna as an alternative, hoping to replace Ravindra Prasad. Surprisingly, Nagarjuna himself proposed Ravindra Prasad as a deserving candidate, and eventually, everyone agreed. Subhash Singh also endorsed Ravindra Prasad's candidacy. Consequently, Ravindra Prasad was unanimously selected for the role of future Prime Minister.

The meeting also involved an analysis of the state-wise situation. In Telangana, Maharashtra, and Chhattisgarh, former chief ministers' names were confirmed for party leadership positions. In Bengal and Gujarat, former opposition leaders were chosen as the Party Leaders or potential Chief Ministers.

The forthcoming election was acknowledged as a significant test for the BLP. Nagarjuna emphasized the need to remind party members of the sacrifices made by Rajendra Kaul and Pratibha Kaul, while Ravindra Prasad remained silent on the matter.

All party members were urged to collaborate harmoniously as a team.

&&&&&

08.10.2032 to 10.10.2032

The RashtriyaVicharmanch Party (RVP) conducted a two-day conference in Goa, commencing with a tribute to the martyrs in war anddeparted workers over the past three months. It was announced that monetary compensation would be provided to the families of the workers, and those who wished to pursue a career in politics would be warmly welcomed.

Ashok Chadda was re-elected as the party's leader and would continue in this role for the next three years.

Several individuals aspired to be the Prime Minister, including Ashok Chadda and Namrata Rupani, a former leader in the dissolved Lok Sabha. However, the unexpected proposal of Mahant Surajnath, the Chief Minister of Uttar Pradesh, was put forth by some chief ministers and Rameshwar Singh, the leader of the Rajya Sabha.

Rameshwar Singh, who had once vied for the PM's position, began to believe that Mahant Surajnath was a more compelling orator and could deliver inspiring speeches. In Rameshwar Singh's view, Surajnath was a superior choice, and he was determined to prevent Ashok Chadda or Namrata Rupani from becoming the next PM if he couldn't secure the position for himself. The issueof candidacy ofSurajnath Mahant was extensively deliberated, yet a unanimous decision on the PM candidate remained elusive.

Suraj Nath expressed his willingness to undertake any responsibility entrusted to him by the party, without insisting on the PM's position. Due to his popularity, the respect he commanded from the masses, and his exceptional oratory skills, he was appointed as the leader of the election campaign. The selection of the PM candidate would be determined at a later stage.

&&&&&

26.10.2032 to30.10.2032

A video featuring Rajendra Koul, which had been released by Afghanistan, suddenly went viral in India. It had fallen into the hands of international media during the Indo-Pak war. When the censorship on mass media was lifted, one of the Indian channels broadcasted it, and soon it was aired on all channels. While the faces were clearly visible, certain physical gestures were intentionally blurred.

Some YouTube channels even displayed the complete exposure of Rajendra Kaul's sexual escapades. This revelation about their beloved leader came as a profound shock to the people of India.

Leaders from the BLP went to court, claiming that the video clip had been doctored and should be banned. The Court ordered an investigation to determine the source of the video release. The channels were instructed to announce that the videos had originated from Afghanistan. The court did not immediately ban the circulation of the video but ruled that objectionable content in the video should be censored and made inaccessible to minors.

A former leader of the DeshbandhuSwabhiman Party (DESWAP), Devashish Sarkar, appeared on television and asserted that the video was genuine and not manipulated. He went on to suggest that the video had been used for blackmailing Rajendra Kaul and facilitating Lalita Chatterjee's rise to the position of Prime Minister in 2029. The BLP and DESWAP parties had suffered reputational damage at that time. Now, Devashish Sarkar had joined the RVP due to his resentment over being excluded from the former state cabinet.

&&&&&

05.11.2032

case challenging the imposition of an emergency by the President has Abeen registered three months ago and is now up for hearing on this datein the Supreme Court. The Supreme Court has decided that a constitutional bench, comprised of Supreme Court judges, will determine the constitutional validity of the President's orders in this matter.

Several major issues were brought up in the case:

Whether the President has the authority to dissolve the lower house of parliament, known as the Lok Sabha.

Whether the Constitution grants the President the right to dismiss the cabinet of the central government.

Additionally, there was a debate over the composition of the judicial bench that will hear this case. The question raised was whether the bench should consist of nine judges or thirteen judges.The Chief Justice of the Supreme Court has ruled that the constitution bench will be constituted three months from the current date, indicating that it will take some time before this case is officially heard and decided by the Supreme Court.

&&&&&

15.11.2032 to 20.11.2032

Avdhesh Singh and his associates were found 'Guilty' by a military court-martial and subsequently sentenced to the death penalty. They were in Military jail. The military court's verdict stated that Avdhesh Singh was responsible for the death of the former Prime Minister, Rajendra Kaul, as he harboured ambitions of becoming the Prime Minister himself. Avdhesh Singh had undergone treatment for substance (drug) abuse and psychological disorders. In a lucid state of mind, he was presented with a video confession and compelled to accept responsibility for the murder of both Rajendra Kaul and Pratibha Kaul.

Following this judgment, some leaders took the matter to the Supreme Court. Avdhesh Singh's son, Rajnarain Singh, who was still incarcerated, appealed through his legal representatives. In response, the Solicitor General of India supported the military court's decision, citing Avdhesh Singh's confession. Rajnarain's legal team requested access to the evidence. They were informed that due to its sensitive nature and the fact that it was conducted during the Emergency period, it posed challenges. However, the lawyers remained steadfast in their demands. Subsequently, a discussion on the video evidence transpired. The legal representatives of Rajnarayan Singh persisted in their request for the video. Eventually, the video recording of Avdhesh Singh's statement was shown in court to them. Once this video went public, it once again tarnished the reputation of the BLP .

&&&&&

17.11.2032

Sunaina Dutt, the sibling of Suresh Dutt, secured a party nomination for the Pune assembly constituency. She caused a significant outcry, accusing the Bharatiya Lok Shakti Party (BLP) of being responsible for her brother's demise. This led to a surge of public resentment against the BLP, particularly in the state of Maharashtra, where the incident involving the arson and death of Suresh Dutt's residence had occurred.

&&&&&

1.12.2032 to 31.12.2032

The country saw peaceful elections, with the exception of sporadic instances of violence in Bengal, Telangana, Bihar, and Maharashtra.

Ravindra Prasad from the BLP and Mahant Surajnath from RVP emerged as prominent campaign figures.

&&&&&

04.01.2033 to 09.01.2033

The election results were announced, with RVP securing 291 out of 542 seats and emerging as the victorious party. There was an election conducted forthe leader of Lok Sabha.Members (parliament members) elected MahantSurajnathwith 195 votes in favour of his appointment as the Prime Minister, while Namrata Rupani received 96 votes. This election was marked by a spirit of camaraderie.

BLP secured 112 seats, while DESWA only managed to secure 9 seats. The remaining seats were won by various regional parties.

In the state Vidhan Sabha elections, RVP claimed victory in Bengal, Maharashtra and Gujaratwhile Chhattisgarh and Telangana were won by BLP.

&&&&&

10.01.2033 to 11.01.2033

A proclamation was made from the Rashtrapati Bhavan that the Emergency had come to an end. The swearing-in ceremony of the new cabinet took place in theAshoka Hallof theRashtrapati Bhavan. It was a simple ceremony, with no public invitees. Mahant Surajnath took the oath of the Prime Minister. Namrata Rupani was sworn in as the Deputy PM. Rameshwar Singh joined the cabinet as a home minister.

&&&&&

14.01.2033

The Prime Minister had received an invitation to lunch at the Rashtrapati Bhavan. Trital had already arrived there with his family. Vijaya had brought some specially crafted sesame laddoos(sweet dish)for the President, prepared with cashew and almond powders and jaggery. The President complimented the laddoos and inquired whether she had also brought some for the PM. Vijaya nodded in agreement. Vijaya and Trital respectfully paid their respects by touching the feet of the President and his wife, Vinaya, and exchanged warm Makar Sankranti greetings, marking the Indian festival.

Mahant Surajnath arrived alone. Contrary to conventional etiquette, President Shiv Narayan Singh waited in the State Drawing Room for the arrival of the Prime Minister. When Mahant Surajnath finally arrived, he humbly bent down to touch the President's feet, and in response, the President warmly embraced him. It was an emotional moment for both of them, and tears welled up in their eyes. They exchanged heartfelt Makar Sankranti greetings.

Mahant Surajnath paid his respects to Vinaya by touching her feet and said, "*Bhouji*,(Sister-in-law) I seek your blessings." She replied with a touch of humour, "After so many years, my brother-in-law is seeking my blessings." Her remark brought a smile to everyone's faces. She then offered the sesame laddoos to the Prime Minister.

For an extended period, the Prime Minister and the President engaged in a conversation on a sofa in a quiet corner. The President eventually invited Trital to join themafterward.

After some time, Vinaya invited them all to the dining table for lunch. She informed the Prime Minister that she had arranged his favourite sesame-jaggery-roti. He expressed his gratitude.

The Hanuman Chalisa played on an Alexa device. Madhubala joined them in the chanting of the Hanuman Chalisa, and lunch was promptly served.

&&&&&

The End

AUTHOR BIO

Name   --- Anant Joshi
Education --- Batchlor of Engineering , BE (Mechanical)
Occupation --- Retired from Coal India Ltd. 2009

Literary   Contribution -----
a) One poetry book in Marathi language – Ek aavegalamrutyu
b) One novel in Hindi Language   -- Gita chaligai
c) One novel in Marathi   -- Beg your pardon
   This novel translated and published into three languages.
   English , Hindi and Bangali
   Links on Amazon
   1) Marathi novel—https://amzn.eu/d/g1YV2L2
   2) English novel ---https://amzn.eu/d/a5630J
   3) Bengali novel --- https://amzn.eu/d/35nIImu
d) One   novel in Marathi   -- On the banks of
   Damodar

   This novel translated and published in English and Hindi

Links on Amazon
   1) English – https://amzn.eu/d/3p2zb3C
   2) Hindi -- https://amzn.eu/d/8wIMN8I

e) One novel in Marathi   --- FacebookchyaKavitavarun